THE L

ANN BENNETT

In memory of my dear sister, Kathy, who sadly didn't get to read this one.

PROLOGUE
PHNOM PENH, 1975

From where she sat, on a blanket on the tiled floor of the porch at the front of the old French Embassy building, Colette had a view of the street beyond the compound through the wire fence. She watched the boy soldiers marching past, weighed down with oversized machine guns they could barely carry, the armoured cars roaring through, burdened with schoolboy troops shooting randomly in the air. And all the time there was a steady stream of refugees fleeing the city with their worldly possessions loaded onto carts, prams and bicycles. She could see too, the crowds of Cambodians clamouring at the embassy gates, shaking the bars, pleading with the security guards, their eyes desperate. It was their last hope.

The huge lawn of the compound was crowded with people too, camping out on blankets under the ornamental trees, surrounded by their possessions crammed into bags and boxes. The smoke from a hundred cooking fires blackened the air, mingling with the smoke from the buildings set alight by the Khmer Rouge.

They had been camping on that porch for ten days now, she and her Cambodian housekeeper, Achariya, lying side by side on the same blanket under the stars. They had come to Phnom Penh, fleeing the influx of Khmer Rouge soldiers in their home village near Angkor Wat, seeking refuge like thousands of others in the French Embassy. But now they were here they felt trapped, alongside all the other random westerners in their fashionable clothes, playing the Beatles on portable gramophones, drinking their way through the stock of embassy wines and spirits. There seemed to be no escape. Certainly no escape through the city that was overrun with unpredictable and undisciplined Khmer Rouge soldiers, and now food and water were running out on the compound too.

The embassy staff sat in their offices constantly on the phone to foreign governments seeking refuge for those in the embassy. They would occasionally emerge from their rooms, wiping the sweat from their furrowed brows to confer in the marble hallway, but for days there had been no breakthrough and it felt like stalemate.

On the tenth day, a convoy of trucks arrived and was admitted through the gates. Someone said they were there to take foreigners out to Bangkok. Those waiting in the embassy flocked towards them, but guards stepped forward to control the crowd.

'Only those with foreign passports, or wives of foreigners,' they said gruffly, shaking their heads and waving away the many Cambodians in the crowd, the hope in their eyes extinguished in an instant.

'Come,' Colette said, picking up her bag and taking Achariya's hand.

'It's hopeless,' Achariya said hanging back.

'We must at least try,' Colette said, pulling her towards the truck.

The crowd surged around them and they pushed their way through the press of bodies towards the back of the truck.

'Passports,' the guard said, clicking his fingers, when they squeezed to the front. Colette produced her French passport and Achariya her Cambodian one. The man shook his head.

'Sorry, only foreigners can leave. Go back, lady, so others can pass.'

Colette clung to Achariya's hand.

'But I can vouch for her,' she pleaded. 'She is with me. I will look after her.' But the man shook his head again and pushed Achariya back. People surged around them, elbowing them in their desperation to reach the truck. Colette clung onto Achariya's hand but eventually they were pulled apart. Panic seized her. How could she leave this woman who had served her faithfully for more than thirty years, had been her friend, who had sacrificed so much for her. Should she stay behind too, try to protect her?

'Go! Madame, you need to go. I will be alright. I'm not in danger here!' Achariya urged and Colette felt herself being carried by the crowd towards the back of the truck and pushed up and over the tailgate. More people surged over the tailgate behind her and her view was almost blocked, but she fought her way to the back of the truck and peered out as the truck drew away. In the stark sunlight she caught a brief glimpse of Achariya's red and yellow sarong in the seething crowd before bodies closed around it and it disappeared from view. She turned back into the truck, her heart heavy with guilt and the searing pain of loss.

1

FRANCE, 1995

Colette turned the key in the lock of the little museum, put it in her handbag, and set off down the village street towards her home. The museum was now closed for the winter season, so her days volunteering there were at an end for the time being. She felt a sudden surge of freedom, a lightness in her step, imagining what the next few months held for her. It reminded her of being young again, like the end of the school term, the promise of long days of freedom ahead.

She smiled to herself, thinking back to the conversation she'd had earlier with Elise, her fellow volunteer, who had asked her what she would be doing through the winter months.

'My husband and I are thinking of motoring down to Spain, to chase the warm weather,' Elise had said.

'Sounds wonderful,' said Colette absently.

'And what about you? Do you have plans?' Elise had asked.

Colette cleared her throat. 'Well yes, I have actually. I'm planning a trip to Cambodia.'

The other woman's eyes widened. She'd looked startled, shocked even.

'Cambodia! Colette! But isn't there a war going on there?'

'Not now. It's all but over. They've been welcoming tourists again for the last couple of years. Things will probably be a bit basic in places, but I don't mind that.'

Elise visibly shuddered. 'You *are* going on an organised tour I take it?'

Colette shook her head, suppressing a smile. She enjoyed gently teasing her rather staid companion. 'No. I'm going alone.'

Again, that incredulous stare. 'Alone? But, Colette, dare I say it, you're not a young woman anymore. Are you sure you'll be safe?'

Colette laughed. She was almost seventy-five but didn't feel or look her age. 'Quite sure, thanks. You see... I used to live in Cambodia. I know the country well.'

'Oh, of course. I remember now. You mentioned that's where you developed your interest in antiquities. You did tell me about it a long time ago. But even so...'

'There's no need to worry about me, Elise,' Colette said, patting the other woman's hand. 'I can look after myself.'

'Well, I sincerely hope so. Do take good care of yourself. I suppose, when you've lived abroad somewhere like that, you will always be curious to go back.'

It was Colette's turn to shudder, as if something from the past had just surfaced and prickled down her spine. She forced a smile but said nothing. It wasn't just curiosity that was calling her back; there were things she'd left unresolved in Cambodia, things she needed to find out about, things she needed to settle.

She arrived back at her picture-perfect cottage of honeyed stone that nestled just behind the village square and let herself in through the front porch. Her tabby cat, Bijou, rubbed himself against her legs and, crooning to him gently, she opened a tin of cat food and dished it out for him. Glancing out of the kitchen window into the garden as she straightened up, she smiled. The gardener was picking berries in the neat vegetable plot next to the lawn, working methodically, putting them into a basket on his hip. He waved at her genially.

How pleasant life was in this sleepy backwater in the Dordogne, how kind and gentle and welcoming the villagers were. But even though she'd known this village since childhood, when her mother and father had bought this house as a retreat from the city, it had never felt quite like home. Her heart and body still yearned for that villa on the Tonlé Sap lake near Angkor Wat, where she would wander out onto her balcony at dawn to watch the floricans and ibises rise in a huge, graceful flock as the morning sun burned the mist off the water. For the past twenty years she had been watching and waiting for an opportunity to return. She had read the international news assiduously every day, dismayed at the reports of continuing bloodshed, *her* heart bleeding for the many wounds inflicted on that far off country that she still considered her home.

She'd waited for two decades now to have a chance to go back there. For the first five anxious years, while Pol Pot and the Khmer Rouge's murderous regime had a stranglehold on the country, it was completely out of bounds to westerners. But then the breakthrough had come in 1979 when the Vietnamese army toppled the Khmer Rouge. She wondered then how long it would be before she could return, but there was another fifteen years of famine and infighting until at last she had read that tourists were beginning to trickle back in the early nineties. Despite the fact that the country was still far from settled, Colette decided it was time to return. After all, she wasn't getting any younger. She'd been planning her trip for a couple of months.

She pushed the kitchen window open and shouted to the gardener. 'Are you coming in for a glass of wine, Jean-Luc?'

It had become a tradition at the end of his day when Colette came back from the museum, for them to share a glass of Bordeaux and catch up with gossip as the light faded outside. Jean-Luc was a handsome, well-built man, his skin burned chestnut by the sun. He was about Colette's age and was always ready to entertain her with an anecdote and a twinkle in his bright blue eyes. They had a comfortable, familiar relationship – they were old friends – but Colette had never wanted to take it further even though she'd been sure for a number of years that Jean-Luc would have needed little encouragement. She was far happier alone, she was quite sure of that now.

Today they spoke about the arrangements for the place while she was away. Jean-Luc had agreed to look after the cottage and the garden, to water the houseplants, to feed the cat. And in the morning he would drive her to the station to catch the Paris train, the first leg of her long journey to Phnom Penh.

After he'd left, she went up to her bedroom with the sloping roof and dormer window that overlooked the picturesque town square. She pulled out her suitcase from under the bed. She had almost finished packing, just a few last-minute things to add before she set off for the airport the next morning. She went over to her little bureau in the corner of the room and took out her photo album. She turned the pages carefully – some of the photographs were very old and fragile now. She eased a couple of them out of their clips and slipped them into a thick envelope. She decided she would put that in between the leaves of a book in the suitcase to make sure the photos didn't bend. She was worried about damaging them but needed to take them with her. As she did this, she examined the photographs again, just as she had many, many times over the long years since she'd left Cambodia.

Looking at them again brought back her motives for going back there at the first possible opportunity. She remembered that, as the truck had drawn away from the French Embassy that fateful day back in April 1975, she'd vowed to return as soon as she could. Now she looked down at the photographs of her villa on the lake, its gleaming white paint, its graceful colonial lines, the verandas and sweeping roofs, such a contrast to the wild, ragged jungle that surrounded it. Then there was the picture of her and Henri standing on the bridge over the moat at Angkor Wat, arm in arm, that first year they had arrived in Cambodia after their wedding. And one of the two of them sitting outside the club in Phnom Penh, cocktails in hand, smiling broadly. Then came the one of Colette standing beside her housekeeper and friend Achariya, on the veranda at the villa, their arms linked. There were a few photographs in that album that she rarely had the courage to contemplate, just looking at them filled her with guilt. Some she barely looked at as she slipped them out of their clips and into the envelope, but there was one she dwelled on longer. It was of a young Cambodian girl who stared solemnly out of the photograph with huge eyes. Colette stared back at the image for a long time and traced her finger around those delicate features. Then, with a sigh, she slipped it into the envelope with the others. Now that she was going back there, it seemed somehow easier to look at those haunting images. And there was no getting away from it, it was time to face up to the past.

2

PHNOM PENH, 1995

The flight from Paris to Phnom Penh was long and exhausting, but Colette, wedged into her economy seat, still found it impossible to sleep. Her mind was going over and over the events from the years she'd spent in Cambodia and anticipating what the next few weeks might bring. When she first got off the plane she was bowled over by the blast of sudden, intense heat. She'd forgotten how it felt for every inch of your body to be covered in beads of sweat, your face glowing, your hair damp from the steamy air.

The taxi from the airport took her along the wide main road that passed the French Embassy. She stared out at the sprawling buildings, curious about the place where she'd spent those terrifying last weeks as Phnom Penh fell to the Khmer Rouge, but nothing appeared to remain of the old place. The building had been completely transformed, with stark white modern blocks bordering the road, the compound surrounded by a high brick wall. It was nothing like the shabby, colonial building in its extensive lawns that had been her home and home to many other desperate people during that tense period when the Khmer Rouge stormed the city. She was relieved in a way that things looked so different. It meant the memories and the pain they brought of that exodus in 1975 were not quite as sharp as they would have been had the place not changed so much over the years.

In contrast, central Phnom Penh had not altered as much as she'd feared. There were still those languid open spaces, the tree-lined boulevards and their French-style buildings that reminded her so much of Paris. She was gratified that all that had remained. The taxi continued along a wide road lined with blossom-laden trees that ran parallel to the wide Tonlé Sap river. They were heading for the enormous hotel, the Cambodiana, a landmark in its own right. Colette would have preferred to stay at the Hotel Royale of course, where she and Henri used to go for a sundowner or to meet friends when they were staying at their villa in Phnom Penh, but the place was far too expensive for her now. Besides, she was curious about the Cambodiana. She could remember back to when the giant monolith was being built by Prince Siaonhouk in the 1960s, on stilts on land reclaimed from the river. It had only operated as a hotel for a few years though – when Siaonhouk was overthrown, it became an army barracks. She recalled hearing how refugees had flocked there to escape from the Khmer Rouge in 1975. She was curious to stay in this building that had played such a significant part in the history of the city.

The taxi swung in under an elaborate arched entrance and approached the huge white hotel with its red Khmer-style roofs. They drove through formal gardens towards the building and, as Colette looked up at the great edifice, she had a real sense of coming home.

Attentive staff checked Colette in and showed her up to her room on the fifth floor. The room had a huge picture window that completely covered the entire front wall. As soon as the porter had left her bags and shuffled away with his tip, she went to stand at the window, to gaze down at the lazy, brown river that stretched as far as the eye could see. Here was where two great rivers, the Tonlé Sap and the Mekong merged to become one huge confluence. To her left she could see the tree-covered island in the middle of the expanse of water that separated the two rivers. It all felt so familiar now, but she had forgotten how bright the tropical colours were – the trees with their flame-red flowers, the bright magenta bougainvillea, the emerald green of the rice fields they'd driven through from the airport.

She sat down on the wide, comfy bed and resisted the urge to lie down and close her eyes. Instead, she opened her suitcase and took out the envelope that she'd sandwiched between the pages of a guidebook. Now she was here it somehow seemed easier to look at all the photographs. It had been so hard at home in France. Cambodia had felt so remote, almost unreal then. The photograph she had resisted looking at before was of a man, but she took it out and contemplated it now. He was a Frenchman with classic dark hair and dark features and with a dashing smile, too dashing... She looked at it for a while and the longer she looked the more it seemed as though he was looking back at her. It was a trick of the camera angle, but like the Mona Lisa, his eyes seemed to follow her. She put the photo away quickly, shuddering involuntarily. She swapped it for the one of the young Cambodian girl. The girl had only been twelve or so when the photograph was taken. Looking at it now, all these years later, Colette realised that the girl had that defiant look in her eyes, even then.

She sighed and slipped it back in its envelope. 'Where are you now, Sophia?' she murmured and fell back against the pillows, finally too exhausted to keep her eyes open.

She awoke before dawn the next morning, and went straight to the window to watch the sunrise. The grey clouds that hung above the distant horizon gradually became tinged with pink, then the first rays of sharp white light pierced the horizon. She watched it spread and grow brighter and bigger and higher in the sky and its reflection shimmered in the wide river until it was so bright that it was impossible to look at it anymore. She recalled how she would sometimes watch the sunrise over the lake from the villa on Tonlé Sap lake. Henri would come and stand beside her and lay his hand on her shoulder and ask; 'Glad you came?' She would beam up at him. His question didn't need an answer.

After breakfast she went out of the hotel's marbled front entrance, under the great portico and asked one of the waiting cyclo riders to take her to the old French Quarter. He looked at her, puzzled. She stared back, realising that they might not call it that anymore. She sighed. So much had changed in the last twenty years.

'Alright. Do you know the old post office?' she asked.

He nodded enthusiastically. 'Of course. Of course. Old post office. Not far, madame.'

She climbed on board and he began pedalling vigorously out of the hotel grounds and towards Sisowath Quay, the road that ran parallel to the river, heading north to the part of the city where the French had their homes in colonial times. They passed the Palais Royale with its red and gold roofs and soaring golden pagodas and it warmed Colette's heart to see this astonishing monument intact and as beautiful as it ever had been. She'd worried that the Khmer Rouge would have destroyed everything.

Then they were moving parallel to the river, past the French colonial buildings that lined the waterfront with their pillared balconies and shuttered shopfronts. It had the feel of a seaside promenade with the palm trees waving in the warm breeze and the cries of boatmen floating up from the water.

They passed the Foreign Correspondents' Club, a beautiful yellow and white building with wide, open balconies overlooking the river and Colette remembered the many happy evenings she had spent in the upstairs bar there, whiling the time away talking to journalists who had come to report the Cambodian revolution.

Colette was astonished at how the city appeared to have

recovered from its tumultuous recent past. The orderly main road, with its pristine gardens in the middle of the carriageway, the coconut palms lining the waterfront, the tall line of plane trees on the other side. The city had been as peaceful and orderly as this when she first arrived in 1939, although of course there had been far fewer motor cars on the road. But looking around at the impassive faces of the people strolling beside the river or riding their cars or motorbikes, it was almost as if its peace had never been interrupted by those bloody, brutal years of war and turmoil.

They reached a street market and turned inland, away from the river. Colette looked with fascination at the stalls overflowing with colourful fruit and produce, inhaled the delicious cooking smells that wafted over to her. Now they were passing through some narrower streets with shophouses and low rise older buildings. They reached the old post office, another yellow and white building with an elaborately decorated façade.

'Here, madame,' said the cyclo rider proudly, stopping the cyclo and getting down from his seat.

'Thank you,' she said getting out nimbly. 'I know my way from here.'

She paid him and added a generous tip and he pedalled off. She felt a sudden sense of freedom such as she'd not experienced in over twenty years. She took a deep breath of the steamy air and looked around with satisfaction. The house she was looking for was a few blocks away from the post office and as she set off down the road she wondered if it had survived. There was so much new building here now. Modern apartment blocks, what looked like a school behind a high wall, in amongst the old shophouses and crumbling colonial villas set in their ample compounds. After she'd been walking for a few minutes the streets opened out onto an area of open green land – some municipal gardens with a fountain in the middle. She remembered this too now.

Beyond the gardens, the streets closed in on her again. She

noticed an air of energy, of frantic commerce everywhere about her. Every old shophouse was occupied by a thriving business. She sensed people desperate to get ahead, making up for the lost decades. She rounded a corner and there it was. The villa that Henri had brought her to as a young bride in 1939. It was square and imposing, its white stucco walls with arched, shuttered windows, a portico and a balcony with a veranda underneath and tall railings around its plot. Cars were parked inside the front garden and the wrought iron gates were open.

Colette stood on the road in front of the entrance wondering, remembering. She was relieved the house had survived but it didn't look very lived in. She moved closer and noticed a plaque beside the gate that read, "Mekong Bank". It was the headquarters of a bank! Perhaps that meant she could go inside. With trepidation she walked through the front gates and towards the building. The old teak front doors were no longer there. Instead, at the top of the stone steps were some plate glass doors. She mounted the steps and pushed them open.

Inside was a cavernous hall tiled in marble and lined with glass-fronted tellers' counters. She stopped and looked around her, disconcerted. They must have ripped out most of the internal walls of the house. But looking beyond the counters she saw a flight of wide stairs leading to another floor. The memories came flooding back. Those were the stairs Henri had carried her up precariously as they both laughed uproariously, the day they had first arrived, and on the very spot she stood they had once entertained guests by the light of a glass chandelier. Standing there now, she could almost hear their voices above the murmur of customers and bank staff. But there was another voice too, calling her name from the stairs, urging her to follow with barely suppressed laughter. 'Colette, come on won't you...'

'Madame, can I help you?' a uniformed bank clerk smiled into her face, mildly anxious.

'Oh no, thank you,' she replied, flustered. 'I made a mistake.

I'm in the wrong place.' And she hurried out of the swing doors which buffeted to and fro, into the heat of the morning.

THE NEXT DAY, a taxi took her along a stretch of still, mirror-like water where buffalo wallowed amongst submerged trees, past farmland with straggly palm trees soaring from the fields, through villages of stilted houses, past orchards, plantations and stretches of ragged jungle. She stared out at flat, emerald-coloured rice fields, wide brown rivers, ponds choked with lilies, and she was reminded of how much she'd missed the beauty of the Cambodian countryside during her years in France. They drove on past groups of schoolchildren going home on their bicycles, past temples set amongst palm trees where monks wandered in their saffron-coloured robes. Finally they arrived in Siem Reap, the little town nearest to Angkor Wat. Colette stared wide-eyed at the building works going on; hotels were going up everywhere.

'Angkor is a UNESCO site now,' the driver said with a smile. 'Many people will want to come here. Which hotel you staying at?'

'We can go to the hotel later,' she said. 'Could you take me to the temple first?'

He shrugged and drove on the four more kilometres or so through the suburbs of the little town, past more villages and farmland until the buildings thinned out and the road ran through a spinney of soft mimosa trees then on through thicker forest. Then the road that previously Colette had only known as a dirt track, ran alongside a lake. It finally opened out into huge sandy car parks where coaches and minibuses were drawn up and there were some booths issuing tickets.

And there it was across the lake. Angkor Wat, the huge, sprawling temple complex, its perfectly symmetrical lines and Khmer towers reflecting in the wide moat. It was what she'd been yearning to see with body and soul for twenty years and now it was here spread out before her in all its majesty. She leaned on the moat wall and breathed in the hot, steamy air and stared across at the ancient building, taking in the splendour and the beauty of the place. And as she did so, she became overwhelmed by the joy of being here once again and her eyes filled with tears.

3

PARIS, NOVEMBER 1931

The day that Colette's father took her to the Paris Colonial Exposition of 1931 changed her life for ever. Papa was a cultured man, and despite being an engineer and industrialist engaged in the manufacture of motor car parts, he took care to ensure that his only daughter grew up with a fine appreciation of the arts. She remembered the day of the expedition for the rest of her life. It made a particular impression on her because her mother was ill that day and couldn't come along, so it was just the two of them who set off from their apartment off the Champs Élysées towards the exhibition site at the Bois de Vincennes. Colette loved having her father to herself. He worked long hours at the office and when he was at home was either preoccupied or busy with his work and it was rare that she got an opportunity to be alone with him.

She recalled standing in a crowd that lined a wide boulevard. On the other side of the road stood a line of soldiers. They stood to attention, motionless, in their full regalia, watching President Doumergue as he was driven in an open-topped limousine escorted through the crowds by cavalrymen on white horses. The enthusiastic cheering of the huge crowd, the band music, the atmosphere, the lavish and exotic displays, all cast a spell on Colette that would last a lifetime.

After the opening ceremony, Colette and her father wandered around the various displays arm in arm. There was an area of the vast exhibition dedicated to each colonial possession of the French empire; they walked through full-sized replicas of Algerian mosques, marvelled at Tunisian souks, Indochinese pagodas, a Madagascan church that looked incongruous under palm trees. Also on display was bountiful exotic produce from every corner of the empire as well as goods produced for export such as latex and rubber, silks, carpets, jewellery and ceramics. Colette, a sheltered schoolgirl of eleven who had never been outside France, was entranced by everything on display.

'I'll always remember today, Papa,' she said clutching her father's hand, and he rewarded her with one of his rare smiles. It lit up his whole face and reached right to his eyes.

But the thing that really took her breath away that day was the astonishing life-sized replica of the Angkor Wat temple in Cambodia, complete with its own moat on which floated delicate pink and white water lilies. They stood hand in hand on the far side of the moat awestruck, just taking in the size and scale of the extravagant building. Then, as they crossed the moat on its wide walkway, Colette stared up at the temple with its exotic carvings and Khmer lines and she knew.

'I want to go there one day, Papa,' she said squeezing his hand. 'I'd like to see the real one.'

Her father laughed.

'Cambodia?' he said, his voice indulgent. 'There's nothing much there, ma petite. It's not really a place anyone would voluntarily travel to.'

'But *that's* there, isn't it? Angkor Wat? Surely *that's* worth seeing?'

They moved on together through the cloistered passageways and out into the central courtyard of the temple to admire its beauty from another angle.

'Other parts of Indochina have much more to offer than Cambodia. Annam, Cochinchina, Tonkin. The cities are said to be beautiful and the countryside has been put to good use. It produces enough rubber to make us all rich. If you ever go to Indochina my little one, that's definitely where you should aim for.'

He patted her hand to indicate that the subject was closed.

But Colette never forgot that temple; its cool symmetrical lines and mystical beauty had sent chills down her young spine. She cut a photograph of it out of a magazine and pinned it up on her bedroom wall and would stare at it and dream of being there, wandering through its cool cloisters sheltered from the tropical sun.

Years later, when she left her gentile private school and started to learn shorthand and typing at secretarial college, she sought out an antiquities evening class at the Sorbonne. She enrolled, excited to be able to deepen the knowledge that her long-held passion had led her to explore.

So, every Wednesday evening for several years, even after she'd started work as a secretary in an accountant's office, she made her way up to a chilly, bare, upstairs classroom in St Michel to join a small group of eccentric enthusiasts, who shared a common love of antiquities. They were taught by a classically odd-ball professor with wild hair and pebble glasses. Despite his appearance, he was an excellent and inspiring teacher. He took them through the rudiments of antiquity and archaeology, explaining everything in minute detail, in a way that brought the subject to life.

Colette was the only woman there. Her classmates all seemed interchangeable; dull, middle-aged bachelors who had trouble relating to the real world, but whose eyes would light up at a story about the dimensions of the pyramids at Giza or the facts behind the construction of Machu Picchu. Together they learned about the treasures of Ancient Greece, Ancient Egypt, the history, technical details and facts of various archaeological sites around the world. Colette absorbed all this information like blotting paper, aware that the friends she'd made at secretarial college and the group of young men they hung around with in bars in the Latin quarter at weekends would laugh if they knew how she spent her Wednesday evenings. They would certainly make fun of her classmates, of that she was sure, so she was very protective and secretive about her Wednesday evenings.

But much as she relished those lessons, she was really watching and waiting for the big prize: an opportunity to learn more about the excavations and restoration of ancient temples in French Indochina. That image of Angkor Wat from 1931 still burned in the back of her impressionable mind.

Finally, that opportunity came in the shape and form of Henri Boissière, a youngish, enthusiastic archaeologist, who had travelled home to Paris from Cambodia to take part in an academic symposium at the Sorbonne and had agreed to speak at one of the Wednesday evening classes. He lectured the class about his recent work as part of the team recovering Angkor Wat from the jungle and restoring it to its former glory. His talk was inspiring, all about how the original French archaeologists in the 19th century had stumbled across the jungle-covered ruins of an Angkor temple and had painstakingly chopped down trees and cleared away the undergrowth to reveal the fabulous structures underneath. Henri spoke for an hour, conjuring up exotic and fantastical pictures of the treasures buried in the Cambodian jungle. To Colette it all seemed impossibly romantic, and the whole time he talked, she sat there at the back of the class, spellbound. By the time he'd finished, she was half in love with him.

At that time Henri was a gawky, awkward, rather introverted academic in his mid to late thirties who had by then given up any hope of romance or marriage and whose whole life revolved around his work. He lived and breathed archaeology and his one true and enduring love was the temple of Angkor Wat.

After the talk Colette stood patiently aside, waiting for Henri to answer questions from the other students. When she got to the front of the queue, he looked up at her. A blush quickly formed on his pale cheeks and he looked away. Colette was too focused on her subject to notice the effect she was having on him. She plunged in and began asking him questions about the restoration project. Soon, he forgot his awkwardness and was answering with a passion that matched Colette's own. The answer to one question sparked another, then another, and by the time he had finished answering them the rest of the class had drifted away.

They progressed naturally on to a nearby bar-brasserie and carried on drinking red wine and talking about the glories of Angkor Wat well into the evening. When Colette finally arrived home, starry-eyed, far later than usual, her mother was sitting anxiously at the kitchen table in her dressing gown waiting for her.

'Papa and I were so worried about you, Colette! We thought something might have happened to you.'

'Something did happen to me, Maman,' Colette replied, her eyes shining.

Henri's shyness didn't stop him sending a note to Colette asking her out the next evening and once again the evening after that. Colette was delighted to spend time in his company and more than happy to show him something of Paris. He'd left France for Cambodia shortly after he'd left school and was little more than a boy. He had grown up in Marseille so hardly knew the city himself. Colette was careful to avoid taking him to the areas that she knew her friends frequented. So, they stuck to the more expensive restaurants nearer the Champs Élysées and the Rue de Faubourg St Honoré where she knew they wouldn't be spotted.

During those long, intimate evenings, Henri told her all about Cambodia and his life there. It seemed to consist mainly of days spent restoring and rebuilding Angkor Wat and evenings alone in his villa on the lake watching the wildlife. He had the occasional foray into Phnom Penh to report to his superiors in the colonial government and to get a taste of city life.

'Don't you ever get lonely?' she asked, and he laughed and shook his head.

'I love my job. It's all I ever wanted to do, so it's like a dream come true. And I love the country too.'

'Oh really?' Colette told him what her father had said to her about it on the day of the exhibition all those years ago. Henri laughed again.

'Lots of people think of it like that,' he replied. 'And it's true. The French don't exploit Cambodia like they do the rest of Indochina. It's a deliberate policy. Cambodia is thought of as more of a buffer to protect the rest of the French empire from landgrabs from Thailand than a place to plunder. I'm glad most people see it that way, actually.'

'Why is that?'

'Well, that way it will remain the domain of those who love it best and won't be in danger of becoming a popular destination. That way, we aficionados who know it and love it can keep it all to ourselves.'

'Tell me more about it,' she said and Henri obliged. As he spoke, his normally quiet features became animated and his dark eyes shone with pleasure. Caught up in the excitement of the moment and in the pictures he was painting with his words, Colette thought this man with the dark, enigmatic eyes was the most beautiful human being on earth.

'It's an exquisite country,' he told her. 'The people are kind. They are completely open and welcoming. They live the lives of simple Buddhists, and the rhythm and pace of life there is gentle and soothing. The countryside is stunning too – with jungle-clad hills in some places, and with great lakes with the most fantastic wildlife in others. You should really come and see it one day.'

'I'd love to,' she said, returning his smile, taking another sip of wine.

She was aware that he was falling in love with her. He had the same look in his eye that she'd observed in the eyes of a couple of the young men she and her friends sometimes met up with. She knew she stood out from the crowd, with her natural ringlets of red-gold hair, her alabaster skin and her willowy figure. But Henri's look was far less loaded with lust, far more genuinely romantic than those of the gauche young men in her crowd. And although she didn't feel quite the same way in return, she was falling under the spell he was casting about his life in Cambodia. And to Colette, Henri himself was inextricably linked to that magic.

But on the fourth evening over dinner, he brought her down to earth when he put down his knife and fork and said, 'I'm afraid to tell you, that I have to leave Paris the day after tomorrow.'

'Oh?' Colette's heart sank. How would she survive without these delicious, absorbing evenings in the company of this fascinating man, talking about Cambodia and the magical world of antiquities?

'Yes. It's the last day of the symposium at the Sorbonne tomorrow and I'm booked on a ship from Marseille in two days' time. But I can't say I'm looking forward to leaving Paris now.'

'But you're going back to Cambodia, surely that's what you want?'

'Well, yes,' he said slowly. 'But we will have to say goodbye. And you've given me a reason to want to stay here.'

She smiled at him and their eyes locked together for a long

moment, and then, to her surprise, he took her chin in his hand, brought her face towards his, and kissed her full on the lips. It was a passionate, long, lingering kiss and she began to wonder if there were hidden depths to Henri Boissière that he'd been keeping from her after all.

On the day he left for Marseille she took the morning off work and went to say goodbye to him at the Gare de Lyon. Her heart twisted with sadness when she saw him making his way across the concourse in a raincoat and hat and carrying a suitcase in each hand. He looked so vulnerable somehow, someone she'd like to take care of.

They walked together down the length of the long platform. Henri stowed his luggage in the first-class compartment of the train then he came back onto the platform to say goodbye. Once again they kissed and this time she saw that Henri had tears in his eyes.

'This is so hard,' he said. 'You know I'm in love with you, don't you?'

She nodded and looked down shyly, not able to meet his eyes. 'Do you think you could ever return that love?' he asked.

'Of course,' she said, lifting her eyes to his and kissing him on the lips again. 'I love you too,' and looking at him, his eyes brimming with love for her, remembering the stories he'd told her of Cambodia and Angkor Wat, she could almost believe it was true.

'I can't bear to part with you,' he said, then he hesitated and she could tell he was struggling with something.

'I was thinking of a way we could be together,' he went on. 'And there is a way. Would you marry me, Colette? I've never met anyone like you before and I don't think I could survive without you. If you say yes, I will arrange for you to get the next boat out to Cambodia and we will be able to marry in the Catholic church in Phnom Penh.'

She was stunned by his words. She'd thought about going out

to visit him in Cambodia but she hadn't thought he would ask
her to share his life there. Not so soon anyway. She hesitated, her
mind spinning. She didn't want to hurt him, but she wasn't sure
she could accept. This was all so sudden.

The whistle blew and the guard shouted for passengers to
board the train.

'Well?' his eyes were full of hope.

'I don't know...' she said. 'I need time.'

His face fell. 'I know. It was unfair of me to spring it on you
like that, but I've thought of little else since I met you. The offer
will remain open until you make your decision. Write to me
when you've made up your mind.'

He slipped a card into her hand, kissed her tenderly again
and got onto the train. Then, with clouds of black smoke and
steam billowing out across the station, much hissing and puffing
and another blast of the whistle, the great locomotive began to
move forward and gather speed. Colette ran alongside Henri's
carriage waving and blowing kisses until she reached the end of
the platform. She carried on waving until the train was out of
sight. Then, with a heavy heart, walking back towards the
concourse, she glanced down at the card he'd slipped in her
hand.

*M. Henri Boissière, Villa du Lac, Chong Khneas, Siem Reap,
Cambodia* was printed in fine, flowing script. The very names of
the places conjured up an image of Henri's white-painted villa
with its wide, shady verandas overlooking the great lake and
something inside her clicked. She knew she wanted to be there
with him, watching the birds rising from the water in the first
light of dawn.

Instead of going home she hurried straight to the offices of a
shipping agent and found out the name of the ship sailing from
Marseille to Kampong Som in Cambodia the next day. She asked
the agent to check the passenger list for a Henri Boissière. When
it was confirmed, she asked if she could send him a telegram.

'Of course, Mademoiselle. We can telegraph it from this office. It will arrive instantly.'

She dictated it to the agent there and then.

'My dearest Henri *stop* Thank you for your offer *stop* The answer is yes *stop* I will book my passage to Cambodia right away. With all my love, Colette.

4

ANGKOR WAT, CAMBODIA, 1995

Colette was deep in thought, staring across the moat towards the temple of Angkor Wat, remembering the day that Henri had introduced her to the temple for the very first time. They'd been fortunate enough to be completely alone there, wandering through its passages and prayer halls side by side, their footsteps echoing in the silence. It had been an incredible, life-changing experience.

'You want guided tour, madam?'

She started back to the present, and the memories melted away. A Cambodian tour guide stood in front of her, smiling a broad, betel-stained smile.

'Not just now thank you,' she said. 'I'll come back soon, though. I just wanted to see the outside today,' she returned his smile. 'I've just arrived in Siem Reap and it's been a long time since I was here.'

'The morning time is better. Temple will be closing shortly. I will be here,' he said bowing his head. 'Temple is opening at ten o'clock in the morning.'

'It may not be tomorrow,' she said, reluctantly. 'But I will come back very soon.'

'Not tomorrow, madam?' he put his head on one side, frowning, clearly unable to imagine why a tour of the temple wouldn't be the very first thing someone did when they arrived in Siem Reap.

'There's something else I need to do before I come back,' she muttered, half to herself.

'Very well, madam. See you another day.'

She wandered back to the taxi and asked the driver to take her back into Siem Reap.

'Could you recommend a hotel please? I'm afraid I don't know their names anymore.'

'Only one hotel fully open at the moment, madam,' the taxi driver said. 'Many others being built, many being refurbished. Many old ones have closed down. I can take you to the Grand Hotel d'Angkor.'

'That sounds expensive,' she said warily. It was where she used to go sometimes in the evenings to meet other ex-pats. She remembered it as easily the most luxurious and pricey place in Siem Reap.

'Not too expensive, madam,' the taxi driver smiled, watching her in the rear view mirror. 'Nothing in Cambodia is too expensive.'

'I suppose not,' she smiled back. Like many other Cambodians he was probably of the view that all westerners were wealthy, and to most Cambodians she supposed they were. Only Colette was on a budget. She'd scrimped and saved for this trip and hadn't bargained on staying anywhere so grand. But, if it was the only place available...

She wondered if anyone would remain from the staff who used to serve her when she would go with friends for cocktails or an evening meal. Would they still be here, or had the revolution swept them away too? Would the hotel still be undamaged even after years of war and bloodshed?

As they swept in through the entrance she was relieved to see that the building appeared unchanged, its opulent white frontage presiding over immaculately kept gardens. They drew in on the wide, sweeping drive and stopped under the giant portico. As Colette went up the front steps and the porters scurried about with her luggage, she was comforted to see that the beautiful building remained intact. It looked just the same as it had in the old days – if anything it looked even more pristine now.

She checked in under the glittering chandeliers of the marble lobby and was shown up to a beautiful, light, airy room that over-looked the swimming pool. She wandered out onto the balcony and leaned on the rail drinking in the beauty of the evening. The light was fading now, the sun streaking the sky red and pink, gradually dipping behind the palm trees beyond. A few swim-mers were pounding through lengths in the long pool below her. She breathed in the warm air and sighed deeply. It was so good to be back here. Soon she would return to the temple and have a proper look around, but before that, she needed to look for some-one. See if they were still here after all the turmoil of recent years.

She also promised herself that before she started out on her quest, she would have an early morning dip in that inviting pool. Colette was no stranger to swimming. During the summer months, she would often take an early morning swim in the unheated village pool in her Dordogne village. The pool here was different, though. It was bright blue and sparkling clean, instead of grimy, concrete-coloured. Here there were no stray waterweeds and the water was likely to be perfect body temperature.

That night, after a solitary dinner in the elegant dining room, she went to bed early but found sleep eluded her despite the comfort of the sumptuous bed. She was beset with visions from the past. Faces swam in and out of her mind – Achariya, Henri, as well as the two others she could never forget and whose photographs she had brought with her. And not only people, places came to her too in her half-waking state. The villa in Phnom Penh, lit up for a dinner party, and the villa on the lake too, its lights dancing on the black night-time waters of Tonlé Sap. What had happened to it? Had it been pulled down by the Khmer Rouge, overtaken by jungle, or was it still standing, occupied by squatters perhaps?

She recalled the day she'd left, standing on the balcony, staring in horror at the black-clad soldiers with their red bandanas jumping over the fence and powering across her grounds, holding their guns aloft. She'd never forgotten the feeling of sheer panic that had overtaken her, seeing them running towards the house. They were after her. She knew it. For a split-second she was paralysed with shock and fear, but then she sprang into action, grabbing a bag, tearing down the stairs and climbing nimbly over the bars of the veranda into her little motor launch, then setting off along the edge of the lake, keeping under the cover of the reeds, her heart in her mouth, listening for a shot to ring out that could end it all.

She woke with a start, drenched in sweat, her heart pounding. She looked around the room and the present returned to her with a profound sense of relief. They weren't coming for her anymore. She was safe now.

Before breakfast, true to her word, she went outside in her bathing costume and swimming hat, modestly shrouded in a bathrobe. There was no one else in the pool when she dived in and began her swim, but by the time she'd finished, half an hour later, there were several other pre-breakfast swimmers. She got out and a lifeguard approached her with a towel.

'Thank you,' she took it from him and then recognised his face. 'Narith! Is that you?'

'Madam! Madame Boissière!' He broke into a broad smile revealing broken teeth, lines around his eyes showing his age.

'You're still here!'

'Of course, madam. I came back.'

'I'm so pleased to see you. Where did you go?' she asked rubbing her hair with the towel.

His face fell and he shook his head sadly. 'We were all forced to leave Siem Reap.'

'Can you tell me where you went?'

Again, he shook his head and his eyes clouded over with memories. 'They were dreadful times. We were forced to march north to a different district. We had to work in the fields. There was not enough food. Many, many people died.'

'I'm so sorry, Narith. What a terrible time you must have had.'

He nodded. 'It was... very bad, madam. Guerrilla soldiers came and took over this hotel during that time. They burned all the furniture for firewood. They treat the place very badly. And after they left, Vietnamese soldiers lived here. It is only in the last year that the place has been rebuilt.'

'I wonder if you know... do you remember my old house-keeper, a lady called Achariya?'

Narith frowned, deep in thought for a moment, then his face cleared. 'Of course, madam. She was often with you in the town.'

'Yes. We were friends. We went to Phnom Penh together in April 1975, but we were separated at the embassy and she wasn't allowed to leave the country with me. I've tried to contact her over the years but with no success. Do you know if she is still living here?'

He shook his head. 'So sorry, madam. I not know. Many people didn't come back. Many sadly died. I haven't seen Achariya since before the revolution.'

Colette fell silent then, wondering about her old friend, plagued once again by that guilty feeling she'd carried with her for twenty years. Should she have stayed and protected her friend? Would they have survived if she had? An image of Achariya's face disappearing into the crowd as the truck drew away from the embassy came back to her. The last image she had of her faithful friend.

'You want water, madam? Tea?' Narith asked.

'Nothing for me thank you,' she said, pulling the towel

around her, suddenly chilled despite the warmth of the morning.

Later, Colette took a taxi from the hotel and asked the driver to take her down to the little settlement of Chong Khneas. They drove through the jungle on a flat, dirt road for a few kilometres and then the trees cleared and the lake came into view. Tonlé Sap. How she'd dreamed of it over the years, and here it was, unchanged, stretching out in front of them, its waters as still and silent as ever. They reached the water's edge and the taxi pulled up in front of a rickety wooden jetty. Colette paid the fare.

'You not go back to hotel later?' the driver asked.

'Maybe later on. I might be here for a couple of hours.'

'I wait,' he said decisively. She wasn't surprised. A well-heeled westerner was a rare meal ticket for the taxi drivers around here, so no wonder he wanted to hang on to her.

She approached the jetty and shaded her eyes against the fierce sun. In front of her, bobbing on the surface of the lake, were a dozen or so wooden structures. Most were painted bright blue and most looked dilapidated. She knew that some were dwellings, others were shops. There was even a church with a wooden cross fixed to its gable. A little way away, she knew there was a floating school for the children of the lake dwellers.

The village looked the same as it always had. Perhaps there were a few new dwellings here now, but Colette was relieved to see that it had survived the years of turbulence unscathed. Achariya had lived here in one of these floating huts, but try as she might, Colette couldn't remember which one it was.

An old woman in a conical hat was poling a long canoe-like boat stacked with fruit and vegetables past the jetty. She must be going to sell her produce in the market in another floating village a little way north on the lake. Colette waved to her and the old woman brought her boat up to the jetty.

'Good day to you, mother,' Colette said in her best Khmer, marvelling at how the courteous phrases were coming back to her. 'I'm looking for someone I used to know.'

'Yes, my dear. And who is that?'

'Achariya. Do you know her? She used to live in one of these floating houses.'

The old woman furrowed her brow for a moment then looked back at Colette with her sharp, brown eyes.

'Achariya not live here any more. She live further away now, on other side of lake.'

Colette's heart lifted in relief. She thanked the old lady and watched her go on her way, skilfully dipping and twisting her pole, propelling the boat forward until it had disappeared out of sight amongst the reeds. Achariya had survived. All those years Colette had spent punishing herself for leaving her behind at the embassy; all those years she'd wondered what had happened to her friend. She'd written letters that had never been answered, she'd even tried contacting the French Embassy about Achariya but without success, but now she could put all that aside. Her next task would be to find Achariya and speak to her, find out what happened to her during the revolution, try to make up for those lost years of silence between them.

She had little idea how she would find where Achariya was living now but the important thing was that Achariya was alive and was still here, living on Tonlé Sap. She stood on the side of the jetty and scanned the area. The place seemed quiet. Perhaps people were out at the market, most of the village children at school, but there were a couple of young men, little more than boys, a little way along the bank, preparing to launch a small craft. She approached them and said good morning, again in Khmer. They straightened up and greeted her politely. She asked them if they would be able to help her find someone. The boys looked at each other and shrugged.

'I will pay you,' Colette said. 'For your time, and for the fuel for the boat.'

The boys agreed. They launched the boat and brought it to the jetty. Colette stepped aboard. She explained that the person she was looking for was called Achariya and that she used to live in one of the boathouses in this floating village but that she'd moved away.

'But if you don't know where she is, we won't be able to find her,' one of the boys said.

'We can ask at these houses. Someone might know where she's gone. She used to live here.'

The boys shrugged again and the boat set off towards the floating village. As they got closer, Colette could see how shabby these floating homes looked, their roofs patched with corrugated iron, platforms repaired with different coloured strips of wood. Some owners had made little gardens with pot plants on their platforms, on others washing was hanging out to dry, limp in the hot, moist breeze. The first couple of boathouses they approached were clearly empty, on a third a dog on a leash barked furiously at them baring its teeth, but at the fourth an old woman pottered out onto the deck as they approached.

'Do you know a lady called Achariya?' Colette asked. 'She used to live here in Chong Khneas.'

The old woman thought for a long moment, shading her eyes against the sun. Then, she spat a stream of betel juice into the water.

'Achariya. Yes. She used to be here. She moved away a couple of years back. She got sick and went to the medical centre across the lake. Another family lives in her house now.'

'Thank you, mother,' Colette said, anxiety rising inside her chest at the mention of Achariya being sick. She turned to the boys.

'Do you know where the medical centre is?'

'Yes. It is a few kilometres south of here,' one replied. 'We could take you there, but...'

'I will pay for the fuel, please don't worry about that. I would be very grateful if you could take me.'

'All right. It will take about half an hour.'

They set off southwards, pulling out into the middle of the lake to catch the best currents. Soon they were skimming the surface at speed, the banks on either side a green blur. Colette strained her eyes to try to see where her villa had once been, but she could hardly make out the bank, let alone any buildings that might be on it. They passed more floating houses, some ancient-looking mangrove swamps, fishermen in stationary boats casting their nets, lily beds where buffalos wallowed. A flock of huge white florican birds flew past them gracefully, their wings beating in unison. Colette leaned back in the boat and closed her eyes, breathing in the warm, fresh air. She turned her face to the sun and remembered how she used to do that on the veranda at the lake villa. It was almost as if she was back there again, but now her pleasure was tinged with worry. How sick was Achariya? What was wrong with her? Would she even be there still?

It didn't take long to reach the medical centre: a floating, square hut painted blue like many of the other buildings. The boys tied the boat up at the dock and helped Colette onto the jetty.

She went in through the glass doors feeling a little nervous. The waiting room was full of people, mainly women with babies and children. It was noisy, there was a lot of chatter and many of the children were wailing at the tops of their voices. She made her way across the floor, stepping over the people who were sitting there, to the desk. She asked the receptionist if she knew a woman called Achariya. The woman nodded and smiled.

'I know her. She comes into the centre every week for her medication.'

'Are you able to tell me where she lives? I'm an old friend from long ago. I've come back to find her.'

'She lives in the third houseboat along from here. You can walk there along the jetty. She is always pleased to have visitors, but I warn you, she is very sick and very weak.'

With her heart racing, Colette thanked the woman and went

outside. She told the boat boys she would be a little while, then made her way along the uneven jetty to the third boathouse along from the medical centre. It was a small structure, clearly only meant to house one person. It was in very poor repair; the boards creaked and buckled under Colette's weight, and as she made her way towards the door, she noticed that the plants in pots outside had withered and died.

Feeling very anxious for Achariya now, Colette knocked firmly on the door.

'Hello, Achariya?' she called. 'It's me, Colette. Colette Boissière. Do you remember me?'

There was no reply so she tried again. 'It's Colette. I've come back from France to see you.'

Colette put her ear to the door and could just make out a faint voice saying, 'Come in, the door is a bit stiff.'

She pushed the door which creaked and scraped open and she stepped inside. It was dark in the hut. Ragged curtains were draped over the windows. The air was stifling and it had the sickly, cloying smell of a sickroom.

'Achariya?'

'Madam?' the voice from the corner was barely a whisper. Colette quickly crossed the hut to the figure in the bed and dropped to her knees beside it.

'It's me, Achariya.'

Colette put her arms around Achariya's fragile frame and held her to her. She could tell that her old friend was weak, perhaps sliding towards death. Her bones felt fragile, as light as a child's.

'It's good that you've come. I always wondered if you got back to France.' Achariya spoke in a halting, rasping voice, struggling for every word.

'I did. I did. And I've been living there ever since. But I've often thought about you and wondered what happened to you. I'm sorry you are so unwell, Achariya.'

'It cannot be helped. My heart is not so good. The result of all those years of starvation. It means that I need to rest most of the time or my heart will give out.'

Those words cut through Colette like a knife. Years of starvation! That was all her fault. If only she hadn't left Achariya at the embassy...

'I'm so sorry,' she muttered, tears in her eyes.

'You must not blame yourself, madam.' She felt Achariya's bony hand taking her own. How well Achariya knew her, even after all these years. 'Why don't you draw back the curtain a little, so we can see each other.'

Colette did as she suggested and sunlight flooded the dusty hut. She looked down at her old friend and saw how thin she looked, how her skin was stretched over her face and how sallow and lined it was.

'Your hair is grey now,' Achariya remarked smiling. 'Like mine.'

Colette wiped the tears away and smiled. 'We're not young anymore, are we?'

'You're right. Many years have passed.'

'Now, is there anything I can get you while I'm here? Food? Drink? Medicine?'

Achariya shook her head and with a twinge of guilt Colette reflected on how the tables had turned. She remembered how Achariya used to wait on *her* and how she'd hardly given it a second thought at the time; Achariya would serve her breakfast, lunch and dinner every day, cook whatever she wanted without a murmur of complaint.

'There's nothing I need, madam. I have enough food here. I don't eat much, and I have medicines until the end of the week when I will go along to the centre.'

'I could come back and go along there for you.'

Colette saw that Achariya was smiling, her still white teeth glinting in her sallow face.

'I would like that, madam. I would like that very much,'

Achariya said. 'I don't have long now, and I'm glad that you've come back. It means that I can go in peace.'

'Oh, don't talk like that, Achariya. You'll get better, won't you?'

Achariya shook her head. 'The doctors say I don't have long. I have been sick for a long time now.'

'Is that why you moved away from Chong Khneas?'

'Yes. To be nearer the medical centre. This little hut is all I need.'

Looking at her friend, Colette was filled with pity and sadness and the guilt she'd been carrying for years came back with full force. Achariya's illness was her fault. It was her fault that Achariya had spent years starving under the Khmer Rouge and was so sick now. But there was something Colette needed to ask her, despite those guilty feelings.

'Achariya,' she said kneeling beside the bed again and taking Achariya's hand. 'I came back especially to see you, but there's someone else I need to find too. I wonder, did you ever see her or hear anything of her?'

'Who, Sophia?' Achariya asked, her voice harsh, and the light went out of her eyes. She picked at her bedding with her free hand.

Colette nodded. 'Yes. I need to find her too. She is part of the reason I came back.'

Slowly, Achariya shook her head. 'I have never heard or seen anything of her,' she said. Colette caught her breath. This was a fresh blow.

'I wonder if she survived the revolution,' she said after a pause.

'Ha!' Achariya injected some of her old spirit into her voice and even managed to sit forward in the bed. 'That one! Nothing could destroy her, not even the Khmer Rouge. She will have survived, for sure. It's just a question of tracking her down.'

5

CAMBODIA, 1939

A s the French ocean liner neared the Cambodian coast and the port of Kampong Som, Colette stood impatiently at the rail, staring at the horizon, willing the land to come into sight. She couldn't wait to get her first glimpse of the country that would be her home. It had been a long, arduous journey, at least three weeks on board, enduring rough seas and cramped conditions, and in the latter stages, as they drew further east, the fierce, stifling heat.

They had called in at Saigon and Haiphong and she'd been able to go ashore for a few hours in each city and get a taste of what Indochina was all about. She'd taken a cyclo around Saigon to take in the sights and had been astonished at the beauty of this tropical city, with its opera house and huge, graceful colonial buildings, its customs houses and cathedral. The fact that all this was set amongst temples and pagodas added to its charm, and the palm trees and tropical scenery under bright blue skies made it doubly enchanting. She recalled what her father had said about this being the best of what Indochina had to offer.

But Henri had told her that Cambodia was different to Annam. The people were more laid back, the pace of life less frenetic. And standing on a street corner in Saigon, watching the endless traffic speed by, tooting and honking their horns, and the energetic efforts of the street sellers and cyclo riders to get trade, she realised what he meant and was looking forward to the more relaxed pace of Cambodia. She gripped the ship's rail as the horizon thickened and darkened and gradually she began to make out the shapes of land and buildings. A small town came into view. White buildings with red roofs above an astonishingly white beach, which curved around a huge bay contrasting with the blue of the South China Sea. On either side of the town the beach was fringed with palm trees and seemed to stretch for miles in each direction. She gasped at the beauty laid out in front of her. It was everything she'd been hoping for.

When the boat finally docked in Kampong Som harbour, Colette scanned the dockside for any sign of Henri. He'd promised he would be there to meet her. Her heart was beating frantically – with excitement and with pent-up nerves too. She hardly knew this man that on an impulse she'd agreed to marry, give up her pleasant, settled life and sail halfway round the world to be with.

Her parents had been aghast when she'd told them of her plans and had tried to persuade her against going, but being an adored only child, she got her way in the end. When she'd departed from Gare de Lyon they'd embraced and cried together and she was glad that she went with their blessing.

She and Henri had corresponded regularly during the two months between his departure and her own. In each letter he had described life in Cambodia and the work he was doing at Angkor Wat. He wrote with obvious enthusiasm for the country and for his vocation. He'd also spoken of his love for her and of how he was looking forward to their life together. She'd had no qualms about giving everything up to marry him. Her friends at the secretarial college had been astounded, if a little envious and admiring when she broke the news.

'Colette, you really are a dark horse! How have you managed to keep all this a secret from us all these months?' But they wished her well and gave her a great send off one evening in the bars and nightclubs of Montmartre.

She'd convinced herself that she was doing the right thing and that it was what she wanted, even though she acknowledged to herself that it was a giant leap in the dark and an enormous gamble.

'You can always come back, you know, anytime you want, if it doesn't work out,' her mother had said to her tearfully as they packed her trunk together in her bedroom overlooking the Champs Élysées. 'There will always be a home for you here.'

She embraced her mother with tears in her own eyes, but said, 'I know it will work out fine, Maman. Please don't worry about me. And you and Papa will have to come out and see us before too long. Henri says there's plenty of space. He has two homes, you know. A house in Phnom Penh and a villa on a lake near Angkor Wat.

Now, craning over the rail, shading her eyes against the sun, she finally caught sight of him. He was leaning against the bonnet of an open-topped car that was parked beside the customs sheds. He was shading his eyes too and scanning the ship's decks, clearly looking for her. Her heart gave a curious twist of recognition when she saw him. He was dressed in a linen suit and white solar topee and looked cooler and more at home than anyone else in the sweating, seething crowds on the dock. There, passengers were descending from the boat and standing around bemused, while hawkers, porters and coolies surged around them. The whole scene was a mass of noise, sweat and confusion.

Colette walked down the companionway, followed by a porter with her trunk and the moment she stepped onto the dock there was Henri in front of her, beaming broadly.

'Colette! My love! I'm so happy you're finally here.'

He enveloped her in his arms and kissed her full on the lips, ignoring the disapproving stares of the middle-aged French women passengers nearby. Then he led her through the crowd to the car, the porter following with the luggage. He drove her through the streets of the small port town to a quiet hotel. Drawing up on the front drive, the hotel porters came rushing out to greet them and take their luggage.

'We will drive up to Phnom Penh tomorrow,' Henri said. 'I can't wait to show you the villa there, but tonight we can stay here. It's quite a long drive. Several hours.'

The hotel was quaint and charming, set in the quiet back-streets amongst palm trees, with shady verandas overlooking luxuriant gardens. Colette was suffering from the heat so the owner switched on the overhead fans on the veranda.

'You must be exhausted,' Henri said. 'It's a long trip from Marseille.'

'I'm just glad to be here,' she said a little awkwardly. They were both nervous, and the conversation between them was stilted at first. But when they ordered their food and the waiter brought a bottle of champagne to the table and they'd both had a glass or two, conversation flowed more easily and they began to regain some of the intimacy they'd had during those few evenings in France. By the time the champagne was finished, everything around had taken on a rosy glow for Colette and when Henri suggested they go to their room, she quickly agreed. There, in the sweltering heat of the Cambodian afternoon, beneath the mosquito nets and under the whirring ceiling fans, they finally sealed the bond they had first entered into on that Paris station platform two months before.

The next morning they set off after an early breakfast of crois-sants, pains aux raisins and freshly brewed coffee, on the long road to Phnom Penh. They drove out through the outskirts of the little town and onto the dusty open road. With the wind in her hair, the sun on her face and the memory of the night before in her mind, Colette was overwhelmed with joy at finally being in Cambodia and starting out on her new life.

Once they had left the straggly outskirts of Kampong Som behind them and were out in the open countryside, Colette had her first glimpse of rural Cambodia close up. She was enchanted by what she saw; villages of stilted bamboo huts nestled amongst the palm trees, where cattle, chickens and pigs wandered freely between the houses, and emerald rice fields bordered by grassy embankments, where people in conical hats worked and water-birds waded on spindly legs. They drove through patches of jungle with enormous teak trees soaring above the undergrowth, where luxuriant and brightly coloured vegetation flourished in the wild. She had read about the beauty of the country but her first encounter with it took her breath away. They passed golden stupas and temple halls and columns of monks walking with begging bowls, their bowed heads shaved, clad in saffron-coloured robes, they passed mirror-like lakes where buffalo wallowed, and crossed fast-flowing rivers on rickety wooden bridges.

There was little traffic on the road, the occasional bullock cart hauling a precarious load of straw or logs, the odd pony cart ferrying children to school, but more often the locals were riding dilapidated bicycles and wobbling across the road as they stared at the motor car and the passing strangers.

To Colette this was a real adventure. It felt as though she and Henri were intrepid explorers, discovering an exotic, alien land for the first time. Sometimes Henri would turn to look at her and take her hand when he wasn't changing gear. He would smile at her and she would smile back, basking in the warmth of his gaze. It was wonderful to be alone with Henri after so many months of waiting and in some ways she wished the journey could last for ever. But another part of her couldn't wait to get to Phnom Penh, to see the sights of the city and spend her first night in Henri's Phnom Penh villa. The real prize at the end of her long journey would be Siem Reap and Angkor Wat. Henri had told her they would spend a couple of days in Phnom Penh to help her acclimatise and to buy supplies, before driving on to his villa on the lake. She couldn't wait to be there and to see for the first time the ancient temple that she'd spent so much of her life imagining.

They entered the city through streets of wooden stilted houses. Colette was surprised to see that there was little motorised traffic even here in the capital city. There were ox-carts and horse-drawn taxi-cabs trotting along the dusty roads. They drove through markets, teeming with life, stacked with exotic fruits and vegetables, jewellery and colourful silks. Food-sellers were cooking over open fires, filling the air with aromas of mouth-watering spices. They passed a couple of temples and an incredibly elaborate building with a golden roof.

'That's the royal palace,' Henri remarked, swerving to avoid a bullock cart. Then they were driving through the French quarter where the buildings were beautifully proportioned.

'It's just like Saigon,' Colette said, looking around in awe, remembering the opera house and other beautiful French build-ings in that city. They drove through streets lined with shop-houses, heaving with life, and passed a wide-open square with large gardens in the centre. Then Henri was turning in between some iron gates and crunching to a halt on a gravel drive.

'This is it,' he said. 'Our home in Phnom Penh.'

Colette stared out at the beautiful, square, white-painted house, shaded by plane trees, with its deep verandas and shut-tered windows. She was filled once again with joy.

'Come on inside.' Henri vaulted down and came round to open Colette's door but she was already out of the car and crossing the drive, walking towards the front door. Two servants came out to meet them, Kiry, the cook and Som the houseboy. They gave her broad smiles and bowed deeply. Colette didn't know quite how to react. No one had ever bowed to her before, but she smiled graciously, bowed her own head deeply and thanked them.

Inside the cool, marble entrance hall she stopped and stared. There was a galleried hallway above. Was this all hers now?

'Oh, Henri. This is marvellous. I hadn't imagined anything so grand,' she said.

'Come. I'll show you round,' he said and whisked her around the ground floor. A high-ceilinged dining room hung with crystal chandeliers, a large drawing room, all tastefully furnished in silks in muted colours.

'Come and see the upstairs,' Henri said and as she walked towards the wide, sweeping staircase that rose towards the gallery, Henri scooped her up. She shrieked with laughter and reminded him they weren't married yet and he just laughed too and carried her upstairs.

'It's a good job I'm used to lifting heavy rocks at the temple,' he joked and she swatted his arm.

There were two guest bedrooms, a bathroom and a master suite. Everything was beautifully furnished and immaculately clean. The master bedroom opened out onto a balcony over-looking the gardens opposite. There was a four-poster bed shrouded in mosquito netting. Beside the window was a velvet chaise longue and in the corner a dressing table. On it were laid silver hairbrushes and combs.

'I bought that especially for you,' Henri said and she smiled at him, touched at how thoughtful he was.

'Come here,' he said, holding his arms out and she went to him. He took her in his arms and kissed her tenderly, and they sank down on the bed together, inside the mosquito netting and made love for the first time in their new home.

Afterwards, Colette drifted off to sleep and when she awoke there were dark shadows in the room and through the open window she saw that the light was going from the sky.

'You slept for a long time, ma petite,' Henri said stroking her hair. 'But we must get up now. I thought we could have dinner at the French Officers' Club. I can't wait to introduce you to all the other expats.'

'All right,' she said a little reluctantly. She would have preferred to spend a quiet evening at home together, but she was flattered at Henri's enthusiasm to introduce her to his friends and didn't want to spoil the moment by objecting to his plans.

When they'd bathed and dressed, Henri drove them the few hundred metres to the club in a pretty yellow building over-looking the wide Tonlé Sap river. The bar was on the first floor. It had airy balconies which caught the breeze from the river. Henri found them a table by the window and ordered champagne. One by one people came up to be introduced to Henri Boissière's attractive new fiancée. Colette soon found her jaw ached from smiling and repeating the same platitudes over and over again. There was the French Resident of Phnom Penh, Charles Leroux, a tall, distant man with an impressive moustache,

'Delighted to meet you, my dear. My wife, Fleur will be in soon. She will show you the ropes. You must come and dine with us soon,' he said vaguely, before melting away.

Then Henri introduced her to several administrators and their wives, a couple of journalists, the head of the forestry department and a few rubber planters.

'Oh, I didn't realise rubber was produced in Cambodia,' Colette said, shaking the hand of Olivier Baudoin, a stocky, muscular man.

'It's mostly over towards Cochinchina, but we have a couple of plantations in Kompong Cham province too. That's where I'm based. I'm just down in Phnom Penh for some R&R. Cambodia came a bit late to the Indochina rubber party, but things are booming now.'

Henri ordered food and by the time the hors d'oeuvres of king prawns arrived, Colette was feeling a bit squiffy from the amount of champagne she'd downed to dampen the nerves she'd felt at being introduced to all these strangers. She wasn't normally shy, but found the influx of new people on top of the exhaustion from the journey and being plunged into a completely new environment had shaken her confidence a little.

Henri took her hand over the table. 'Don't worry. You'll soon get to know everyone and people here are mostly really friendly.'

'Mostly?' she asked sharply, but he just smiled and tucked into his food.

When they'd finished their meal, Colette noticed a ripple of activity at the door and a stylish woman appeared through the huddle of people. She was striking. Tall, her dark hair cut short in the latest Parisian style, she wore a low-cut grey dress that floated around her slim figure. She made a B-line for Henri and Colette's table.

'Henri, old boy. You told me your fiancée was young, but you didn't tell me how beautiful she was. Hello, my dear. I'm delighted to make your acquaintance.'

She held out her hand rather imperiously and Colette took it automatically.

'This is Fleur Leroux, the Resident's wife,' Henri said. 'Fleur, this is Colette, my fiancée.'

After they'd shaken hands, Fleur said, 'Can I come and sit down with you for a little while, my dear? I'd like to get to know you and to explain the lie of the land here. Cambodia can be quite tricky to navigate for a newcomer.'

Henri stood up. 'I'll leave you ladies to it, then,' he said and moved away towards the bar.

Fleur slid into the seat next to Colette and lit a cigarette. She offered the packet of Gitanes to Colette who shook her head.

'I gave up the day I boarded the ship. I'm trying to be good.'

'Ha!' Fleur laughed with a hint of derision. 'You have to take what pleasures you can in this place, my dear and booze and ciggies are amongst the least harmful of those, I have to tell you.'

Colette found it hard to keep the polite smile from vanishing. 'Whatever do you mean?'

'Let's just say, life can get a little boring in this backwater. I don't want to disillusion you on your very first day, but I wouldn't be doing you any favours by sugaring the pill. As I said, we girls have to take our pleasures where we can.'

'Oh,' Colette said in a small voice, feeling deflated. It was hard to understand what Fleur might mean, looking around her at the bustling bar full of Europeans who looked as though they were enjoying themselves, and outside at the twinkling lights strung between the lampposts, that cast pools of glittering light on the waters of the Tonlé Sap river. 'It seems quite enchanting to me,' she replied, meaning it.

'Yes, well, it's your first day,' Fleur said, picking tobacco from her tongue. 'And I agree, the country does have a sort of superficial charm at first. But it wouldn't be fair not to warn you. For all its charm and the apparent friendliness of the natives, Cambodia does have its dark side too.'

'Dark side?' Colette asked, alarmed. She looked round for Henri, but he was engaged in conversation with one of the rubber planters at the bar.

'Yes. Well of course the French Government exploits the natives and the country mercilessly. The peasant farmers pay the highest taxes in Asia and there's a hell of a lot of resentment. One of the French tax collectors was beaten to death in a remote village a couple of years back. You mark my words, there's deep unrest beneath the surface here.'

'No! Oh, how terrible,' Colette said, genuinely distressed, and what had started out as a light, pleasant evening full of promise had suddenly turned sour. She looked back at Fleur's face with its heavy makeup and knowing look, one elegant eyebrow arched, and wondered if the hasty decision she'd made to give up her life in Paris and rush out here, had been the right one.

6

PHNOM PENH, 1939

The next morning they set off early to drive to Siem Reap. Colette was subdued on the journey and stared out vacantly as they passed through the outskirts of Phnom Penh without registering much about her surroundings. She had barely slept. The words of the Resident's wife had chilled her to the core and kept going round and round in her mind. She was plagued by images of a crowd of villagers setting upon the French tax collector, first surrounding him, then beating him to the ground, kicking him and hitting him with sticks. How could this have happened here, in this quiet, gentle, welcoming back-water of French Indochina? But eventually, exhausted, she'd fallen into a restless sleep but had awoken with a start. One of the shutters had come loose and was banging against the wall of the house.

She got out of bed and went over to the window. It was raining hard outside, but inside the bedroom it felt airless and close, so she pushed the shutters back and peered out. It was rain like no rain she'd ever seen before. It was as if a solid wall of water was pouring down in front of the window, soaking the balcony and splashing off the roof onto the drive. The skies were dark but occasionally a fork of lightning would crack through the blackness, turning the park opposite and the surrounding buildings a ghostly yellow for a second. Colette stood there, mesmerised. She was tempted to go out onto the balcony and experience it to the full but held back, not wanting to get soaked to the skin. Every so often a gust of wind would blow the rain in her direction and before long her hair and shoulders were wet through, but still she stayed where she was. She couldn't tear herself away. She'd never encountered anything like this before.

She had no idea how long she stood there by the window watching the rain. The street outside was deserted, but at one point under the light of the flickering streetlamps she saw a little family struggle past pulling a hand cart filled with clutter. They were dressed in rags, obviously destitute. Mother, father, two tiny children, their heads bent against the driving rain. Colette had seen beggars the day before in some of the villages and a couple on the pavement outside the Officers' Club, but this scene really brought home to her the poverty that surrounded them, despite the richness of the natural environment and the luxury in which the exp-pats lived.

Her heart went out to that little family and Fleur's words came back to her once again, 'For all its charm, Cambodia does have its dark side too.' She was beginning to see the truth of those words. She was half-minded to grab some money and run out into the rain to hand it to them, but the next second she felt Henri's arms enveloping her and his lips on her neck. 'Come to bed, chérie, you'll catch your death of cold standing here. You're all wet. Let me fetch you a towel.' And she'd allowed him to lead her away from the window, to take off her wet nightgown, dry her hair and body tenderly and to wrap her in a towel.

'You're very quiet, chérie,' Henri said now, glancing across at her in the passenger seat.

'I'm sorry. I'm just thinking about some things that Fleur said to me.'

'What did she say?' he asked, his voice half amused, half curious.

'She said that despite its charm, Cambodia has its dark side, and that there's a lot of discontent amongst the peasant population.'

'I wondered what she was saying to you. You looked quite distressed when I glanced over at one point. I wish she didn't have to be quite so blunt.'

'Is it true? That there's a lot of simmering resentment?'

Henri sighed. 'This is a colony, Colette. We French are not here for humanitarian reasons. We need to make money from the enterprise so we can afford to keep the place running. There is bound to be some resentment from the locals. But it is nothing like the situation in Cochinchina.'

'What's happening there?' she asked in alarm.

'There has been rioting in the rubber plantations over the past few years. I can't say I'm surprised. The big estate owners like Michelin exploit the coolies terribly. And now they've had enough.'

'Fleur mentioned that a tax collector was killed recently in Cambodia, though.'

'I shouldn't have left you with that woman! It was your first day here and I thought she might have some tact. There are two sides to that story. Rumour has it that the collector was taking liberties with the villagers, that he showed no mercy to those too poor to pay, that he'd made some very harsh decisions. So, you see, there are often different ways of looking at things. There's a lot going on beneath the surface here.'

'Is it like that in Siem Reap?' she asked.

Henri paused, slowing down to let a herd of goats driven by a small, ragged boy cross the dusty road.

'Throughout Cambodia the locals have to pay their taxes. Some struggle, and you'll have seen beggars in Phnom Penh who've had to give up their land, but the Siem Reap region is very

fertile. Life is easier for people there. And they can make money
fishing on Tonlé Sap or working on the restorations at Angkor
Wat. So, on the whole you won't see beggars there and people are
content.'

Colette let out a sigh of relief and turned her attention to the
countryside. They were just passing a village temple with a huge
golden buddha that soared into the sky, its surface glinting in the
sunlight. Monks knelt at its feet, holding lotus blossom as offerings. Her heart lifted at the beauty of the scene and she soaked it
up, putting her qualms aside.

At last they rolled into the settlement of Siem Reap. It was a
small town of mainly stilted bamboo structures set amongst palm
trees with a few French properties dotted around, some municipal buildings and a huge hotel.

'Our place is a few kilometres out of town, but this is the
local centre where we can come to the market and to drink at
the hotel,' Henri explained. 'They built that at the beginning of
the thirties, anticipating an influx of tourists to see Angkor
Wat.'

'And has that happened?'

'It did for a couple of years, but lately people haven't travelled
as much because of the situation in Europe.'

'It *is* very worrying,' she said, biting a nail, thinking of her
parents in Paris. She'd read the papers with mounting alarm over
the past couple of years, seeing pictures of German troops
storming through Austria and Czechoslovakia, wondering where
Hitler's aggression would lead.

'Yes, it is indeed. The latest reports are that there's a build-up
of German troops on the Polish border. If Hitler does have the
gall to invade Poland, it will certainly lead to war.'

'How terrible...' and again she thought about her parents,
their tear-stained faces on the platform at the Gare de Lyon. But
the night before she'd left, her father had taken her aside and
said, 'It's good that you're going to the Far East. Best to get away

from Europe at any cost at the moment. Things are going to get very sticky here.'

'But what about you and Maman, Papa?' she'd asked, worried by his words.

'No need to be concerned about us. We're getting old now and stuck in our ways. We would never leave Paris. No, it's your life that matters, Colette.'

She thought about how they'd promised to come and visit her, but how that might not be possible if war broke out.

They were now driving through deep rainforest on their way to Tonlé Sap. She shuddered looking around her at the luxuriant but all-pervasive undergrowth dripping with moisture. She noticed a snake slither off the road and into a clump of bamboo. Again, she shuddered and wondered if she'd done the right thing coming here.

But her spirits lifted when the strip of jungle came to an end and they were driving through rice fields again, their flooded surface reflecting the sun. The road ahead was made of red soil, contrasting starkly with the greenery that surrounded it.

'Not far now,' Henri said and she could see from his eyes that he couldn't wait to show her the villa. They continued along the dusty road. Now either side of it looked like marshland or flood-plains, with reeds and mangroves growing in the shallow water. Buffalo wallowed in muddy puddles, surrounded by wading birds.

'In the hot season these plains are dry,' Henri explained. 'It is much more beautiful in the wet season. You are coming at the best time of year. In the dry season the villa is sometimes left high and dry.'

There was a bend in the road and then they were driving between the flood plain and the Tonlé Sap lake itself. Colette leaned over to look properly and gasped at the beauty of the huge, glittering stretch of water, stretching as far as the eye could see, interspersed with verdant green islands, patches of water lily and mangrove swamp. Waterbirds waded or flew in flocks above the water. On the far, blue horizon the lake melded into the sky. They passed a group of rickety huts which were actually afloat on the water, where people were cooking out on their platforms or lounging in hammocks watching fishing lines, where small children swam and played in the water.

'You didn't tell me about this?' Colette said. 'Are there a lot of these villages?'

'Yes. There are several settlements like this around the lake. Most of the people who live here are of Vietnamese origin. They were brought to Cambodia by the French to build roads and other infrastructure. They are sometimes resented by the locals for that. That's why they have to live on the water. They are not allowed to own property here.'

'Oh,' she said, staring at the shabby, floating homes, wondering about the hardships the inhabitants were suffering. Was this another aspect of the dark side of this country that Fleur had talked about?

But she didn't have long to ponder that thought. They plunged on through another patch of jungle and when they emerged from the trees the villa was there in front of them. Built right on the edge of the shimmering water, so close it could almost be floating on the lake. It was bigger and grander than the house in Phnom Penh, painted white with deep, shady verandas on all sides, large windows and an imposing porch with pillars either side of a portico.

'It's beautiful, Henri,' she said and he beamed with pride. He drove through the open gates, through the well-kept grounds and drew the car up in front of the porch.

Just like in Phnom Penh the servants came out to meet them. A cook and a houseboy, a gardener and a kitchen maid. Henri introduced them and Colette shook hands awkwardly and they all bowed and curtsied when they took her hand and dropped their gaze to their feet.

'I've also engaged a housekeeper for you,' Henri said. 'She's coming tomorrow. She will be good company for you. She's about your age, actually.'

'Oh?' Colette looked at him with consternation. Hadn't she got him for company? Why would they need to pay someone for that?

'Don't worry. You'll like her. She speaks good French,' he said, misunderstanding her concern. 'Now, come on inside. I'll show you around.'

For the second time in twenty-four hours Henri proudly walked her around his residence. He told her that he actually owned this house – he had bought the land and had it built to his own design. The other house in Phnom Penh was provided to him by the colonial government because of his position of Chief Archaeologist.

'I don't know why the house they provided is in Phnom Penh rather than here, when here is where I work,' he said, laughing. 'Typical chaotic French bureaucracy. But I took matters into my own hands a few years ago and bought this stretch of land from a local farmer. The architect who designed the Grand Hotel D'Angkor in Siem Reap helped to draw up the plans and a lot of the construction workers from the hotel came to build the house. It all fell into place rather well, actually.'

'That's an understatement. I'd say it's magnificent,' she said, wandering around the galleried hallway with its polished oak floor and high ceilings, running her finger over the artefacts on display.

'Come into the drawing room. There are beautiful views of the lake from there.'

He opened some double doors and led her through into a huge square room furnished with comfortable looking sofas and armchairs and lined with bookcases. All along the opposite wall, French windows opened out onto a wide veranda and even from where she stood in the doorway, see could see that the view of the lake was breath-taking, the blue water stretching into infinity.

'Oh, Henri,' she said following him out onto the veranda and leaning on the rail. 'I never imagined it was as beautiful as this.'

He drew her towards him and kissed her full on the lips. 'It's all the more beautiful now you're here to share it with me. I'll get the houseboy to bring us tea out here and we can sit and enjoy the view.'

They sat down in a couple of planter's chairs, cooled by ceiling fans and Colette feasted her eyes upon the beauty of the surroundings. She'd been trying to picture what it might be like ever since she'd first met Henri, but now she was here she completely understood why he loved the place so much. It was not just the view, but the whole ambience of the place that came from overlooking this expanse of peaceful water. The villa seemed to soak up a sense of calm from the water itself.

Later, they walked around the grounds and Henri showed her some of the specimen trees he'd planted and the pond with a fountain in the middle of the drive he was very proud of. Then he showed her upstairs and as in Phnom Penh Colette was enchanted by the master suite and how Henri had bought her a dressing table and chaise longue to relax on.

'You are so thoughtful,' she said, kissing him. 'Thank you for everything.'

They went out onto the balcony where there were some cane recliners and another stunning view of the lake. From here there was a view of a small island a little way out on the water.

'You can see the cranes nesting there in the right season,' Henri told her.

'How marvellous!' she said, leaning on the rail and watching the teeming birdlife on the water. She closed her eyes and all she could hear was the calling of the birds and the lapping of the water beneath the verandas of the house. But then came another sound. The sound of a motor car approaching the house at speed.

Henri's face clouded over. 'Whoever can that be,' he said and strode to the edge of the balcony to see. Colette went with him and watched as a small, red, open-topped sports car burst through the front gates, and skidded to a halt in front of the house.

'Damn him!' Henri said. 'I will have to go down. I won't be long.'

'Who is it?' she asked, alarmed.

'Oh, just one of my assistants. I told them not to bother me.'

He disappeared into the room and she heard his steps running down the stairs. From her vantage point she watched as a dark-haired man vaulted out of the car and ran towards the house. He was taller and younger than Henri, lithe and agile.

'Boissière!' he shouted as he mounted the front steps.

Then she heard Henri's voice, raised in anger. 'What the hell, Gilbert, I told you not to disturb me this weekend, didn't I?'

'There's been an accident at the temple, sir. Quite serious I'm afraid. You'll have to come back with me.'

7

ANGKOR WAT, 1995

The guide Colette had met on her first day in Siem Reap hadn't forgotten about her. He was sitting on the wall of the bridge over the moat, smoking a cigarette and swinging his legs, when she arrived by tuk-tuk the day after she'd been to see Achariya.

'You came back!' He greeted her with a broad smile and jumped off the wall to join her.

'I waited for you. Now, come, let me show you the temple,' and he waved her onto the wide bridge. Colette allowed herself to be ushered forward and as they crossed the moat surrounding the great temple, he started telling her the history of the Khmer empire. She wasn't listening. She knew all this already. Her eyes strayed to the magnificence of the building before them and its five symmetrical, conical towers. She experienced a spine-tingling moment. Just looking at this ancient, mystical temple, which must be one of the most beautiful buildings in the world, filled her with wonder.

She remembered how it had been when Henri had brought her here for her first official visit, the day after they first arrived at the lake villa. She'd paused on the bridge then too, just taking it all in, shivers going through her at the mystical splendour of the place, just as they were now. Now the guide ushered her towards some wooden steps that protected the worn stone ones underneath and must have been constructed for visitors. She recalled vividly scrambling up broken stone steps previously, laughing as Henri half-lifted her, remembering the feel of his strong hands on her waist.

Inside the elaborately pillared cloisters of the outer chambers of the great temple, she followed the man as he guided her round, pointing out important frescos on the wall, telling her the history behind the carvings, showing her the many extraordinary reliefs depicting apsaras or heavenly nymphs. They were intricately worked, and had now been restored to perfection. She recalled how most of these stones had been covered in moss and lichen when she'd first visited and Henri had told her how his team were painstakingly restoring the frescos by removing the lichen that had built up over the ages, but that they had to take great care not to damage the artwork by doing so.

She followed the guide through several layers of corridors, that intersected cleverly to allow the light and breeze from the central courtyard to illuminate and ventilate the whole interior. Every so often they would come across a primitively carved statue, standing alone on a plinth, and the guide would explain that this was the god of such and such and that it was revered by certain people for certain purposes. Colette was in awe of how much more restoration had taken place since she'd last seen the temple. She wondered what had happened to it during the revolution, but her answer came soon enough. The guide pointed her to some round holes that scarred one of the frescos.

'These are bullet holes made from a gunfight during the revolution,' he pronounced solemnly and Colette shuddered at the sacrilege involved in shooting at such a sacred and mystical place. Looking into the man's eyes now she wondered what he had suffered during those turbulent years, but didn't want to bring back painful memories by asking him.

They emerged through the maze of corridors into the central courtyard of the temple and Colette gasped in surprise. When she'd first seen it, this area had been filled with a tangle of trees and undergrowth. Under Henri's initial supervision it had been carefully cleared, but that restoration had taken decades and hadn't even been completed when she'd been forced to leave in 1975. Now it was a large, open area, exposing the inner walls of the temple complex. In the middle was a large pond that had been positioned to provide a perfect reflection of the temple towers, adding depth to the scene and another perspective of its beauty. The pond was bursting with white flowering lilies and surrounded by ornamental palm trees.

'Can I sit here for a moment?' she asked overwhelmed by the beauty around her. 'I just need to take it all in.'

'Of course. You take photos, madam?'

'Soon. Not just now.'

For now, she just wanted to digest the perfection that surrounded her and to make some sense of the memories that were besieging her. She sank down on the stone steps and the guide wandered away tactfully to give her some space. Then, the memories really started coming back. She recalled the first time she'd come through that entrance into the great courtyard. It was actually the day before her first official visit, and the sky was already losing its light by the time they'd arrived late on that first afternoon. There was no pond in the courtyard then, just under-growth, tumbledown ruins and big, stagnant puddles that attracted snakes.

She'd jumped in the car with Henri when he'd set off from the villa to follow Luc Gilbert back to the temple on that first evening. Henri was tense and white-faced. His knuckles were white on the steering wheel and Colette sensed that anger simmered under the surface as he drove.

'I know Luc Gilbert,' Henri fumed. 'He won't have been taking proper safety precautions on the site despite promising me before I left. He is slapdash, he wants instant results.'

Colette remained silent and fixed her gaze on the taillights of the car ahead. Henri had not mentioned Luc Gilbert to her before. She was surprised about that and also surprised at the apparent antipathy between the two men. Henri followed Gilbert's speeding car as it skidded round bends and accelerated over the bumpy, unmade road. He was concentrating so hard, Colette didn't want to distract him with conversation so they passed the journey in silence.

At last, they arrived in front of Angkor Wat and she'd had her first glimpse of the astonishing ruin. It was all the more dramatic in the charged circumstances of the visit. There it stood in the fading light, its elaborately tiered roof illuminated by the setting sun in reds and golds. They'd got out of the car and rushed over the bridge and scrambled up the rough steps and into the temple. When they'd reached the inner courtyard, they saw straight away that something calamitous had happened. A wooden scaffold that had been erected against one of the inner walls had collapsed. It lay in splinters on the ground amongst a pile of fallen rocks and stones. A group of men clad only in sarongs and loin cloths were clustered around something on the ground and two other men sat miserably on nearby rocks, bleeding from wounds on their limbs. The whole scene was eerily lit by hurricane lamps propped up on poles.

Colette hung back feeling helpless. She knew nothing about first-aid, and she was ashamed to admit that the sight of blood made her faint. She sat down, in the very spot that she was sitting now, some fifty-six years later, and watched helplessly as the drama unfolded right before her eyes. Luc Gilbert sauntered after Henri towards the huddle of men but instead of going further into the centre of the group, remained standing on the edge. Colette watched breathlessly. In a few minutes the bodies parted and two men emerged carrying another man between them, his body floppy, his head lolling about. Henri followed them, his head bowed. He paused and spoke to Luc Gilbert. Colette couldn't hear what they were saying but she could see from their gesticulations and body language that it was a tense exchange.

Then Henri took down one of the hurricane lamps and came over to where she was sitting.

'I'm so sorry about this, my love. Something terrible has happened. A rock fell on a man when the scaffold collapsed. He must have died instantly of head injuries. I will need to go and speak to his family. They live very close by. I will take you back to the car. Would you wait there for me?'

'Of course, but I could come with you.'

'No, that's a kind offer, but it would be better if I went alone. I shouldn't be too long.'

He took her arm and by the light of the hurricane lamp, guided her back through the echoing passages of the temple, the light flickering eerily, lighting up hidden passages and recesses, creating strange, dancing shadows.

'I'm so sorry, Colette,' Henri said when they emerged onto the bridge. 'It's so unfortunate that you are seeing Angkor Wat for the first time in these dreadful circumstances. I will bring you back here tomorrow and show it to you properly.'

'It really doesn't matter, Henri, just concentrate on that poor man.'

'I know... I know, it's truly terrible. Nothing has ever happened like this before.' In the lamplight she saw that his face was ravaged with grief. 'I hold myself responsible.'

'You mustn't do that. You weren't here when it happened, after all.'

'But I am the chief curator and archaeologist. I'm responsible for everything that happens on the site.'

They had reached the car now. He opened the passenger door and she climbed inside. Henri leaned in and kissed her tenderly, then set off across the patch of scrubby land. He was following the group of men that were carrying the body of the dead worker back to the little group of huts on the other side of the clearing.

Colette watched him go, then sank back against the leather seat of the car, exhausted by the shock of what had just happened. The light was almost gone from the sky but as she looked at the temple, another hurricane lamp came bobbing across the bridge towards the clearing. To her surprise it approached her car. Her heart sank as she realised it must be Gilbert. He stopped beside the car and held out his hand.

'I'm Luc Gilbert,' he said. 'How do you do? You must be Boissière's fiancée.

She shook his hand a little reluctantly and he held hers for a moment longer than necessary.

'I'm Colette,' she said.

'I'm so sorry you've had to witness this. Boissière shouldn't have let you come.'

'It was me who insisted on coming,' she said coldly.

'Of course. You look like a woman who knows her own mind. This is such an unfortunate turn of events, but I'm afraid Boissière's tenure as chief curator of Angkor Wat is rather jinxed.'

He put his elbows on the top of the car door and leaned in to speak to her.

'Oh?' the hair rose on the back of her neck. Whatever could Gilbert mean by that?

'It's hardly surprising really, when you think about how he came by the job,' he went on, 'But of course, you know all about that, don't you?'

'He was appointed. Three years ago, that's all I know.'

Gilbert gave a hollow laugh. 'He was assistant curator at first. To a great man. Pierre Samuels. Of course, your fiancé had a lot of potential, but he was promoted before his time in extraordinary circumstances.'

Despite not trusting this man, Gilbert had piqued Colette's interest.

'Whatever to you mean?' she asked.

'I'm really surprised you don't know this. Pierre Samuels was killed. Set upon in the forest and beaten to death by robbers. He was carrying the wages for the site workers. A considerable sum. Everyone knew he brought the wages in cash from the bank in Siem Reap on a Friday evening. Some opportunists took their chance.'

'That's truly terrible,' she said, realising that her hands were trembling with shock. It *was* strange that Henri hadn't told her that story. Perhaps he hadn't wanted to unsettle her, or to put her off coming here to be with him. Once again Fleur's words returned to her. *Cambodia has its dark side.*

'So, you can see what I meant now. Henri was promoted ahead of his time in extraordinary circumstances.'

Colette didn't know what to say in response, so she remained silent. She was uncertain about Gilbert's motives in revealing this information, but what was quite clear to her was that he hadn't got Henri's best interests at heart.

'Well,' Gilbert said. 'I'm sorry to be the bearer of bad tidings. I can see that I've unsettled you. I will leave you in peace now. I'll wait in my own car until Henri comes back. I wouldn't want to leave you here on your own after dark.'

She watched him get into his own car that was parked in front of Henri's. Gilbert was right. He had unsettled her. What with the shock of the accident, the walk through the dark temple and Gilbert's revelation, her heart was hammering against her ribs. It didn't start to slow down until she saw the light of Henri's hurricane lamp bobbing across the clearing.

Fifty-six years later she was still musing over that first encounter with Luc Gilbert. From where she was sitting on the temple steps she could see the spot on the far wall that his team had been repairing when the scaffolding had collapsed. She shuddered, even in the heat, thinking about that evening. The events had tainted her first encounter with Angkor Wat and had stayed in her mind to that day. She knew it had unsettled Henri deeply. He'd been subdued when he'd returned to the car and had driven home in virtual silence. He'd taken the death of a worker on his watch to his heart and held himself fully responsible. Through the ensuing weeks Colette would know when it had returned to his mind because that anguished look would come upon him. She supported him as best she could through it, and through the process of negotiating the best compensation payment possible for the family of the dead worker, but the episode cast a dark shadow over their wedding and the first months of their marriage.

8

TONLÉ SAP, 1995

On Friday morning after breakfast, Colette took a taxi from outside the Grand Hotel d'Angkor. She asked the driver to take her to the Tonlé Sap lake. This time, instead of stopping at the little settlement of Chong Khneas, she asked him to take her on around the lake to the floating community where the medical centre was.

She walked along the rickety jetty past the centre to the third hut, just as she had two days before. She stopped a few paces from Achariya's hut, surprised at the scene before her. Achariya was sitting outside the door in a battered chair. She was dressed in a yellow sarong and her face was turned towards the sun, a beatific smile on her face.

'Good morning,' Colette said, approaching and Achariya's eyes snapped open.

'Madam!' she made as if to get up but Colette gestured her to stay where she was. 'I wasn't sure that you would come.'

'Of course, I was going to come. I said I would, didn't I?'

'You did, but... but...'

'Didn't you trust me?' Colette settled herself down beside Achariya on an old wooden bench.

'It's not that, madam, it's just that when you came to see me the other day... afterwards I just couldn't believe it had actually happened. I began to think it must have been a dream.'

Colette laughed at her old friend's words and patted her hand. 'It wasn't a dream, Achariya. In a dream we might not have grey hair! Now, I've come to help you along to the medical centre to collect your medication, just like we agreed. And believe it or not I am actually real.'

'Well, thank you for coming. Sometimes the neighbour helps me along to the medical centre, but she has had to go out fishing today. Her husband is sick. I would have had to go alone. And that is difficult for me now.'

'Shall we go now? Shall I help you up?'

Colette helped her get out of the chair. Achariya rose stiffly and Colette handed her the walking stick that was hooked over the railings of the hut. Achariya moved forward slowly, leaning heavily on the stick, and Colette walked on the opposite side with her arm around Achariya's waist to help her along. Progress along the uneven boards of the jetty was slow and difficult. As they shuffled forward, Colette reflected on how things had come full circle since she'd last been in Cambodia. Achariya used to look after *her* then and tend to her every need. Colette had accepted this with barely a second thought. How strange those times had been. Having lived in France for the last twenty years, doing her own cleaning, cooking, washing, shopping and household chores, it felt very odd to think that she had once had servants who had done all those things for her. She'd been so pampered that if she didn't want to, she'd hardly had to lift a finger. And that wasn't all. Achariya had put herself at risk on more than one occasion to help Colette. She was acutely aware that she probably owed her old housekeeper her life. She was glad to be able to help Achariya now, albeit in this small way.

They reached the glass doors of the floating medical centre. Colette pushed them open and held them aside while Achariya shuffled through. The place wasn't quite as busy as it had been two days ago. Colette helped Achariya to the desk and the nurses there took her details and gave her a box of pills to take away.

'You're the lady who came in the other day, aren't you?' one of the nurses asked and Colette nodded. 'It's so nice that Achariya has people to help her. She has no family at all you know.'

Colette looked at Achariya in surprise. No family? She'd had so many brothers and sisters before that Colette had lost track of their names. They'd all lived together with their parents in that floating house over in Chong Khneas. Colette even remembered that Achariya had been fond of one of the fishermen who'd lived a few huts along, a widower. Colette had expected them to marry. Had that never happened? Whatever had become of them all?

'What happened, Achariya?' she asked and Achariya shook her head and pursed her lips as if to fend off tears.

'Not here,' she mouthed, and Colette helped her out of the medical centre and back along to her hut where they sat down outside in the warm breeze from the lake.

'Can I get you anything? Something to eat and a drink perhaps?'

Achariya nodded, catching her breath. 'That would be most welcome, madam, Thank you. There are some food stalls back past the centre. Could you get me some fried rice and some sugar cane juice?'

'Of course. Whatever you want,' Colette said, quickly finding her purse and hurrying along the jetty to a row of food stalls that were set up on the waterfront to cater for the fishermen and their families. She bought rice and sugar cane juice, which was handed to her in a hollowed-out bamboo shoot. She also bought a bottle of water for herself. It was extremely hot and humid on the lake that day and she wasn't used to such temperatures.

Back at Achariya's hut, she found a plate and fork and dished the rice out of its plastic bag. There was an old folding table on the deck so she put it in front of Achariya's chair and set the food and drink out for her.

'I never thought you would be doing this for me one day, madam,' she said and Colette laughed.

'I've been thinking about that myself. I used to take everything you did for me for granted. You might be surprised to know that I look after myself now.'

Achariya's face dropped. 'You have no servants?'

Colette shook her head and Achariya shook her own head in dismay.

Colette sat down beside Achariya and waited until she'd finished her food. Then she said gently, 'Achariya, can you tell me what happened to you and your family in the revolution?'

Achariya dabbed her mouth with a tissue and said, 'My family are all gone now.'

'Gone?'

'They are all dead. Mother, Father, three brothers, two sisters. The Khmer Rouge took them all.'

'Can you tell me what happened to you after I left in 1975? I'd like to understand. I thought about you every day, you know.'

'I can tell you, madam, but it is a long story. And a sad one. Do you have time?'

'Of course I have time. I came back to Cambodia specifically to find you. I really want to know what happened to you and your family, if it isn't too painful to talk about.'

Achariya turned her face towards Colette and the depth of sadness in her eyes was immense.

'It *is* painful, madam, very painful, but that won't stop me telling it. These stories have to be told.

'After you'd left the French embassy in that convoy of trucks, the Khmer Rouge soldiers made all of us Cambodians who had been with westerners line up. I was terrified. I thought that they would kill us for associating with foreigners and for trying to leave the country, but they just pushed us around a bit and stole all our cash and jewellery. Then they pointed to the north and told us to walk out of the city and to keep walking until we found somewhere in the countryside where we could stay and find work.

'So that's what we did. Carrying our luggage, we walked out of Phnom Penh on the main road. We joined a great column of people who were already walking north. The column stretched a long way ahead into the distance. It was miles long and as we walked, people joined behind us too. We walked for a long time. People got sick and dropped out. Some collapsed by the roadside, unable to go on.

'We were many weeks on the road, heading north. At night we would sleep on the grass or in the undergrowth beside the road. People carried their possessions on their backs and also their babies. The air was filled with the sound of babies and children crying. A few people tried to make a break for it from the column, running across open fields or into the jungle. They were caught and beaten by the Khmer Rouge and brought back, their faces bruised and bloody.

'Khmer Rouge soldiers were a constant presence on the road. They were stationed at every crossroads and in every village that they hadn't burned to the ground. Sometimes tanks would patrol the column to make sure people weren't trying to escape. Some collapsed and died by the roadside and their bodies were left to rot where they had fallen. Babies were born in the ditch as the column marched past. The Khmer Rouge supervised villagers who'd been ordered to give us food and water on the route. But the food and water they provided was insufficient fuel for a day's marching and we always went to sleep hungry, our stomachs crying out for food. Some of us ate berries we found by the road, grass and leaves too when we were desperate. Before long many of us were suffering from diarrhoea and had to run for the bushes each time our watery bowels gave way.

'It was a terrifying, miserable trek. I hardly spoke to any of the others on the march. We were all subdued, unsure of who we could trust, terrified that others might be reporting back to the Khmer Rouge, afraid of saying the wrong thing. Gradually, as time went on, some people were told to stay in the villages and the marching column grew shorter. But I was instructed to keep moving, to keep on marching north.

'I was one of the last people to reach my destination. The village where I was ordered to stay was little more than a small settlement, mud and bamboo huts on stilts surrounded by rice fields. The Khmer Rouge soldiers there, just boys really, told me and another woman to find a place to sleep in the communal dormitory in the middle of the village. They took all our clothes and burned them and gave us black tunics to wear, like everyone else. There was hardly any room for us in the dormitory. Almost the entire floor was already occupied by female workers who like us had arrived from the cities. This was the women's hut. Women and men, husbands and wives had been separated when they arrived and sent to different dormitories. Their children had been taken from them too.

'Rumour had it that the children were being indoctrinated by the Khmer Rouge to deny their parents and to deny the history of Cambodia and everything they had learned to that point. Certainly, whenever we came across any of the children, they turned their noses up at us, scorning us. Children as young as ten were put in charge of the work parties on the fields. They were cruel, always on the lookout for people who were slow or were taking a rest. They would point them out, yelling at the tops of their voices to alert the Khmer Rouge soldiers who would come and beat the unfortunate workers who were simply too weak through lack of food or sickness to work quickly.

'The day after our arrival we started work in the rice fields. I had never done anything like that before. As you know, I was a housekeeper, used to cooking and cleaning indoors. Because of my upbringing, I knew how to fish but that was the limit of my experience of farming. Now I was given a bucket and told to weed the field. This meant bending down and finding the weeds under the water. I had no idea what a weed was and what a rice plant was. Everything looked the same to me and I was often picked upon by the children in charge of the work parties. I have scars on my back from the lashes I was given by the Khmer Rouge soldiers for not working hard or fast enough.'

Colette could barely take it in. Tears came to her eyes picturing what poor Achariya had been through. Again, she felt the full weight of responsibility on her shoulders. If only she'd been able to ensure that Achariya could leave. But she was struck too that Achariya's experience had been shared by a large percentage of the population. Everywhere she looked there were people who must have been through similar things. And yet they'd picked themselves up and carried on with their lives, hardly speaking about the past, looking to the practicalities of the present, making a life for themselves and thinking about what the future might bring.

'The night-times were the worst,' Achariya went on. 'As I said, there was little room to sleep in that hot hut, but no one would go outside to sleep on the ground. Snakes were everywhere and if you went out to relieve yourself in the night you were in danger of stepping on one and getting bitten. That happened to more than one woman in the dormitory. One died from the snake venom and the other had to have her leg amputated by the camp doctor, who wasn't a doctor at all. She died later, from blood poisoning.

'We worked long hours, from dawn until after dark. We weeded the rice fields, and we harvested the rice and planted new rice plants the following year. We ploughed the fields, dug ditches and repaired the nearby riverbank. We also grew vegetables but there was never enough food to eat. We all grew thin and weak, shadows of our former selves. All the time we tried to avoid the snakes that lurked in the water in the rice fields and under bushes. Most of us came from the cities and were no good at farming. Every day was a struggle and full of heartache. I was missing my family desperately and wondered what had become of them. I could only imagine that they were somewhere else, in another godforsaken village, doing exactly the same as I was, day in, day out. I missed you, madam and I missed my fiancé Youkimny with all my heart and soul. There was no way of finding out what had happened to any of them. All the women I worked with were in the same position, missing their family and in anguish about what might be happening to them. The mood was one of sadness and depression. Many people talked about taking their own lives, and some did, hanging themselves by their sarongs from trees in the jungle in the dead of night.

'In the evenings, we were forced to attend meetings where the Khmer Rouge leaders came to teach us about communism and to preach hatred and sow discord. We were told to distrust people with an education or who lived in cities, or even those who wore glasses. We were encouraged to spy on one another and tell on our neighbours if they breached any of the rules. We were told to forget our families and our homes and whatever we'd been taught before we came to the countryside. It made everyone suspicious and that made it difficult to make friends amongst the other women. Each and every one of us was looking out for ourselves.

'We carried on like that for years. Day after day was the same and one blurred into the next. No one told us what the date was but we knew from the cycles of the monsoon and the progress of the harvests roughly how long we had been there. Women died from malnutrition, from malaria and other tropical illnesses. We were left to bury them in a patch of wasteland behind the hut. Sometimes we were sent to fields further away from the village to prepare them for harvest but these fields were even more dangerous than the ones in the village. Fighting had taken place in those fields during the civil war. More than one woman stepped on a landmine and had her legs blown off, dying in agony and distress out there in the fields with no medical attention. Once again, we carried their bodies back to the village and buried them on the wasteland behind the hut. The graves were shallow and we lost track of how many people were buried there.

'After a long time had passed, we began to hear the sound of fighting in the nearby mountains. The rumble of guns and shells. We wondered what was happening but no one told us anything. Was it another civil war? Were people rising up against the Khmer Rouge as we would have done if we'd had a chance? The Khmer Rouge soldiers guarding us seemed to be getting nervous and jumpy. More than once they shot at people who they thought weren't working hard enough, killing them stone dead right there in the fields.

'But one day we woke up and they were all gone. They'd taken all their possessions and their guns. We were ecstatic. There was no sign of them anywhere. We wondered what to do and that day no one did any work. We began to relax, to chat to each other as we'd never done before.

'The next day, some Vietnamese soldiers arrived in the village. They had tanks and guns, but they were smiling and friendly towards us. They didn't speak our language but they were able to make us understand that they had overthrown the Khmer Rouge and that we were free at last. We looked at each other, wondering what to do. A few of us, whose homes were in the south, decided to start walking.

'Again, we walked for weeks. It was harder than the march north because we were weak from four years of brutalisation at the hands of the Khmer Rouge. The roads were very bad, full of potholes and washed away by the monsoon in some places. We often saw dead bodies by the roadside, rotting away, both humans and animals. We cared for each other as we had never done during the Khmer Rouge years, though. Sometimes we managed to get a lift for a few miles from a lorry or cart. Eventually, we came to a goods yard on the edge of a town where men were loading trains. We managed to climb on board a goods train going south. We stayed on that train for two days and to our joy it finally arrived in Phnom Penh.

'When we walked through the streets of the city we were distraught by what had happened to it. Buildings had been ransacked, destroyed or burned to the ground. The Khmer Rouge had tried to rip the heart out of our beautiful capital. But some buildings still remained – the city palace, some of the French buildings including the embassies. I walked past the French Embassy, peering in, thinking for some strange reason that I might see you there, madam. But the place was deserted like many other buildings in Phnom Penh.

'I left my companions in the city to look for their families and I walked on to Siem Reap alone. It took me several days and when I arrived, the place was unrecognisable from four years before. Just like Phnom Penh, buildings had been ransacked, burned to the ground. Jungle had taken over houses. The only place that looked to have remained was the Grand Hotel d'Angkor, which by then was occupied by Vietnamese soldiers.

'There weren't many local people left. Someone told me that they had all been marched north as I had and were only just beginning to return. I walked on to Tonlé Sap, hoping that my family would already be there. Our little house was still floating on the water although it was on the tilt and half of it had been submerged. I got on board and started to fix it up straight away. I wanted to make it good for when my family returned. I worked for days. I scrubbed and washed and mended the boards and the broken bottom of the boat. I even painted the outside again. Soon I had the place looking as good as it had before we left.

'I waited and waited. Neighbours began to return and told me what had happened to them in the north. Their experience was similar to mine. They had been forced to work in the fields, just as I had, in similar conditions. Stories began to emerge about my family. One by one I found out how they had died. Two had been killed by stepping on mines. My mother had died of malaria, two of my sisters of starvation. My fiancé had been shot trying to escape. My father had been tortured to death because he was found reading a book. None of them had survived. I was numb with grief. I spent days alone in the house, just lying there, crying for everyone I had lost.' The old woman paused and gave a shuddering breath.

'I'm so very sorry,' Colette said, 'how awful for you. How on earth did you manage to go on?'

'Thank you, madam.' She took a sip of sugar cane juice. 'One day, I was so hungry, I was forced to get up. My father's fishing boat was moored to the house. I took it out with his nets and spent a day catching fish. I caught far more than I needed so I gave the rest to my neighbours. I went out every day after that. I found that the activity helped me to move on. I needed some sort of routine. I caught so much that I was able to supply our little community and sell some of the fish at market. I began to get money from that and to save it up. I had no one to spend the money on, but I took satisfaction from helping others and from saving. It gave me purpose and I thought that one day I might not be able to go out fishing any more. I was right. A couple of years ago I had a heart attack. I needed the money I'd saved for my medical care. The doctors told me that the years of starvation had weakened my heart irreparably and that I shouldn't work any longer. I sold my house and boat to another fisherman and came to live here. I use the savings I put by to live on and to pay for my medicines. But it is no life really. I mourn for my family and my fiancé. Nothing has been the same since the Khmer Rouge took over and brought this country to its knees.'

Colette took her hand and looked into her eyes.

'Thank you for telling me your story, Achariya. I feel so very humbled by it. It is truly amazing that you survived and that you had so much resilience. I wish I could do something for you to make amends.'

Achariya gripped Colette's hand in return and smiled. 'You came back to find me, didn't you? That means the world to me, madam. It has made me realise the power of friendship and it has restored a little of my faith in humanity. It has also made me think that there might be some point in carrying on living after all.'

They sat together in comfortable companionship well into the afternoon. Colette told Achariya something of her life in the Dordogne, but there wasn't much to tell. Hers had been a boring, if comfortable existence.

'I was always waiting for a chance to come back here,' she said. 'As soon as I read that visitors were coming back to Angkor Wat, I booked a ticket.'

'And you've come back to a country that has changed a lot,' Achariya said.

'That's true,' Colette said, 'By the way, do you know if my villa is still standing? I couldn't see it when I came over here by boat the other day.'

'It is still there. But it is derelict and overgrown now. I think some of the Khmer Rouge might have lived in it for a while. Mangrove swamps have grown up in front of it, hiding it from view. That's probably why you couldn't see it from the water.'

'How do you know it's still standing?'

'I used to go over sometimes when I was fishing, just to look at it. It reminded me of the old days ...'

They were both silent for a few moments, musing on those years. Then Achariya said, 'If you'd like to go over there, I know a boatman who could take you. He knows the lake like the back of his hand. He knows all the channels and backwaters. You would be safe with him.'

'Really?' Colette asked, her heartbeat speeding up. 'I'd love to go.'

'Then go along to the pier and ask for Boran. He will probably be back from his fishing by now and sitting having a drink with friends. He shouldn't charge you much. A few riels only. Go and find him quickly, before he goes home.'

Colette got up, kissed her friend's cheek, then made her way back along the jetty to the pier. A few fishermen were sitting around a food stall, drinking and chatting. She approached the group and asked for Boran. A man stood up.

'Achariya told me you would know your way across the lake to the old villa on the other side,' she said.

He put his drink down and came over. 'I do. Do you want to go there? It will cost you twenty-five thousand.'

It sounded a lot but after a quick calculation Colette realised it was quite reasonable. She agreed and he motioned her to follow him to his boat that was tied up at the pier.

She sat on a wooden bench in the middle of the boat. It was still wet from his catch. The little boat smelled strongly of fish, but it had a powerful engine and soon they had left the huts at the side of the lake behind them and were powering across the water towards a mangrove swamp on the other side. She didn't remember that being there. It must have grown since she left. They reached the swamp and Boran slowed the engine to a slow put-put and guided the boat into a little channel between the mangrove trees. She wouldn't have known the channel was there, it was so well hidden in the reeds. Some waterbirds, disturbed by their arrival, took off noisily. After a few minutes a steep bank came into view ahead of them. Boran pulled the boat round so it was aligned with the bank.

'Villa is just up there,' he pointed through the undergrowth. 'I wait for you here.'

Colette hesitated. After all the talk of snakes she'd heard that morning, she wasn't keen on striking out through the long grass in her sandals, but she'd come all this way and she wasn't going to miss this opportunity. She heaved herself out of the boat and, gritting her teeth, clambered up the bank. At the top, she realised she was above the mangroves. She straightened up and looked ahead of her and her heart lurched with recognition. There it was, covered in creepers and ferns, its walls blackened with lichen, but the shape of it was unmistakeable. The graceful proportions, the wide, sweeping veranda that was now falling in on itself. Henri's lake villa that he'd built in 1937. She walked towards it through the long grass and as she did so, she realised that her face was wet with tears.

9

TONLÉ SAP, 1939

The first few weeks of Colette's life in Cambodia passed in a whirlwind of preparations for the wedding. She and Henri decided to marry in St Joseph's Cathedral in Phnom Penh, a church with two impressive square towers, very much like a French provincial cathedral. Colette found a dressmaker in a back street in Siem Reap and asked for a simple, calf-length gown in ivory silk with minimal trimmings. She didn't want anything fancy. Within a few weeks of her arrival in Cambodia, Britain and France had declared war on Hitler's Germany, so she didn't feel that an elaborate occasion or an extravagant dress was appropriate.

Fleur Leroux, whom she happened to bump into in the club each time she returned to Phnom Penh with Henri, tried to persuade her otherwise.

'What difference does it make?' Fleur said through a cloud of smoke, 'War or no war, it's still your wedding and a cause for celebration.'

'Just think of all the people suffering in Europe. My parents for example. I'm worried about them. I had hoped they might be able to come out here for the wedding, but there's no chance of that now. It would seem odd to have a huge wedding when they can't be there.'

Fleur shrugged. 'It's a shame about your parents, of course. But the war won't come here, for sure. So, I don't think anyone would be offended by you having a proper celebration. In fact, it's rather expected. God knows, life is dull enough in the outpost...' she finished wistfully, staring out over the wide river below.

But Colette stuck to her guns, insisting on a low-key ceremony with the minimum of fuss. The reception would be at the Grand Central Hotel, Phnom Penh and the following day she and Henri would return to Angkor Wat. He was too busy at work to take time off for a honeymoon. Virtually all the expats in the community were to be invited. Fleur helped Colette to draw up the guest list and they had almost finished, with fifty names on the list.

'What about Luc Gilbert?' Fleur asked biting the end of her pen.

'I'm not sure about him,' Colette said. 'To be honest, he and Henri don't seem to get on at all.'

'Yes, so I've heard,' Fleur said with a raised eyebrow. 'But you can't possibly leave him out. He really is the life and soul of any party round here. You'd be really missing out if you didn't invite him.'

Colette sat forward and lowered her voice. 'You know that it was his fault that the scaffolding collapsed at Angkor and a man died on site?' she said. 'He wasn't following safety protocols and he hadn't checked that all the ties were in place before he ordered the men to climb up onto the scaffold.'

Fleur stubbed out her cigarette and lit another one. 'I heard a rumour about that. But Luc is a passionate man. He must have been eager to get results, plunging ahead regardless of the rules. People know very well that excavation and archaeology are dangerous occupations. Those workers would have known that too.'

Colette stared at her, appalled. 'That doesn't excuse it, surely,' she said. 'A man died. Irrespective of whether he was French or Cambodian. What difference does it make?'

Fleur smiled indulgently and blew a long stream of smoke in the air. 'It's obvious you are new to the colonies. In time you'll come to understand that the lives of coolies are cheap in Indochina. That's what the French empire is built on.'

Colette didn't reply to such an inflammatory statement, but she did give in and invite Luc Gilbert to the wedding. After all, he was Henri's assistant, and it would look very odd if he was left out.

In the weeks leading up to the wedding, Henri was pensive and distant. He seemed to have retreated into his shell. Colette knew he was worried about the accident but she couldn't help feeling a little pushed out and sad too that he wasn't full of joy about the upcoming wedding. It felt all wrong that they weren't sharing that fully.

Henri had wanted to suspend Gilbert from site duties, but the Ministry of Works in Paris wouldn't allow it. They sent out an inspector from Hanoi who conducted a cursory investigation into the incident and made some safety recommendations but fell short of recommending disciplinary action against Gilbert. Henri made it his business to negotiate a fair settlement with the Ministry for the family of the worker. This was all on top of a heavy schedule of excavations and restorations that he was supervising each day. He would leave the villa just after dawn and not return until after dark.

Colette began to wish that he worked shorter hours, but she knew that his work was important, so when she started feeling left out, she tried to suppress those thoughts and make the most of what her new life had to offer. Indeed, she was growing more and more fascinated by the enigma of Angkor Wat herself. She would sometimes get a pony cart or motor-cyclo to take her from the villa up to Angkor Wat during the daytime. There, she would wander through the echoing corridors until she came across Henri at work with his team. She would spend a few hours with him there, watching the painstaking work as the men uncovered magnificent sculptures and friezes from centuries of dirt and undergrowth. The daily discoveries they were making were astonishing. It was fascinating to watch, and Colette began to understand why Henri was so obsessed with his work.

During those early days she was also trying to get to know her new housekeeper Achariya. When they'd been introduced on Colette's second day at the villa, Achariya had been painfully shy, and although Colette had done everything she could think of to make her feel welcome, the girl seemed very ill at ease and reluctant to engage in conversation.

'Give her a chance,' Henri told her after a difficult day when Colette had made no progress in getting Achariya to speak. 'It's early days yet. She's never been in service before.'

'She doesn't seem to want to talk at all. She's so shy, she doesn't even look me in the eye,' Colette said despairingly.

The day before, she'd gone into the kitchen where Achariya was preparing vegetables for the evening meal. The young housekeeper had stood there stiffly at the table in her starched grey uniform with its white apron, chopping away. The gardener had been in there chatting away with Achariya but he scurried off when he saw Colette approaching. Achariya gave Colette a wary look when she came in and sat down at the kitchen table.

'What are you making for dinner tonight?' Colette ventured. Achariya answered in monosyllables, that she was preparing a vegetable gratin to go with their lamb cutlets.

'Do you like cooking?' Colette asked and Achariya simply nodded and whispered, 'Yes, madam.'

'Do you cook at home?' Colette persisted and Achariya said 'sometimes' once again in a whisper. Through persistent questioning, Colette managed to glean that Achariya lived on the lake in a floating house, that she had several brothers and sisters and that her father was a fisherman. In the end, she gave up and left the kitchen, silently despairing.

Each day she carried on trying, but she had no luck until the breakthrough came in an unexpected way.

Colette was upstairs, putting some clothes away in her bedroom one morning, when she heard the scrunch of gravel as a car drew up on the drive. She went out onto the balcony and her heart sank. It was Luc Gilbert's sports car and he was already at the front door, ringing the bell. She heard Achariya cross the tiled hall and open it. Colette paused at the top of the stairs, listening, astonished. Luc Gilbert and Achariya were conversing in rapid Cambodian. Their voices rose and fell and to her surprise she heard them both burst into spontaneous laughter.

She went downstairs slowly. The conversation carried on. Then Luc spotted her and said something to Achariya. Achariya spun round, lifted her eyes to Colette's then, head bowed, hurried to the kitchen.

'Good morning, mademoiselle,' Gilbert said. 'I came to thank you for your kind invitation and to accept it. It's very nice of you to invite me. I know things haven't been easy between your husband and me lately and I assume that it was you who made the decision to ask me to your wedding.'

Colette raised her eyebrows, neither denying nor confirming his assumption. She certainly wasn't going to tell him that it had been Fleur who'd argued his case.

'Would you like to come in and have a coffee?' she asked politely, 'I was just about to have one out on the veranda.'

He smiled, a little triumphantly she thought. 'I'd like that very much.'

'Come this way then,' she said crossing the hall and pausing at the kitchen door to ask Achariya for a pot of coffee for two.

Tonlé Sap was particularly beautiful that morning, sun glinting on the water, floricans wading in the reeds in front of the villa, mist rising over distant trees on the far bank.

They sat down opposite each other in the planter's chairs.

'Your maid is a real personality,' Luc said. 'We had quite a chat. She virtually told me her life story.'

'It's funny,' Colette said. 'But she will hardly talk to me. Henri said she spoke perfect French but she will hardly speak it at all.'

'You know,' Luc leaned forward and spoke quietly. 'I think she might find it constraining to be dressed in a maid's uniform like that. If you asked her to come to work in her own clothes, I'm sure she'd be much happier. That happened to me with one of my servants once. She was transformed when she was wearing her own clothes. There's something about that uniform that reinforces the servant-master relationship and puts a damper on natural conversation.'

'Do you think so?' Colette asked, surprised. 'She seemed to talk to you though.'

'I was speaking in her language. That's different. Why don't you give it a try?'

At that point Achariya came out with the tray and there was an awkward silence while she put the coffee pot and milk on the table, set out the cups and saucers and poured the coffee. Colette hoped she didn't pick up on the fact that they'd been discussing her.

'You speak the language very well,' Colette said when Achariya had left and he laughed.

'I've been here a long time. It pays to be able to speak the native tongue. I was in China before, learned Mandarin too.'

'China! How romantic,' Colette said, sounding far more enthusiastic than she intended.

She glanced at him to see his reaction and saw an earnestness in his eyes that she'd not noticed before. She'd not really looked at him properly before though. He'd been around when she'd visited the temple but he'd kept his distance and of course on that first, fateful evening, it had been dark when he'd come to speak to her. She realised now that he was rather striking looking, with chiselled cheekbones and beautiful dark eyes with long lashes. She put that thought away quickly though, feeling disloyal to Henri who, she quickly reminded herself, was equally good looking in his own way.

'You could describe it as romantic I suppose,' Luc said, leaning back in his chair. 'I was in Yinxu. It was jolly hard work. That's how I remember it. But we made some fabulous discoveries. Old manuscripts. Priceless...'

'The Oracle scripts? How fascinating.'

He looked at her with surprise and a creeping respect. 'You know about them?'

'Yes, I used to take evening classes in archaeology. We studied them there.'

'Incredible! I had no idea.'

'And how long have you been in Cambodia?' she asked.

'A couple of years less than your husband.'

Colette sensed rivalry in that remark but she didn't respond.

'I've seen you up at the temple several times,' he said. 'Is that to pursue your interest in archaeology or is it that you just can't keep away from your dashing fiancé?'

Colette raised her eyebrows. 'Actually, I'm particularly interested in Angkor Wat,' she said, keeping her voice smooth, 'I've been fascinated by it since my father took me to the Colonial Exhibition in Paris in 1931.'

'You were there?' He leaned forward. 'I was there too. A gauche young man. It was one of my first jobs. I was an usher, opening the gates on the Angkor Wat display and ensuring a steady flow of visitors. I might have seen you. How extraordinary!'

'And did that give you an enduring fascination with Angkor Wat too?' she asked.

He thought for a moment, his fingers together at the fingertips. 'You know what, I've never thought of it that way before, but I suppose it must have done.'

He didn't stay long after that, and as she saw him back to the front door and stood in the doorway watching him drive away, she reflected that there was more to Luc Gilbert than she'd gleaned from Henri's remarks about him and that perhaps she should give him a second chance. But as his car disappeared into the trees on the jungle road, a question came into her mind that refused to go away. Why had he come to the house to accept the invitation, when he could have simply spoken to Henri at work about it? There must be a reason for that, she thought, but not one she could think of at that moment.

She went back into the house and spoke to Achariya.

'There's no need for you to wear the uniform tomorrow,' she said and Achariya's eyes widened in surprise. 'I think it would be better if you came to work in your own clothes.'

Achariya immediately brightened, a broad smile spreading across her face, showing gleaming white teeth. 'Thank you, madam. I would like that very much.'

So, the next morning, and every morning after that, Achariya came to work in a colourful sarong, her hair wrapped up in a contrasting headscarf. It seemed to relax her, make her brighter and happier and from that day on, there were no difficulties in communication. In fact, once Achariya started chatting, there was no stopping her. She told Colette all about her family. She was the eldest of six children – three boys and three girls. They all lived together in a floating house in Chong Khneas. Her father worked as a fisherman, selling his catch in the market in Siem Reap. Her mother would often go out with him too. Her parents had come to Cambodia from Indochina, hoping to make a better life for their family, and in a way they were, but because of their nationality they couldn't buy a property on land and had to live on the water. The children couldn't go to school, but the community had set up their own floating school there on the lake.

'One of my brothers and two of my sisters go to school there. We have to pay for it, so those of us old enough to work help with the fees. My parents hope that through education, the younger ones will have a better life. But the school struggles. I used to go there to teach French, but now I'm working...'

Colette felt a sudden rush of sympathy for this young woman, so brave and persistent, so devoted to her family. 'You could still go if you like. You don't have to come here every day.'

Achariya's face lit up. 'If I could have two hours one morning each week, it would be a real help.'

'I wonder,' Colette sent on, 'Perhaps I could come along too one day. I don't have much to do here, and perhaps I could speak French to the children too? After the wedding, of course...' she said hastily.

'I will ask the teacher. I'm sure they would love that,' Achariya beamed.

The wedding was the following Saturday. It all passed in a blur of happiness. Walking up the aisle alone, Colette reflected on how lucky she was to have found love with Henri, to be able to share his life here in Cambodia and support him in the fascinating and important work he was doing at Angkor Wat. She was lucky too that the French community was friendly, and had welcomed her with open arms as one of their own. She was beginning to feel a part of it already. She'd all but forgotten Fleur's words of warning about the dark side of Cambodia. But then she remembered her parents, living with the fear and uncertainty that war would inevitably bring and sadness washed over her. It was the one blemish on that otherwise happy day that they couldn't be here, and she wondered when she might see them again. Henri was ahead of her then. She straightened her shoulders and forced the sad feelings away. Today was her day and she wasn't going to let gloomy thoughts spoil it for her.

They travelled by an open topped car to the reception at the Grand Central Hotel. Local people stood on the pavements waving and smiling, some even threw flowers. At the reception they ate a light wedding breakfast of seafood salad followed by steak. It was all washed down with lashings of champagne. Afterwards, as the light faded outside, they danced to a string quartet in the ballroom, lit by sparkling chandeliers, and as Henri took her in his arms for a waltz, Colette thought she would burst with happiness.

But later on, she went out onto the hotel balcony alone to get some air, and had an unsettling experience. She leaned on the balcony parapet and stared up at the stars. She could hear boatmen on the nearby river, the sloshing of the water against the quayside, the horns and bells of traffic in the city. She became aware that she wasn't alone, in fact, she could smell cigarette smoke. She turned, alarmed. Luc Gilbert was sitting in a basket chair in the corner, one leg crossed over the other, smoking a cigarette and watching her. She gasped in surprise.

'I wondered when you'd notice me,' he said, his eyes taking in the shape of her body in her silk dress. 'Has anyone told you that you look ravishing today?' Warmth crept into her cheeks and she felt conflicting emotions. Shame and humiliation, but there was something else there too, she didn't want to admit it but she felt flattered by his words. He laughed and stood up and came towards her. Instinctively she moved aside, but there was something compelling in the way he looked at her.

'I can't help feeling that you and I have an awful lot in common,' he said, coming close.

She could feel his breath on her skin and to her horror it made her tingle all over. She wanted to pull away but it was as if she was pinned there, unable to resist, unable to move. Her eyes were drawn to his and their gaze was locked together for a long moment before she tore herself away and rushed back into the ballroom, her heart hammering. Henri approached, relief spreading over his face.

'Ah, there you are, Colette. I was looking for you. Are you quite alright, chérie? You look quite flushed. How about another dance?'

10

TONLÉ SAP, 1939-40

After the wedding, life in the villa on the lake settled back into a comfortable routine. Henri continued to work long hours.Colette minded less about that now but sometimes still, she would feel a prickle of resentment that she took second place to an ancient temple.

She looked forward to Achariya arriving by bicycle each day. They would exchange their latest news and Achariya would tell her about her family and what they were up to. Two or three times a week Colette would travel up to Angkor Wat and watch Henri at work. She always took the team some food that she and Achariya had cooked up that morning – steamed pork buns or chive cakes that were local delicacies. The team always made her feel welcome and were keen to show her their latest discoveries. On those occasions she carefully avoided bumping into Luc Gilbert. If she spotted him somewhere in the distance she would turn and walk the other way. She'd tried to put him out of her mind after the wedding. She didn't want to confront the maelstrom of emotions the thought of him provoked.

On the second week after her marriage, Achariya took her to the floating school at Chong Khneas. Henri had some old bicy-

cles stored in a shed behind the villa and the gardener had
cleaned one up for her. The two of them cycled the short distance
to the little settlement and then took a boat from the jetty out to
the school which was a little way north around the shore of the
lake. Colette felt self-conscious entering the classroom full of
Cambodian children of all ages. Thirty faces turned to stare at
her round-eyed as she walked with Achariya to the front of the
class. She noticed how bare the classroom was. There were no
pictures on the wall, no desks or chairs even, all the children sat
cross-legged on the floor. The only furniture was a teacher's desk
at the front and a blackboard. But there was an air of quiet
studiousness in the room and it was immediately clear that the
children were eager to learn.

The teacher introduced Colette to the class and told them
that she'd come to help them with their French. Then, the
teacher and Achariya took it in turns to ask Colette questions
about France and about her life there. The children listened,
spellbound by her answers. She took care to speak slowly and
clearly. At the end of the session some of them put their hands up
and asked her questions too in faltering French, which she was
glad to answer.

'Will you come again next week?' the teacher asked when
Colette was leaving.

'Of course. I'd be honoured to.'

'The children loved it. It will really help them. There's
nothing like hearing a native speaker to make progress in a
language. We are very grateful to you, madam.'

On the way back to Chong Khneas in the boat, Colette
reflected that it was she who was grateful to the school, for the
opportunity to be allowed into their community and contribute
something to the children, albeit in a small way. She'd noticed
that most French people in the colony stuck to their own insular
world and she was glad that her blossoming relationship with
Achariya was opening up other opportunities for her.

When Henri heard that she'd been to the school he said, 'Oh, you should have taken one of the boats. It would have been quicker.'

'One of the boats?'

'Yes, in the boathouse. I suppose I haven't shown it to you. I haven't had much use for it lately, but I used to enjoy taking a boat out on the lake to fish occasionally.'

'The boathouse?' Again she looked at him, puzzled.

'I'll show you.'

He took her outside and they walked along the edge of the lake towards the far side of the garden to where a group of trees stood on the edge of the property. Colette had never ventured near this thick spinney before. She'd thought it was just a patch of untamed jungle and had kept well clear of it, fearing snakes and other wild creatures. She hadn't realised that there was in fact a narrow, gravel path that wound its way through the undergrowth. They followed it and were soon deep inside the trees. On the other side of the spinney, tucked away and completely out of sight of the villa, was a wooden boathouse painted bright blue in the same shade as many of the local houseboats on the edge of the lake. Henri unlocked the door and they went inside. He flicked on some rather weak electric lights and Colette followed him down a set of wooden stairs to a jetty where two small boats bobbed on the water.

'This one is a rowing boat, and this one has a motor. Not sure if it will still be working, but I'll get Lim to have a look at it. Then I'll teach you how to use it and next time you go to the school you can go straight there by water.'

He turned to her, beaming, and took her in his arms. She put her arms around him too and they kissed. How kind and thoughtful Henri was, always thinking of her comfort and pleasure. For this, she could forgive him his long hours of absence.

The next day, Lim, the gardener, serviced the engine on the larger boat. Henri decided to take the following day off work, it

was a Saturday after all, and after breakfast they walked over to
the boathouse.

'Did you have this built at the same time as the villa?' Colette
asked.

'No, it was here before I came here. The farmer who owned
the land used to use it. That's why it's painted blue. He used it for
household storage as well as boats. That's why there are lots of
cupboards and shelves on the walls.

He went to the front of the boathouse and pushed open the
doors that gave out onto the lake. Then he loaded some fishing
equipment onto the boat and they both got in, settling themselves on the wooden benches. After a couple of pulls on the
starter motor, the engine spluttered into life and they were
heading through the reeds and straight out onto the lake. It was a
perfect day – bright blue skies and a light breeze. The boat
skimmed the surface and Colette turned her face towards the
sun, basking in its warmth. When they reached the middle of the
lake Henri dropped anchor.

'Let's do a spot of fishing, shall we?'

So, they sat there on the middle of the lake, amongst the boats
of the local fisherman, while Henri cast his line. Colette sat back
in the boat, watching the sun playing on Henri's face. She was
relishing being together alone for once, loving spending time
with him. She wished they could have more of these moments
together. It didn't take long for Henri's line to go taut, and Henri
reeled in a huge silver fish with round black markings all along
its body. It flopped around in the bottom of the boat and Colette
hastily drew her legs away. When Henri stunned the fish with an
oar, it lay still.

'That's a trey kray. A beauty. What all the fishermen are after
here. It's the staple diet of Tonlé Sap. We can have it for supper.'
He looked up at her and laughed. 'Don't look so appalled. Come,
I'll show you how to drive the boat.'

It didn't take Colette long to master the controls and by the time they headed back to the boathouse an hour or so later, she felt confident to take the boat out alone.

The following Wednesday, she and Achariya settled into the boat and set off to the school. It felt wonderful to be at the controls, propelling them across the lake without the need for help from anyone. It made Colette feel more at home here – as if she was now a fully-functioning part of the community.

Over the next few weeks though, Henri began to spend less and less time at home. He told Colette that he was on the verge of a great discovery at Angkor Wat.

'We think there's a buried inner chamber. Possibly a sarcophagus under the central tower. It's so exciting. Who knows what riches might be hidden in there!'

He became very nervy, as if he could not settle to anything. He didn't seem interested in talking about anything other than his work. He would arrive home late, gobble his food and collapse into bed, only to get up before dawn to head off to work.

In between visits to the school, Colette carried on going up to Angkor a couple of times a week, but the team were so focused on their digging that she had little to do. They were excavating under the central tower and had dug a pit some twenty metres deep. Henri had discovered some ancient scrolls that indicated the presence of a burial chamber on the spot. But there was nothing to see except piles of earth and stones. On those occasions, she didn't stay long. She would get bored after an hour or so and wander out to the front of the temple, cross the bridge and find a local driver to take her home. She began to feel a little pushed out again by Henri's obsession with his work, although her rational mind tried to put these feelings aside. It was because of his brilliance and his devotion to his subject that she loved him, she told herself, so she shouldn't be surprised that his work should take priority when he was on the brink of a great discovery. But despite these thoughts, still her heart and body craved attention. She knew he loved her, and was frustrated that he didn't show it more.

One day, she managed to stay until late in the afternoon, but could see that no breakthrough was going to be made that day. She wandered out through the maze of passages, feeling deflated. Henri had been deep inside the pit, making exploratory holes with a long chisel in search of an underground door. He'd barely acknowledged her presence and sadness washed through her. She tried to resist the feeling that it was a rejection, telling herself that his behaviour wasn't meant to hurt her. She sighed to herself, hoping fervently that he would get the results he was craving very soon.

When she reached the front of the temple and crossed the bridge, there were no drivers in sight, so she sat down on the wall to wait. Before long she heard footsteps behind her and when she turned round she saw with a start that it was Luc Gilbert.

'Waiting for a lift?' he asked. 'I could drop you home. I'm going back to Siem Reap now. It's the end of the working day for us mere mortals.'

'It's alright,' she said, feeling a blush creep into her cheeks, realising that they hadn't spoken since that odd exchange at her wedding, a few months ago now. The memory of it hovered in the air between them. 'Tonlé Sap is a long way out of your way. I'm sure a taxi will be along soon.'

'Nonsense. It would be a pleasure. Wait there, I'll get my car.'

Luc Gilbert drove along the unmade jungle roads quickly and recklessly. Gripping the door handle, her eyes fixed on the road ahead, it occurred to Colette that he was driving exactly as he'd driven on the night of the accident. She refused to be rattled by it. She realised that his driving reflected his personality, reckless and impulsive, whereas Henri's driving was careful and dependable, just as he was.

They arrived at the lake villa and Luc drew up on the drive with a spray of gravel.

'Here you are... home safely.'

'Thank you,' she said getting out and shutting the car door.

'Aren't you going to invite me in?' he asked.

She glanced at the sky, it was growing dark now, the sun starting to dip in the sky. Who knew what time Henri would be back. A wave of loneliness swept over her. She'd been alone every evening for several weeks now. It would be nice to have some company for once.

'All right,' she said. 'Why not? We could have a drink on the veranda.'

The houseboy brought them Pernod and ice and they sipped their drinks sitting in the planter's chairs, watching the sun go down over the lake.

'It's a truly beautiful spot,' Luc said. 'Boissière certainly makes sure he gets the best things in life. A beautiful home in a gorgeous position, a beautiful wife too. However does he manage it?'

Colette fell silent then, too embarrassed to reply. She stared down at her drink. She couldn't look him in the eye, remembering how he'd come close to her and made her body tingle all over, and on her wedding day of all days. She wished she'd been strong enough not to ask him in this evening. She was regretting it now. This was surely playing with fire.

'If I had a beautiful wife like you at home, I certainly wouldn't be out working all hours,' Luc went on.

'Henri's work is important to him,' she said, not meeting his eyes. Luc was very close to finding out her Achilles heel. 'He's on the verge of a discovery. I understand.'

'You understand, like a loving, caring wife understands, but don't tell me that the passionate woman that lurks beneath that cool exterior doesn't feel a tiny bit neglected sometimes.'

She put her drink down and stood up.

'Thank you for the lift, and it's been nice talking to you, but I think you'd better go now.'

He stood up too, draining his drink. 'Very well. I'm sorry to have unsettled you. But it's only because all this strikes a chord with you that you don't want to hear it. Tell me that it's not true.'

He came up close then and she could smell the cologne on his skin, the Pernod on his breath.

'Kiss me, Colette. I know you want to,' he said, and she took a step back. Her heart was racing. Part of her yearned to be kissed by this exciting, attractive man, but she knew it was wrong.

'I'm asking you to leave now,' she said coldly. 'If you don't, I'll call the houseboy.'

'As you wish,' he said with a knowing smile. He turned and walked towards the door. 'But I can tell you want to. I can feel it in the air. Perhaps another time, then. Goodbye, Colette.'

She walked behind him to the front door, her heart still racing fit to burst, and watched him run down the steps and vault into his car and drive off. It wasn't until his taillights disappeared into the jungle that her heart began to slow down and she was able to tear herself away from the front door.

11

TONLÉ SAP, 1940

After that evening, try as she might, Colette could not get Luc Gilbert out of her mind. She was confused by her reaction to him. She was sure he wasn't trustworthy. He was unreliable, reckless, dangerous even, but there was something visceral that drew her to him, nonetheless. It troubled her that she had these feelings. They had come upon her unbidden and quite unexpectedly. Wasn't she supposed to be a newlywed, deeply in love with her husband, starting out on an idyllic chapter in her life with him? All those things were true, but there was still this thread, running right through her, that seemed to connect her to Luc Gilbert at a level that was deeper than consciousness. And coming at a time when she was feeling neglected and ignored by her husband, made the connection even more tantalising.

As a result of these feelings, she redoubled her efforts with Henri. Each day that she wasn't due at the school she would make sure she went up to Angkor Wat with sweetmeats and pastries. She had to make an effort to avoid Gilbert, who was working with his team on another part of the temple, and she was relieved that he didn't repeat his offer of a lift home.

A dark shadow was threatening their world, though, in the shape of the war. Her parents had written to her from Paris in the early months of the year to say that although France was at war with Germany, nothing much had changed. They later wrote to say that Hitler had invaded Scandinavia and was fighting the British and French in Norway, Fascist Italy had agreed to enter the war on Germany's side and that Germany had invaded Brussels and taken Antwerp. That was in May, a few months ago and then the letters stopped. Colette waited for the newspapers to arrive but the French ones had stopped coming. When she eventually managed to tune into a news station on Henri's ancient radio, over the crackly airwaves she heard to her horror that Paris had fallen to Hitler in June. She was devastated, thinking of her parents right in the centre of that city. How would they cope with Nazis on the streets? Would her father's business survive? Would food be short? It was doubly worrying that there was no news of them and no way of getting a letter to them either.

The following week, Henri came home early one evening. He parked up on the drive and Colette went out onto the balcony to wave to him. He looked up and waved at her, blowing a kiss. She ran downstairs to meet him.

'Is everything OK, Henri?'

'We've managed to locate a chamber at the base of the tower. I've called a halt to work for today. The men deserve a rest. This calls for a celebration, I think.'

He put his head around the kitchen door and asked the houseboy to bring champagne.

'Tell me all about it, Henri,' she said.

Henri's face was wreathed in smiles as he spoke.

'We managed to clear enough earth and stones away from the base of the central tower to open up a chamber there. It was full of bats. Incredible. They all came flying out at us when we breached the wall. Everything in there is covered in bat droppings. There's a lot of rubbish inside too. Fallen masonry, some of it sculpted, some of it just rough stones.'

'That's incredible, Henri. It was worth all the effort then.'

'Yes. And it will silence the doubters. For example Gilbert. He was always against this, saying it would lead to nothing. Mocking my efforts.'

Colette said nothing and looked away, guilt surging through her.

'The amazing thing is, through all the debris in there, you can see that there's a seated Buddha statue inside. Once we've cleared all the old stones out, we'll be able to get to it and restore it. It's truly magnificent. I'm hoping the burial chamber I've been looking for will be underneath this central chamber, but there's a lot of work to do before we get to that.'

He poured the champagne that the boy had left on the table and raised his glass.

'Here's to you, Colette. You've been such a support and strength to me these past few weeks. I'm sorry I've been so distant. I intend to work shorter days now and make it up to you, if you'll allow me to?'

'There's nothing to make up to me, Henri. I know your work is important to you. I would never complain about that.'

Henri was true to his word and over the next couple of weeks he was home early each evening and they would eat their evening meal on the veranda by the light of the setting sun. She would tell him about her day and what had happened at the school if she'd been there, and he would tell her all about his work that day, how they were making progress clearing the fallen stones from the central chamber and getting closer to the Buddha statue and how, once they reached it, they would be painstakingly restoring it to its former glory.

But one day he came home with more sombre news.

'There's been some bad news coming through from Tonkin in

Indochina. One of the fellows had heard it at the Grand Hotel
d'Angkor earlier,' he said.

'Oh? What's that?' she asked, alarmed.

'The Japanese have invaded Indochina. They were trying to
negotiate a deal with the Vichy imposed government in Hanoi,
but the Japs went on the offensive. There's been some fighting
apparently.'

Colette's hand flew to her mouth. 'That's terrible. What does
it mean for Cambodia?'

Henri shrugged. 'Nobody knows at the moment. We're hoping
they'll leave us well alone, but anything can happen. The Japs
have already shown themselves to be unpredictable.'

'Is there anything we can do?' she asked.

'Just keep your ear to the ground. Rumour has it that the Japs
have started to infiltrate Cambodia, that they've established
networks of informants to help them plan an invasion here too.
We just need to be vigilant.'

'That's terrible. Especially on top of the news about the invasion of France. Is nowhere safe anymore?'

Henri put his arms around her and held her tight. 'Here is as
safe as anywhere. And I'll look after you. Don't worry. Oh, and
I've got some good news too... I almost forgot.'

'Go on?'

'This afternoon we discovered a well inside the central
chamber when we cleared away the debris,' he was brimming
with excitement again, 'And our next task is to excavate that. The
burial chamber may well be somewhere beneath it.'

'That's fantastic news,' Colette said, drawing away from him.
She realised, with a sinking heart, that this would probably mean
he would soon start working long hours again.

She was right. The very next day he didn't get back until
after she was in bed, and he was up again at dawn, skipping
breakfast and dashing off in his car. She decided to go up to
Angkor that day and see the chamber. As usual, she and

Achariya spent the morning cooking, then she asked the houseboy to cycle up to Chong Khneas to call her one of the local taxis. By the time she arrived at the temple it was lunchtime. She wandered through the corridors carrying her tins of food and eventually reached the central tower, where she was amazed to see a huge opening in the wall supported by wooden joists. She went right up to it and peered inside. The men were working by flashlights inside the dark chamber, excavating earth from a large hole in the floor. Henri was supervising from the top. When he straightened up and saw her his face lit up.

'Come, come and see the Buddha statue we discovered!' he said. 'Ah! Have you brought some food? We were just going to have a break so it's very timely.'

He guided her across the chamber and showed her a beautiful statue of a seated Buddha on the far wall. Carved delicately in alabaster stone, the buddha figure was cross-legged, in meditation pose, seated on a naga, a huge, curled up snake.

'It's exquisite,' she said, running her fingers over the smooth, cool surface. 'I'm so proud of what you've done here, Henri.'

Everyone trooped outside and sat on the grass to eat the pastries Colette had brought. She looked around at the workers eating happily and chatting away amongst themselves and felt a fresh surge of pride for Henri and his persistence with the project. As well as uncovering priceless treasures, he had provided all these men and their families with a livelihood.

Soon it was time for Henri to get back to work. He kissed her absently then went back inside the chamber. With a heavy sigh she packed up the tins and started to make her way back through the temple. Entering the outer cloister, she saw a tall, slim figure standing in the aperture at the far end. Her heart sped up. She knew who it was, even from the silhouette. The way he held himself, the shape of his shoulders. She walked towards him, unable to stop herself.

'Colette. I saw you were here, and I couldn't resist coming to speak to you,' he said as she approached. She stopped walking.

'I don't think there's anything to say,' she said. 'Now if you wouldn't mind, I need to get through.'

'Before you go, why don't you come and see what I've been doing on the other site? I'd like to show you my work, if you're interested.'

She hesitated. He'd never really spoken about his work to her before apart from to tell her he'd been at Xiping. Her curiosity was piqued.

'What are you working on?' she asked.

'I've finished my work here at Angkor Wat. That was mainly restoring the bas reliefs on the outside of the temple. They tell astonishing stories from the Hindu Mahabharata epic. They're truly works of genius. But that work is finished for now. I'm working on another temple now, a little way from here. It's called Ta Prohm. It's very different to Angkor Wat. Would you like to see it?'

Colette glanced through the open door behind him. There were no cars drawn up outside waiting to take people into Siem Reap. She would have to wait a while anyway. Why not spend half an hour viewing another temple? She suppressed the resolutions she'd made to herself not to speak to Luc, not to think about him. She would have to be careful, she told herself.

'All right,' she said. 'I've never seen any of the other temples yet.'

His face brightened. 'Great. I think you'll love this one. The car is parked under that tree,' he pointed across the clearing and they walked over to it together.

She noticed that he drove more carefully this time. The roads around Angkor were very potholed and uneven, perhaps he was protecting his car. They turned off the main drag between Siem Reap and Angkor Wat and drove down a long, sandy avenue lined with tall, leafy trees, which cast a grey-green light into the car. He drove even more carefully here, slowing right down to manoeuvre over tree roots and rocks. She turned towards him to remark on the beauty of the light and his face was already turned towards her. She caught his eye and looked away instantly, fearing that he'd seen something in her look that she didn't want to reveal.

He drew up at the end of the avenue. 'It's here,' he said, nodding in the direction of some trees. Colette peered. 'I can't see a temple.'

Luc laughed and got out of the car. 'Come on, I'll show you. This temple was abandoned to the elements. Very different indeed from Angkor Wat. I think I love it even more, if that's possible. I hope you'll agree – it's incredible.'

As they walked through the giant teak trees she saw what he meant. In front of them, camouflaged by moss and undergrowth was a square, grey tower, built from elaborately carved stones. Beside it were some tumbledown buildings, but the astonishing thing was that giant trees were growing from the roofs, their sinuous roots winding their way through the rafters, fusing nature with the monument.

Luc led her up some steps and through a series of carved stone arches, which led through a thick wall and into the inner sanctum of the temple. In front of them was an elaborate building with a central tower covered in ornate carvings and bas reliefs. On they walked through more labyrinthine passages containing seated buddhas and statues of lions. The air was hot and steamy and thick with the sound of cicadas and the whoop of monkeys.

Ancient silver trees, with multiple root systems and curtains of creepers, were growing right through the walls. In some places they'd wrapped themselves around the stones and seemed to meld with them, making them as one. They came upon elaborately carved square towers, half collapsed, covered in green moss and lichen. Everywhere they walked, the leaves overhead cast dappled sunlight on the fallen stones.

In some areas there were dangerous rock falls where it was impossible to walk. In one place, an enormous tree was growing on top of a wall, its multiple roots winding down around the wall, and in between them the entrance to one of the passageways. This temple was far less well-preserved than Angkor Wat, far more primitive and raw, and Colette instantly understood Luc's desire to work on it. For some reason the intermingling of the stones with the flora of the jungle made it all the more fascinating.

They carried on, wandering through the sinuous jungle trees and amongst the ruins of the temple. It was astonishing to see how completely nature had taken over the place, but equally how it enhanced its beauty.

'So, this is my project,' Luc said, a note of pride in his voice. 'Others wanted to let the jungle take it over, abandon it to the elements, but I argued to preserve it as it is.'

'I hope you're not going to remove the trees,' Colette said. 'It looks so beautiful like this.'

'Of course not,' Luc said, 'I will restore the buildings, remove some of the debris, but keep it in its natural state. The trees add to its beauty now. They are truly a part of it.'

She looked admiringly at him. This was exactly in tune with what she was thinking.

They reached an abandoned tower and he led her inside. Shafts of sunlight slanted down through the broken roof, spilling down the wall, piercing the darkness. He was standing close to her, too close. She could smell the scent of him, the sweat of the day mingled with his heady cologne. He moved even closer and she backed against the wall, but then his arms were around her and he was leaning in to kiss her. She was astonished, but exhilarated at the same time. Her head was telling her to stop but her heart was soaring with joy. She couldn't help responding to the kiss, opening her mouth and letting his tongue explore hers. They kissed for a long time, then he drew back and covered her face with kisses.

'I've been wanting to do that ever since I first saw you,' he said. 'That terrible first evening. Despite the trauma of what happened, I couldn't take my eyes off you.'

'We shouldn't be doing this,' she said, stepping away from him, her head winning out at last. 'I think we should go back now.'

'As you wish,' he said. 'I will take you back to Angkor, or I'll take you home if you like. I'll do whatever you want. We can take it as slowly or as quickly as you want. I'm happy to play the waiting game. I'm sure that one day you'll come round to my way of thinking and that we will be lovers.'

They drove in silence back to Angkor Wat and she was relieved to see a taxi waiting there. She picked up the lunch cans, which reminded her of the recent lunch with Henri and his team and sent prickles of guilt all through her. She drove off in the taxi without looking back.

The anxiety about a Japanese invasion mounted. Stories filtered through from Indochina about how the Japanese had come to an agreement with the Vichy government, and allowed them to remain in place as long as Japanese troops could be stationed in Indochina.

'They're building up to invade British Malaya,' Henri told her one evening as he read the newspaper on the veranda. 'That's their real prize.'

'What about here? What about Cambodia?'

'I doubt they're interested, although there are still reports of informers flying about. People at the site are full of it.'

She was silent, wondering what anyone would have to gain by informing the Japanese. She knew there were various Japanese ex-pats in Phnom Penh, even a couple in Siem Reap. Were they there to inform on the population, paving the way to an easy invasion? The day before, she'd been in Siem Reap with Achariya and they'd seen a troop of French soldiers march by, rifles on their shoulders. They both stood and stared. They'd never seen that before. It must signal something.

Colette kept away from Angkor Wat for a few weeks. She didn't want a repeat of the incident at Ta Prohm, which she dismissed as a mistake. She redoubled her efforts to be loving and caring towards Henri and for a time things seemed idyllic between the two of them. In the daytime, she stepped up her volunteering at the school, going three mornings a week instead of just one. The teacher was delighted and the children were making excellent progress with their French.

After about a month a messenger riding a bicycle brought her a letter. It arrived during the daytime when Henri was at work. When she glanced at the writing, although she'd never seen it before, she knew who it was from. It was in black ink, stylised, flowing script. She ripped it open.

My darling Colette,

Every day I go up to Angkor in the hope of catching sight of you there. Just a glimpse would be enough, but you are keeping away, hiding yourself away at home. What have I done to deserve this punishment? All I have done is admire your beauty, and steal one delicious kiss. My heart and body are yearning for you. I need to see you and I don't think I'm being conceited when I say I believe you feel the same way. If this is true, come and meet me at my house on any Friday afternoon. It is on Rue de Russeau, behind the old market, number nine. I will be there waiting for you. I know you will come to me one day.

With Love, Luc Gilbert

Colette read the words breathlessly. She recalled the way he had kissed her in the tower at Ta Prohm, the smell of his cologne, the touch of his hands as he held her, the way the shafts of sunlight played on his face. She folded the letter and put it away in her desk. She couldn't act on it straight away. She needed to bide her time, to think about it. She knew what the consequences would be of meeting him, there was no doubt about that. And there would be no going back from that. She needed time to think before taking such a momentous step. To think and to reflect on what it would mean for her, how it might change her life.

THE DAYS WORE ON and she tried to put Luc's letter to the back of her mind. She went to the school to teach the children French, and she went to Angkor Wat to watch Henri at work. On those occasions, Luc was conspicuous by his absence. She tried to make up for her transgressions by being even more attentive to Henri than she'd ever been before. But whatever she did, still, in the back of her mind Luc was there, watching her, waiting for her, willing her to go to him. It was as if they were connected by an invisible thread and he was pulling her inexorably to him.

Towards the end of the month she went into Siem Reap with Achariya to shop at the market. She thought it would be a good way of passing the time and putting her dilemmas out of her mind. She and Achariya often went to the food market in the old French Quarter together to buy food for the following week.

The stalls were busy, and Colette followed Achariya around, listening to her joshing the stallholders, engaging in verbal banter with them. Her own Cambodian wasn't good enough to partake yet, but she was beginning to understand the gist of the words they exchanged.

They had bought vegetables and were at the butcher's stall looking for some cuts of steak. Colette found this stall hard to deal with. The smell of the recently slaughtered animals, the blood-spattered surfaces, the cuts of bleeding meat, so fresh they almost quivered. Today with the sun bearing down it became too much. She walked away to catch her breath and stood on the edge of the market, under the plane trees, taking in huge gulps of air. She leaned against a tree and watched the milling crowds of locals. Then her eyes wandered to an unusual group in the middle of the market. It was a group of men conversing animatedly. They looked very different from the usual customers who frequented the market. It was a group of Japanese men dressed in black. No doubt they were spies, or informants, she thought, sending reports back to occupied Annam. In the middle of the group was a western man... she looked closer and shock washed over her. Yes, it was Luc Gilbert, there was no doubt about it. Henri's words came back into her mind.

Rumour has it that the Japs have started to infiltrate Cambodia, that they've established networks of informants to help them plan an invasion here too. We just need to be vigilant.

Was Luc one of those informants? She stared, making quite sure in her mind that it was him. There he was, speaking openly to a group of Japanese. There could be no other explanation.

When Achariya was finished at the butcher's stall, Colette hurried over to her.

'Let's get home quickly,' she said.

They called a pony cart and trotted straight back to the villa on Tonlé Sap.

Colette couldn't wait to get to her desk in her room. When they arrived she ran upstairs. She opened her bureau, pulled Luc's letter out and tore it into strips. She took them out into the garden and burned them in the gardener's brazier. Then she sat down and put her face in her hands, sighing heavily. She'd had a narrow escape. At least she'd discovered the truth about Luc Gilbert before she'd given herself to him, body and soul.

When Henri came home that evening, she ran to him, flung her arms around him and held him tight.

'What's all this?' he asked, bemused.

'I love you, Henri and I want you to know that,' she said, kissing him passionately. 'And don't you ever forget it.'

'You really are an extraordinary woman, Colette Boissière,' Henri said, drawing her close to him and kissing her back.

A WEEK OR SO LATER, Henri came home from his day's work looking perplexed. She asked him what was wrong. He shook his head.

'Luc Gilbert has disappeared,' he said. 'He hadn't been into work for a few days, so I went round to his house in the old quarter of Siem Reap on the way home to see if he's alright. There was no one about so I went round to the back door. His cook was in the kitchen. He told me that Monsieur Gilbert had left suddenly for France a couple of days ago.'

'For France?' Colette's mouth dropped open in surprise. No one was going to France at the moment. It was practically impossible with the war on. There were no passenger liners at all.

'He has friends in high places for sure,' Henri said. 'Someone like Gilbert will always be able to negotiate himself a passage somehow. Perhaps on a naval vessel or something. I'm most put out he didn't even tell me. I *am* meant to be his boss after all.'

Colette was silent. Perhaps he knew about something particular that had made him leave. Perhaps he'd even gone back to France via Japan?

'Hmmm maybe his wife is sick or something,' Henri mused. 'Perhaps he needed to get back to France right away.'

Shock washed through Colette and she felt her hands begin to shake. His wife? Had she heard Henri correctly? Luc had never alluded to the fact that he was married. She was stunned. That made his advances towards her all the more duplicitous.

'I had no idea he was married,' she said when she'd recovered her composure enough to speak.

'Oh yes. His wife lives in Lyon. She flatly refused to come out to Cambodia. She'd been to Indochina and said the climate didn't suit her.'

'How very strange,' Colette mused.

But a couple of days after that, when Henri rushed home in the middle of the day to tell her that Japanese troops had walked into Phnom Penh and he'd come home to tell her about the invasion, she wasn't at all surprised. It all fitted together perfectly. If Luc had been spying for the Japs, he would surely have got out of Cambodia himself before the invasion.

12

TONLÉ SAP, 1995

Colette stood at the top of the bank amongst the wild grass, staring at the derelict house. It was living proof of the power of the jungle. Trees had sprouted on the veranda and were growing through the roof, wrapping their silver limbs around the rafters. In a strange way it reminded her of the temple at Ta Prohm and how the sinewy trees had completely taken over the buildings there. She recalled wandering through the rambling temple grounds with Luc Gilbert, back in the early forties, admiring the raw beauty of the setting. Now she shook her head in dismay, looking at her old home. It seemed impossible that this decrepit and tumbledown building, covered in moss and lichen and choked with wild trees, had once been that pristine residence with clipped lawns and manicured pot plants, where they used to take tea on the veranda under the whirring fans. The villa had been Henri's pride and joy. Whatever would he say if he could see it now. She shook her head, blinking the tears away.

She thought once again to the last time she'd seen the villa, glancing back frantically from the little motor boat as she sped away over the lake, fearing that at any moment a shot would ring out from the grounds and end it all. She hadn't realised at that time that she would never see her beautiful home again, or at least not in the state it was in then.

She wasn't even sure if the property belonged to her anymore. She knew that the Khmer Rouge had confiscated all private property and banned property ownership in their collectivisation initiative, part of their so-called five-year plan. But what had happened after that? She guessed that no one had bothered with her house and land because it was so overgrown no one would have had any use for it. Standing there, staring at those walls she had once owned, within which so many happy memories had been made, she wondered whether there was any way of finding out. She made a mental note to ask Achariya when she went back across the lake to see her. It was strange, she reflected, she hadn't returned to Cambodia with this in mind, but now she had stood on her old land, she had a powerful urge to own it once again, and if she could, to restore it to its former glory.

She shaded her eyes and scanned the overgrown land behind the house. It was covered in jungle plants, thickets of bamboo, giant ferns, huge spiky bushes with luxuriant flowers. The growth was so dense that she reluctantly decided not to try to walk through it. In the corner of the plot, though, she could see the patch of old jungle that covered the boathouse. It had grown even thicker over the years. She shivered. Was the boathouse still there, shrouded by that solid wall of shrubbery? If it was, its front doors would surely be blocked by the mangroves that had grown up in the shallows of the lake in recent years.

And there, somewhere in the distance, in the very corner of the plot under a spreading banyan tree, was Henri's grave, marked by a simple stone on which was carved an image of Angkor Wat. Was the grave still there even? Had the jungle obliterated it, or had the Khmer Rouge destroyed it in their hatred of the French? She recalled tending it religiously every morning that she was at the villa, until that terrible day in 1975 when she was chased out by the Khmer Rouge. She would bring lotus flowers, bougainvillea, jasmine, whatever was in bloom, and she would kneel beside it and say a little prayer for that good man, who'd given her a new life in Cambodia and who had shown her nothing but kindness and so much love. She would sit there for a while chatting to him, telling him about her day. Shading her eyes now, she tried to make out the banyan tree amongst the greenery but to no avail. She turned away, tears in her eyes. The devastation wrought upon the villa and its grounds had shocked her to the core. It seemed like sacrilege.

She took some photographs of the jungle and of the house then turned back towards the lake. It was heart-breaking to see the place like that, but it had triggered something inside her that drove away her tears. Now she had seen it she knew that something had to be done. It had given her certainty and purpose and she was sure that the decision to come back to Cambodia had been the right one.

The boatman ferried her quickly and expertly back across to Achariya's hut, winding his way between the stationary fishing boats, making sure his wake didn't disturb their lines. She remembered sitting there in the middle of the lake while Henri fished, and the feeling of peace and tranquillity that had stolen over her during those cherished moments.

At the jetty near Achariya's hut she paid the boat man, giving him a handsome tip on top of his fee.

'It wasn't easy to navigate those mangroves,' she said. 'I really appreciate you taking me there. I might want to go again soon.' The man smiled, showing blackened teeth and pocketed the money gratefully.

'Anytime, madam,' he said. 'Just ask for Boran.'

Achariya was still sitting on her deck watching the lake when Colette approached. She sat up and smiled.

'Did you see the villa?' she asked.

'Yes. It's in a terrible state I'm afraid,' Colette said with a sigh.

'Completely overgrown. And it made me think. I'd really like to try to restore it if I possibly can.'

She sat down on the bench beside Achariya. Achariya was smiling now.

'But madam, that would mean you would have to come back and live here.'

'If necessary I would, if that's possible. If not, I could at least make an extended stay. I was going to ask you, though. Do you know who might own that land now?'

Achariya fell silent, thinking deeply for a time. Then she shook her head.

'I really don't know. The Khmer Rouge took everything, but since then, I am not sure what happened. Why don't you go to the town hall in Siem Reap and ask? The officials there will surely be able to tell you.'

'Of course. Yes, I'll do that tomorrow morning. It might be a bit late today by the time I get back.'

'Will you stay with me for a while longer?' Achariya asked. 'I could make some tea.'

'Of course I'll stay. We can talk about the old times. We have so much to catch up on. And *I* will make the tea. You stay right where you are.'

Colette went to Achariya's tiny kitchenette in the corner of her hut, lit the little stove, which was powered by bottled gas, and boiled the kettle. She made a pot of Jasmine tea in a chipped china teapot, put it and two cups on a wicker tray and took everything outside.

'You used to make me tea in the afternoons, do you remember?' she said, smiling at the memory.

Achariya laughed. 'Yes, I would bring it out onto the veranda for you. And at first you only wanted English Breakfast tea with milk, but after a time you began to prefer Jasmine like a local.'

'Of course. It's the perfect tea to drink in Cambodia. I was a complete convert. I still drink it in France, even now.'

When the tea had brewed Colette poured and handed Achariya a cup.

'I was wondering,' she said, pouring her own tea and sitting down, 'whether you've had a chance to think about what we spoke of the other day. Of Sophia. Have you given any more thought to where she might be?'

Achariya was silent for a moment, then she spoke with surprising force. There was a bitter edge to her voice too.

'I wonder why you want to find her. She only caused you trouble and heartache when you were here before.'

'I came here to find you, Achariya, and to find her too. I owe it to her.'

'But why?'

Colette sighed. She had predicted some sort of resistance from Achariya, and knowing that, she'd been reluctant to bring up the subject, but if she was ever going to find Sophia, she needed her help.

'I feel responsible for her, I suppose. I always have.'

'Madam, I know you mean well, but I'm afraid this will only bring you more pain. I have no idea where she might be. As you know things have been chaotic in this country for a long time.'

'Yes, I know. But you are the only person I know here. If you can't help, I'm not sure what to do.'

'Well, if you really want to try, I will ask my neighbours. They have children and relatives who have travelled and who live in different parts of the country they could also ask. We have a big network. We might be able to find someone who knows what happened to her.'

Colette took Achariya's hand. It felt smooth and bony, Achariya had lost a lot of flesh during her illness. Achariya squeezed Colette's hand and patted it with the other one.

'Don't worry, madam, all will be well.'

All will be well... It's what Achariya used to say in the old days when things had become difficult for Colette. Hearing it now brought those days back to her. What a comfort Achariya had been to her back then. How she had looked out for her, cared for her. But those days were gone. Now, Colette reflected, it was up to her to return the favour and to look after her old friend.

THE NEXT DAY, after an early morning swim followed by a hearty hotel breakfast, Colette took a cyclo-rickshaw from outside the hotel. The driver took her to the Siem Reap town hall, a square, modern building a little way out of the town centre. It was cool and echoing inside the marble entrance hall, where huge fans whirred on the high ceiling above. She asked the receptionist if she could speak to someone about land ownership in the district.

A stony-faced official came to see her within a few minutes and ushered her into a meeting room.

'I used to own a villa here. On the lake,' she explained. 'My husband was chief curator of Angkor Wat. He bought the land before independence. I realise that property was confiscated by the Khmer Rouge but I'd like to know how I can get it back. It's very overgrown and the house is derelict, but I'd like to restore it if possible.'

The official didn't smile. 'All land confiscated by the Khmer Rouge reverted to the ownership of the local authority two years ago. So that is the position regarding your land now. It is owned by the Siem Reap District Authority.'

'Yes,' she said slowly, realising that she had to tread carefully. 'I understand that, but is there any way that I could buy the land back? I have some savings.'

Again, he looked at her steadily, his face serious. 'Our new constitution states that only those of Khmer citizenship may own the title to land in Cambodia.'

She stared at him, her dreams melting away rapidly. 'That's very unfortunate,' she said, her mind racing. Did this mean it was impossible for a foreigner to buy land here? Surely there must be some solution.

'So that's the situation I'm afraid, Madame Boissière. Some foreigners find a way around this, but I wouldn't advise it. Those schemes are very risky and you could lose your entire investment.'

'Of course,' she murmured, wondering what he was talking about. She got up from the table, shook his hand and went out of the office.

When she left the cool hall and stepped out into the morning sunlight, it was like stepping into an oven and she gasped as the steamy heat enveloped her. She hadn't expected to be thwarted at the first hurdle. How could she overcome this? Perhaps there wasn't a way, she thought with sinking spirits, perhaps she would never own that patch of land that held so many treasured memories again. She got into the cyclo and with a heavy heart asked the driver to take her back to the hotel.

13

TONLÉ SAP, 1941–45

The Japanese forces didn't come as far as Siem Reap at first. They remained in Phnom Penh, and allowed the pro-Vichy and pro-German French government to stay in position. Henri found out, from speaking to others he met in the colonial service through his work, that the Japanese had agreed to let the French administration remain in place as long as Japanese troops could be stationed in Cambodia and use it as a route through to battlefields in other countries.

At first, Colette's life was affected very little by the occupation. After a few months a small contingent of Japanese troops arrived in Siem Reap and paraded down the main street, but it was a token gesture, a mere show of strength. There was a ripple of fear amongst the locals but things quietened down again quickly. Food became a little harder to get at the market, but Achariya stepped into the breach and brought Colette and Henri fresh fish from her father's catch each day.

'Are you sure you can spare them? I know you have a big family,' Colette asked.

'Of course. Tonlé Sap will feed everyone who needs it,' Achariya replied and Colette felt a rush of gratitude towards her kind and generous housekeeper whom she now counted as a friend.

But within a few months of the Japanese occupation, news of heavy fighting between French and Thai armies near to the Thai border filtered through.

'Thailand is taking this opportunity to assert its strength over territories it has long disputed with Cambodia,' Henri explained. 'They know the French government is distracted by the Japanese occupation and doesn't have the strength to intervene.'

'What does it mean for us?' asked Colette, alarmed. 'It sounds as though the fighting might be quite close to here.'

'Let's wait and see,' Henri said grimly. 'Nothing very much, I hope.'

But the next morning they awoke to a strange, monotonous rumbling sound in the air that built and built until it had become deafening.

'What's that?' Colette sat up in bed, terrified. Was it thunder? There were often fierce storms over the lake, but it wasn't the monsoon season.

Henri ran out onto the balcony and Colette got out of bed and followed him. The sky darkened and a fleet of bomber planes flew over the house, their silver fuselage flashing in the bright sunshine of the early morning. There was a flag painted on the underside of the wings that Colette didn't recognise.

'They're not Japanese aircraft,' she said, puzzled.

'They are Thai planes,' Henri said. The planes were in the distance now, flying north, but as they watched, the undercarriage of each one expanded and huge round objects plummeted down from each. The next second came huge bangs and flashes from the direction of Siem Reap.

'They're bombing the town,' Henri gasped rushing inside and grabbing his clothes. 'I need to get up there, see what I can do to help.'

He grabbed their first-aid box from the bathroom.

'I'll come with you,' Colette said instantly, pulling on trousers and an old cotton top.

'You really don't need to. It could be dangerous.'

'It's no more dangerous for me than it is for you.'

Henri drove the few kilometres into town at breakneck speed. When they reached the outskirts, chaos ensued ahead of them. People were rushing to and fro, terrified, and the road was completely blocked with animals and vehicles.

'Let's leave the car and walk. It can't be far to where the bombs hit,' Henri said.

They walked through the outskirts towards the centre of the little town, pushing their way through the crowds of people who had all come out of their homes to find out what had happened. The fear in the air was palpable.

When they reached the town centre, the extent of the damage was clear to see and shock washed through Colette at the scenes before her. A row of buildings in the main street lay in ruins, fire still raging in some. Elsewhere smaller fires were burning randomly. The fire brigade with their hand-drawn pump was doing its best to douse the flames and other people were throwing buckets of water onto the burning buildings. The air was thick with black smoke and amongst the crowd there was a lot of panic and yelling. People staggered around in the road, stunned from the blast, and a few lay bloodied and still in the middle of the road. Beside them, a cyclo had overturned, its wheels buckled, the rider lying motionless on the ground, blood spreading from his head. Near him a bullock cart lay on its side, one bullock lying still, the other struggling to get to its feet, filling the air with its heart-breaking cries of distress.

Colette grabbed the medical kit and knelt down beside an injured woman. Blood was pouring from her head where she'd fallen on some sharp stones. Colette bathed the wound, fetched her some water from a nearby building and encouraged her to take some sips. Then she bandaged her head, propped her up and moved on to the next person, who lay prone with wounds to his leg. She carried on like this for hours, until there were no more wounded people to treat. Beside her, Henri and others were also helping the injured and when an ambulance arrived from the local hospital, they all helped the porters to carry the worst injured people to it.

Finally, it was over, the fires were out, people were drifting away and Colette sat down by the roadside, exhausted. Henri eased himself down beside her. His face was streaked with dirt, sweat was pouring from his brow, his shirt stuck to his back, but a wave of admiration went through Colette just looking at him. It was only through his quick thinking and selflessness that they were here at all. She slipped her arm around him and drew him close. How she regretted now being swayed by Luc Gilbert. Shame washed through her when she thought about the stolen kiss at Ta Prohm. What had she been thinking of? Henri, this good, kind man, didn't deserve such betrayal. And with Luc Gilbert of all people, possibly a real traitor himself. She went hot and cold just thinking about it.

Exhausted, they wandered back to the car and drove home. Achariya gave a cry of concern when she saw the state they were in and, fussing over them ceaselessly, brought them drinks and fried fish on the veranda. Later, tired from the events of the day, they bathed and went to bed early. They held each other tight, the shared experience of the traumatic day binding them together like never before.

There were no more bombings in Siem Reap but still the rumours of fighting continued. A few weeks later, Henri came home to tell Colette that France had been forced by the Japanese to sign a treaty giving up several provinces in Cambodia to the Thais including Siem Reap.

'This is terrible for Cambodia and for the French regime,' Henri sighed. 'Nothing like this has ever happened to this country before. Do you know that now over half a million

Cambodians are under Thai rule and a third of its land surface. Even Cambodia's rice harvest and fishing at Tonlé Sap belong to the Thais.'

The very next day Thai troops arrived in Siem Reap and patrolled the streets. They forced fishermen on Tonlé Sap to give up a proportion of their catch. Achariya was unable to bring fish to the villa anymore. She was very shamefaced. 'My father says he is sorry but he doesn't have enough now. We barely have enough to feed the family, and he has none to sell in the market.'

'Please don't worry, Achariya. We are very grateful for what you've done for us so far,' Colette assured her, privately worrying about how she and Henri were going to feed themselves. Luckily, at the start of the occupation, Lim the gardener, with great foresight, had dug and planted a vegetable patch at the far end of the villa gardens that was now producing beautiful, ripe fruit and vegetables. Achariya cooked imaginative vegetarian dishes for them each day, ensuring they didn't go hungry. Again, Colette's heart filled with gratitude towards those who cared for them – the gardener and this young woman whose kindness seemed boundless.

Life limped on in that vein for a long time. Their daily routine hardly varied for months. Henri continued to travel to Angkor Wat each day and work on the restorations with a reduced workforce. He was the only Frenchman there now, and Colette and Achariya still visited the school several times a week. They thought it was important to keep a regular routine for the children during these difficult times. There wasn't enough for anyone to eat and they all began to grow thin, including the children in the school. Whenever she could, Colette took them vegetables from the garden. Colette worried for everyone around her, but deep in her heart she knew they were a long way from starving and that many in other countries were having a far worse time in this terrible war than herself.

Colette followed the war through the newspapers that Henri

brought home, the relentless takeover of south-east Asia by the Japanese, the iron grip they had on the people they ruled over there. She read with horror leaked reports of the massacre of thousands of Chinese citizens in Singapore and Malaya. She also read with horror of the Nazi takeover of Europe, their offensives in north Africa and on the Eastern Front. For a long time there was very little news from France, with the Nazi occupation in place in Paris, Colette hoped fervently that her parents were living safely and quietly in the centre of the city. Then, with mounting optimism she read about the way the US and allies took Japan on in the Pacific, and with hope and prayers of the Normandy landings in June 1944 and of subsequent reports of the Allied armies fighting their way south towards Paris. In August she was overjoyed to read that they had reached the capital and then, after a couple of days that the city had been liberated.

Her feeling of joy at this news was tainted with sadness that because of the Japanese occupation of Cambodia, she was unable to contact her parents to check they were safe. So, she went through her days in a state of suspended anxiety that she knew wouldn't reach a resolution until she finally received news of them.

One day though, everything changed. There had been rumblings in ex-pat circles that the Japanese were losing faith in the French regime. Once the Vichy government fell in France, the Japanese acted quickly in Indochina. On March 9th 1945, Colette got up and went out onto the balcony as usual to watch the morning mist rise on the lake. Henri was already downstairs eating breakfast. She heard the rumble of wheels and a loud throaty engine on the road outside. The vehicle came to a halt outside the villa gates and then she heard fierce hammering on the gate. The hairs on the back of her neck stood up in fear and she saw Lim, the gardener, shamble over to open them.

'Open up! Open up! Imperial Japanese Army. All French civilians must report to us.'

Pulling on some clothes, Colette dashed down the stairs. Henri was already at the front door, his lips tight with fury.

'What the hell do they think they're up to,' he fumed storming out of the house and across the drive. But he stopped in his tracks when he saw the Japanese soldiers ranged in front of him, dressed in khaki uniforms, with their guns and bayonets at the ready.

An officer stepped forward. 'You must come with us,' he said. 'If you come quietly, you will not come to harm.'

'And if we don't?'

'Just come with us, Monsieur Boissière. It is the orders of the Imperial Japanese Army that all French civilians be detained.'

'Detained? Where?' Henri stormed.

'Just get your things. You have five minutes.'

Colette saw Henri hesitate but not for long. He turned back to the house clenching his fists.

'I can't believe this,' he said.

'Don't argue. They mean what they say, they will hurt you,' she said quietly, thinking of stories of Japanese atrocities that had filtered out from Singapore, from British Malaya, from Nang King in China. She saw that Henri's knuckles were white, he was making a supreme effort to restrain himself.

She rushed back into the house, ran upstairs and threw a few things into a suitcase. On the other side of the room Henri was doing the same. They went downstairs together and at the front door, Achariya appeared and threw her arms around Colette.

'They can't take you, madam,' she said. 'This can't be...'

'Don't worry, Achariya, we will be back,' Colette said returning her embrace but trying to keep calm. But Achariya carried on clinging to her, walking beside her while she walked down the front steps and across the drive towards the truck. When they neared the soldiers, one of them stepped forward, tore Achariya away from Colette and threw her forcibly to the ground. Achariya looked up at Colette, her face streaked with tears, blood oozing from her lips. 'I will take care of things here for you, madam,' she said, sobbing. 'Please come back soon.'

Colette desperately wanted to bend down and help Achariya to her feet but the soldiers were prodding her forward with their bayonets. A soldier snatched her suitcase and threw it into the truck, then he motioned her to climb up. Inside, seated on the hard benches running along either side were a few dishevelled and terrified looking French people, three men and two women, whose faces she recognised from occasional functions at the hotel at Siem Reap. Two of the men she knew to be rubber planters, the other some sort of official in the local French administration. They each nodded to her but no one smiled. She sat down, and Henri sat beside her. The tailgate was slammed shut and the engine roared into life. Then they were off, bouncing down the jungle road towards Siem Reap, the villa and the lake fading into the distance behind them.

14

CAMBODIA, 1945

The truck rattled away from the villa on the jungle road, jolting and bumping on the uneven surface and amidst her shock and inner turmoil, Colette wondered when they would get to see their home again. Tears kept flooding her eyes and clouding her vision. Tears of fear and frustration. Her mind kept returning to Achariya and the horror of seeing how the soldiers had thrown her to the ground brutally, as if she was less than human. What would happen to her and her family? What would happen to Lim and the houseboy and everyone here in this little community she'd grown to know and love? And what of herself and Henri? What would happen to them? Where were they being taken?

She grasped Henri's hand on the bench beside her and he squeezed her fingers.

'It'll be alright,' he said. 'They always treat citizen detainees better than prisoners of war.'

'But where are they taking us?'

He shrugged. 'At the moment we seem to be heading to Siem Reap. Perhaps they're taking us there, but I'm not sure where they would put us.'

She glanced at the two soldiers stationed near the tailgate, their rifles drawn, and looked away quickly. Their presence sent chills through her, reminding her that this was serious. The Japanese clearly meant business.

Within a few minutes they were rolling through the straggly outskirts of the town. Colette stared out at the empty streets. It was like a ghost town. There was no traffic about or even any people. They passed the food market where the frames of the wooden stalls stood bare. There were Japanese soldiers on every street corner, though, replacing the Thai soldiers who were now nowhere to be seen.

They rumbled down the main street and came to a noisy halt outside the Governor's residence. Two soldiers jumped down from the cab, ran down the drive and hammered on the front door. After some animated discussion, the Governor and his wife came out of the house, carrying suitcases, their heads bowed in shame. Colette remembered seeing them at functions at the Grand Hotel d'Angkor, dressed in finery, drinking champagne and enjoying their privileged position. Now they were shadows of their former selves – an older couple, grey-haired, moving stiffly, prodded on by the Japanese soldiers. It took them a while to climb into the back of the truck and they looked around bewildered. Then the Governor sat down beside Henri, and his wife beside him.

'Hello, Boissière,' the Governor said, shaking his head. 'What a terrible day for the French empire.'

'It is, sir. It certainly is.'

'But we'll be back. Don't doubt it. I hear the French forces are trying to resist the takeover. Just like we tried to resist the Thais in '42. I received reports of fighting in Kampong Cham province earlier, but of course we were beaten back. Didn't have the manpower.'

The lorry started up again and rattled on through the silent town. On the outskirts it stopped at another French home to collect another official and his wife. This man tried to resist, shouting at the soldiers. One of them drew his bayonet and held it to the man's back and then he stopped. When he climbed over the tailgate his face was red with rage.

Then they were on the move again, through the outskirts of the town and onto the bumpy road that ran along beside Tonlé Sap and headed south. Peering out, shading her eyes, Colette was certain she could see their villa on the other side of the lake as they sped past, white pillars rising amongst the tropical greenery, contrasting with the deep blue of the waters of the lake. A lump formed in her throat at the pain of the parting, at the not knowing when she might see her home again.

'They're taking us to Phnom Penh, or so I hear,' the Governor said.

'Why?' Henri asked.

'I suppose they want us all in one place to keep an eye on us. They'll have all the other ex-pats stationed there already.'

'Will they put us in prison?' She could hardly bear to ask the question, but she wanted to know the truth.

'I am not sure of their exact intentions at the moment. I heard that all French officials in Annam, Tonkin and Cochinchina have been rounded up and put in jail. So perhaps we'll go the same way.'

'Oh, please, Albert.' His wife spoke up for the first time. 'Don't alarm people. We don't know what will happen.'

'Best people know the worst so they can prepare themselves,' the Governor muttered but remained silent after that.

Nobody spoke much on the long journey. Colette held Henri's hand and when she got tired she rested her head on his shoulder, although it was difficult to sleep on the hard bench with the constant jolting of the truck, the diesel fumes from the exhaust that blew back at them and the clouds of dust that rose from the unmade road.

She knew this road well. It was the road that she and Henri had driven in either direction many times since their marriage. They had travelled to Phnom Penh to stay in the villa there while Henri attended meetings with the Resident General, to give presentations about his work or to ask for more funds for the project. Those drives had been happy occasions. Achariya had always packed them food and drink to take along, and they would stop and picnic by the roadside in beautiful, remote spots admiring the beauty of the jungle, listening to its sounds. Since the occupation they had gone less frequently, but with the French administration in charge and a very light Japanese army presence on the ground, they came and went between their homes almost as they had before the invasion. She could scarcely believe that now she was being driven along the road as a prisoner. She wondered if it would be possible to escape, to jump down from the lorry and run into the jungle. But that was a wild thought and she dismissed it. Where would she go? The Japanese were in charge now, throughout South East Asia.

They passed remote farms and drove through villages that straddled the road. The locals sat on their porches, staring mutely at their former rulers, now captive, cut down and humiliated. What were they thinking, Colette wondered. Were they filled with joy at the demise of their colonisers, or were they worried about what the future might bring for themselves? Stories of Japanese atrocities preceded them. They might not be the liberators of all Asians that they promised to be.

Colette lost track of how long they'd been travelling. After several hours the lorry drew up on a patch of bare land in the middle of the jungle. The soldiers handed round a bucket of water with one tin cup. Each prisoner dipped the cup into the water and drank thirstily. Then the soldiers lowered the tailgate of the truck and motioned for them to climb down. A bolt of shock went through Colette. Were they going to shoot them all here and now? In this remote place?

'Toilet stop,' the guard said, and relief washed through her. 'Men that side of lorry, women the other.'

They climbed down from the back of the truck, stretching their aching limbs. It was humiliating but necessary to squat amongst the trees with the other female passengers who all carefully avoided looking at each other.

After that the journey continued. Within a couple of hours, they had reached the outskirts of Phnom Penh. Just as Siem Reap had been, the city was unnaturally quiet with only a few brave people venturing out onto the streets. The main life there seemed to consist of packs of wild dogs roaming neighbourhoods unchecked. There were signs of skirmishes here too – burned out cars, upturned cyclos, collapsed buildings. It was as if an army had gone through at speed like a plague of locusts, destroying everything in its path.

They progressed through the city, and eventually entered the wide, tree-lined boulevards of the French quarter. Soon afterwards, they passed the end of the road to Henri's villa. Colette strained her eyes to get a glimpse of the building, but the street was jammed with Japanese army vehicles.

'They've probably requisitioned the place as quarters for their officers,' Henri said grimly, following her gaze.

The truck moved on, turning off a boulevard and into the narrower streets with terraced shop-houses on either side. All the shops were closed and shuttered, the sound of the truck's engine reverberating between the walls. Colette imagined people cowering inside their houses, terrified of the new occupiers of their city and what they might do. Finally, they drew up outside some temporary-looking metal gates that completely cut off the end of one street. One of the officers, the one who could speak some French, got out of the cab and came round to the back to talk to the prisoners.

'This is where you will stay,' he said. 'It is the designated zone for interned French nationals.'

Everyone in the truck exchanged looks, surprised. So, they weren't going to prison after all. They were going to stay in the city in ordinary houses. They got down from the truck, hauling their luggage with them and were ushered through the metal gates which clanged shut behind them. Colette started at that sound. It meant the end of her life as she knew it, the end of freedom. She walked down the narrow street beside Henri, following the other prisoners and, as she did so, a feeling of deep dread and foreboding enveloped her.

They continued along the street, carrying their suitcases, wondering where they were meant to be going. A few paces down the road, a desk was set up in the shade of a tree. Two stony-faced Japanese officials stood behind it. Guards waved them forward and they waited in line to be registered. When it was Henri and Colette's turn, Henri stepped forward.

'Residence papers?' the official snapped without looking up, clicking his fingers.

'Did you bring them?' Colette asked under her breath.

'Of course. I slipped them into my suitcase. It's lucky I did by the looks of it,' Henri said. He fished them from his suitcase and handed them to the official who stamped them with the seal of the Imperial Japanese Army.

'Your accommodation is one room in a flat further down this road,' the official said. 'Number 6B. You are not allowed out of area. Do not go beyond perimeter of the internment zone. You will see a wire fence on the edge. To go beyond that is punishable by death.'

'What about food?' Henri asked.

'There are shops in the zone. You can buy food,' the man replied. 'Now move on.' He waved them aside and turned his attention to the next people in the queue.

Colette and Henri walked along the road, looking at the numbers on the terraced houses until they came to number 6. It was a two-storey shophouse and the downstairs still seemed to function as some sort of shop although nobody was about. Sacks of what looked like rice were stacked on the floor.

Beside the entrance to the shop they found the concrete staircase to the first floor and climbed to the top. In front of them, on a rubbish-strewn landing was a door on which someone had written 6B crudely in chalk. They pushed the door open and inside was a bare room with two grubby, narrow mattresses laid out on the floor, a rickety chair beside the window, a broken wooden chest of drawers and very little else. A fan circled slowly from the high ceiling but even as they stood there it stuttered to a halt, then started up again even more slowly.

The air in the room was dank and moist. The only saving grace was the fact that the window looked out over the street. Colette went to it and pushed the shutters open and peered out. A group of French children ran along the street beneath her, laughing and shouting. They looked ragged and wild. Then, a platoon of Japanese soldiers marched through, bayonets over their shoulders and she drew back into the room quickly.

'It might look as if we're free in here, but there seems to be a heavy Japanese presence,' she said. She sat down on the chair and put her face in her hands.

'It's awful here, Henri. How are we going to manage? There aren't even any sheets on those filthy mattresses.'

'We will cope, ma chérie, don't worry. This can't last for ever and we're surrounded by people just like us. We can surely all help each other.'

There was a knock on the door and an elderly French woman appeared in the doorway. In one hand she held a cigarette that was burning down, dropping ash on the floor. She looked them up and down in a swift, appraising motion. She wore a floral dress and her hair was tied up in a headscarf.

'Bonjour monsieur, madame, I am Madame Leclerc, I live in the flat opposite. If there's anything I can help you with...'

Colette and Henri introduced themselves. 'How long have you been here?' Henri asked.

'Only since yesterday, but long enough to get the lie of the land. The Japs have commandeered all the shops and are charging the earth for food. There's barely anywhere to cook, I'm afraid. There's a stove in the next door shophouse but it seems to serve half the houses in the street so you have to queue. I gave up yesterday and just ate bread for my supper. The lavatory is down the backstairs and out in the yard. It doesn't flush so you have to use a bucket of water. There's a bucket and tap out in the yard. That's the only washing facilities here too.'

'We haven't got anything with us,' Colette said, 'No cooking equipment, only clothes, so we can't really cook.'

'I expect others will help you out... for a fee,' Madame Leclerc said, narrowing her eyes. 'If you need sheets I have some I could let you have for a few francs.'

Colette hesitated but Henri agreed. He followed the old woman out of the room and reappeared with a pile of sheets.

'How much did you pay her?'

'Oh, only a couple of francs. We want to be as comfortable as possible and I know you were worried about the sheets.'

Colette smiled at him. 'You're so thoughtful, Henri Boissèire,' she said. 'I really don't deserve you.'

He took her in his arms and they held each other for a long time, listening to the shouts of the children in the streets, the chatter of cicadas in the trees behind the houses. The marching feet of some soldiers in another street, distant traffic in the rest of the city.

'We'll muddle through, you'll see.'

That evening they ate fried rice that they managed to buy from a French woman cooking a great quantity downstairs on the stove next door.

'Tomorrow we can try to buy some cooking equipment,' Henri said. 'We can't pay this much for every meal.'

'How much money did you bring?'

'Not sure, as much as there was in the house. But it won't last for ever.'

They lay down on the mattresses and pulled the sheets over their faces to prevent being bitten by mosquitoes, but Colette couldn't sleep despite her exhaustion. Several mosquitoes buzzed around on the ceiling above and occasionally she would hear the whine of one near her face as it tried to dive-bomb her. She lay awake, watching the ceiling fan circulate the stale air and listening to the alien sounds of the occupied city.

Her mind kept wandering to Luc Gilbert. Had he really been spying for the Japanese? Where had he disappeared to and why did he leave so suddenly? How had he got out of the country during wartime? She couldn't purge herself of the guilt of that illicit embrace at Ta Prohm because in her heart of hearts she knew that she'd been attracted to him and had been tempted to visit him at his house to take it further. It was only because she'd seen him speaking to those Japanese men in the market that she'd decided against it. She turned and looked at Henri, who was now gently snoring under his sheet, and felt a flood of affection for him. She slipped her arm around his middle and snuggled closer to him, thinking how much closer they had grown lately, how much he meant to her. Just his presence there beside her made her feel safe.

15

PHNOM PENH, 1945

In the morning they got up early. It was too hot and uncomfortable in the room to lie there for long. Colette went down in the back yard to wash. She started to take off her clothes, then glanced up at the windows of the shophouse and, seeing a shutter wobble in one of the upstairs rooms, decided against it. Perhaps she could come down after dark for a proper wash. In the meantime, she would keep her clothes on and just wash her face and hands. When she went back upstairs, Henry had already gone out to look for food. He came back within half an hour or so with some bananas and a mango. He also handed her a knife and some plates which he'd managed to purchase from another internee.

'These were all incredibly expensive,' he said. 'And do you know, I discovered something disturbing while I was out. The Japs run all the food shops for their own profit and fix the prices incredibly high. As well as imprisoning us, they are hell bent on exploiting us too!'

'That's terrible, Henri. But we're their prisoners, they're hardly going to treat us with kindness.'

She began to peel the mango, her mouth watering at the sight of the juicy, yellow fruit and the sweet, delicious smell. She realised that she was very hungry.

'I've a good mind to kick up a stink about it,' Henri said. 'I spoke to some of the other men and they agree. We shouldn't just take this lying down.'

Colette experienced a flutter of anxiety at his words. 'Oh, Henri, please don't go getting yourself into trouble. They are armed, they have all the power. They don't care about us.'

'Don't worry, chérie. I'll be careful, but this is a point of principle...'

After breakfast, he left the house again, hoping to buy cooking equipment. Colette went to the window and watched him walk up the street. She bit her nail nervously, watching him stride away with his head held high and his shoulders squared. She was full of admiration for his courage, but couldn't help worrying for his safety. She lingered awhile at the window, watching the comings and goings in the street. Women walking up and down with buckets of water, sacks of food, children rushing about chasing each other, the sound of their laughter filling the air. The odd feral dog or cat joined the throng too.

There was a knock on the door and when she opened it, she was surprised to see the Resident General's wife.

'Good morning,' she said, holding out her hand for Colette to shake. 'We haven't met formally but I'm Françoise Fournier, we came up from Siem Reap on the truck together yesterday.'

Colette suppressed a smile. Hadn't they squatted together in the jungle to relieve themselves? Surely such a formal introduction wasn't necessary.

'Bonjour, Madame,' she said. 'Would you like to come in? There's only one chair but please sit down and I can sit on the windowsill.'

'Thank you,' Madame Fournier inclined her head graciously and sat down on the rickety chair.

'I've come to ask for your help. One of the other women

approached me this morning, knowing I have a little influence amongst the wives of officials. Apparently, they're thinking of setting up a temporary school for the children here. We don't know how long we're going to be here, but we don't want them to miss out on their learning. Even in twenty-four hours, the children have become a little wild.'

'Poor things, they're probably feeling unsettled at having to leave their homes.'

'Well, it has to be nipped in the bud,' said Madame Fournier, drawing herself up. 'I heard that you teach at the school on Tonlé Sap so you have some prior experience.'

Colette wondered how Madame Fournier had come by the knowledge, then realised that the French community in Cambodia was incredibly close-knit. Everyone knew everyone else's business, especially in a small place like Siem Reap.

'I do teach at the school, but it's only French conversation I'm afraid. All I do is talk. It's not really teaching.'

'Well, it's better than nothing, and needless to say, these ladies are desperate for help. I'd be very grateful if you'd agree. It might help to fill the time too while you're here. Goodness knows, it's boring enough.'

'Alright,' Colette said reluctantly. She had no objection to helping out in some way, but wasn't sure that teaching was the right thing for her.

'Thank you,' Madame Fournier said briskly, getting to her feet. 'I expect to see you in the schoolroom at nine o'clock sharp tomorrow morning. It's at the end of this road on the right in an old latex warehouse. You can't miss it.'

Then she was gone, and Colette was left reeling. What had she just agreed to? She had to hand it to Madame Fournier, she was certainly very persuasive.

So, the next morning, after a breakfast of black tea and banana, Colette set forth up the narrow street towards the crossroads. She'd kissed Henri goodbye with misgivings. She was worried about what he might say to the Japanese about the food situation. It was something he had latched onto and he didn't seem to want to let go of it. Just as he could be with his work when he was onto an important discovery, he could be single-minded and stubborn about other things too.

Sure enough there was an old-fashioned warehouse set back from the road in a courtyard. She walked in across the cobbles jostled by the mothers bringing their children.

A friendly young teacher greeted her at the door. 'Madame Boissière? I'm Yvette André. Thank you so much for coming. I don't know what we'd do without you. Madame Fournier told us that you have a lot of experience.'

'Well, actually...'

'If you wouldn't mind going through to the next room, I've sent all the five to eight year-olds in there in the hope that you'll be able to take that class. They are a little rowdy I'm afraid.'

Colette could see that there was no escape, so, taking a deep breath, she went through to the next room, where about a dozen children were rushing about playing, yelling at the tops of their voices.

She closed the door with a bang.

'Children!' she shouted, and they all stopped exactly where they were and turned to look at her, their eyes wide. 'I'm your new teacher. Now, come and sit down on the floor and we will work out what we're going to do today.'

She had to use great ingenuity to entertain the children and at the end of the morning went back to the room at number 6 thoroughly exhausted. Henri was pacing about the small room, muttering under his breath.

'It's outrageous what's happening here, Colette. I've spoken to the Governor General but he won't do a thing. He's lily livered. Just wants to cave into the Japs and doesn't want trouble. I would have thought he would have more bottle.'

'Perhaps he's afraid for his safety,' Colette suggested but Henri snorted dismissively and went straight out. Colette sat down on the broken chair, worried about this turn of events. She could see that for Henri, this had quickly become an obsession. She hoped he would calm down about it soon because she could only foresee trouble ahead otherwise.

He didn't come back until late afternoon and this time he had brought rice, onions and some meat which neither of them could identify.

'We're going to eat like kings tonight,' he said, a triumphant look on his face.

'How much did you pay for that?'

'Nothing. Precisely nothing.'

She stared at him, her mouth open.

'I waited until the Jap guard had closed the store and disappeared, then I broke in and helped myself. They hardly bother to secure the place. Easy as pie.'

'Oh, Henri. That's so dangerous.'

He laughed. 'It wasn't dangerous at all. No one saw me. And if the Japs won't play fair with us, they can't expect us to play fair with them.'

Reluctantly she went downstairs to the communal kitchen, waited her turn then cooked the illicit food on the utensils Henri had managed to gather together that day. She took it back up to the room on two tin plates. Henri gobbled his down, but despite the rumbling of her stomach, Colette found she had little appetite. She was wracked with anxiety. What would happen if the Japanese discovered that some food was missing? Surely there would be some reprisals? She toyed with the unappetising-looking risotto, plagued by these concerns.

'Don't worry, Colette. Eat your food. I was careful. No one will ever know.'

She ate slowly, having difficulty swallowing every mouthful, wondering how she was going to persuade Henri that stealing from the Japanese was a very bad idea. She knew that if he got away with it this time, he would try again.

She was right. He didn't do it every evening, because sometimes the Japanese kept the shop open until very late, but whenever it closed early, under cover of darkness, he found a way in and stole what he could lay his hands on.

'Why do you do it?' Colette pleaded. 'We have money. We can buy food.'

'It's the principle of the thing, Colette. If they're going to exploit us, I will exploit them, it's as simple as that. And anyway, we don't have much money left.'

The days wore on in their monotonous but tense routine. The French community settled down into its captivity with only a few murmurs of discontent. Most people wanted to keep their heads down and get through it as quietly as possible. Only a few, like Henri, were willing to challenge the authority of the Japanese. And although the guards and soldiers weren't a prominent presence on the street, as Colette had guessed on their first evening, they were ever present. They patrolled the streets at regular intervals during the day and expected internees to stop and bow their heads when they passed. The same rule applied if an internee met a soldier on the street. They were expected to stop and bow respectfully too. If they didn't, and Colette had seen this happening, the soldier would step forward and slap the internee several times on alternate cheeks. This was done to humiliate and subjugate the French, rather than to hurt them.

Against this backdrop of fear and oppression, Colette went to teach at the school each weekday morning. She found the children a challenge. They were far more difficult to interest and to maintain discipline with than the Vietnamese-Cambodian children at the school on Tonlé Sap. Those children were quiet, keen to learn, hanging on her every word, whereas these were ebullient, excitable, difficult to control. She would read them stories, listen to them reading, give them simple sums to do, teach them what she knew about history and geography.

Some of the children were very sweet and compliant, especially the little girls. They would come up to Colette at the end of the morning to say goodbye, melting her heart by putting their arms around her affectionately. She found herself wondering for the first time why she and Henri hadn't conceived and began to long for a child. When they'd first married, she'd been too young to worry about babies and had wanted to experience her new life to the full, but now, she was twenty-five. It was surely time. She determined to speak to Henri about it when she could get him off the subject of the Japanese. It was a long time since they'd had a civilised conversation, she reflected.

This longing for a child increased her distance from the others and her feelings of loneliness. The other women were friendly, especially Yvette the young teacher at the school, Madame Fournier and some of the mothers. To them the camp represented a reason to band together as a community and face adversity as one. But Colette found herself holding back from that. She didn't want to get too close to anyone in case they began to ask questions about Henri's food pilfering activities.

One day, walking to school, she met Fleur Leroux who was heading towards the store.

'Fleur!' Fleur turned towards her and Colette instantly saw that Fleur had suffered immeasurably since they last met. She looked a lot thinner, her face was pinched and angular now and her skin sallow. Her dress hung off her shoulders and her previously immaculate dark hair was grey at the roots.

'Colette! How are you?'

'I'm alright. I didn't realise you were here, Fleur,' Colette said. 'I haven't seen you about.'

'I've been very ill,' she replied. 'Malaria, dysentery, the works. There's no medicine to speak of in here, Charles has had to buy opium for me from the Japs at ridiculous prices. It's been hell.'

'I'm so sorry, Fleur,' said Colette. 'If I'd known I would have come to see you. I could have brought you food.'

'Yes, I heard about Henri's activities. He should be more careful.'

'I know... but if there's anything I can do to help, do let me know.'

'Of course. Thank you,' Fleur said turning away and walking towards the shop with drooping shoulders. Colette reflected on the change in her old friend. What a dreadful time she was having. When would this terrible imprisonment ever come to an end?

Walking to the school, she reflected too on what Fleur had said about Henri's activities. It was not surprising that people were talking about him. If anything, he'd become more daring as time went on. He'd begun to steal not just for Colette and himself, but also for the neighbours. When Madame Leclerc fell ill with malaria, Colette went into her room in the afternoons to make sure she had enough to drink and to cool her down with a wet cloth, but Henri brought her food each evening. When she recovered a little she began to ask where it came from and Henri had to let her into the secret.

'Don't tell anyone,' he said.

'Your secret's safe with me, Monsieur Bossière,' she said, but Colette could tell, from the look in the neighbour's hard eyes, that if she got an opportunity she would exploit her knowledge to the full.

Henri also stole for an elderly couple who lived next door and for others who'd run out of food or had no money left. He would sometimes even bring rice to the school for the mothers to take home with them. The Japanese were aware that food was going missing and were becoming more and more vigilant. They stationed a guard outside the shop in the evenings, but Henri's trick was to slip in the back way while the shopkeeper was distracted, closing up and putting the stock away. He would grab what he could and creep out the way he'd got in.

They'd been there two months when early one evening Colette was waiting in the flat for Henri to return with food for their meal. The sun had gone down over the buildings opposite and Colette was beginning to worry. This wasn't unusual, she normally worried, but it was unusual for him to be this late. She paced up and down their room until she could bear it no longer. She left the room, ran downstairs and hurried up the road towards the Japanese stores, despite the curfew that the Japanese had recently introduced. To her surprise the lights were still on in the store. Japanese guards were swarming around the makeshift building. Her heart did a somersault. Had they seen Henri stealing food? Had they caught him? It didn't look like it because they were still searching, but if not, wherever was he?

She waited in the shadows until the Japanese soldiers finally shut up the shop and marched away to their barracks. Then, slowly and carefully she emerged from her hiding place. Her heart missed another beat. There was Henri coming down the road towards her. She ran to him and flung her arms around him.

'What happened? Where have you been? The place was full of soldiers.'

'I know, I know. I managed to get out and hide in the place opposite until they'd finished. I wasn't able to get any food tonight. I'm so sorry.'

'Don't be sorry! You've had a lucky escape. Promise me you won't try again. They're obviously on to you.'

'Hush! Let's talk about this at home,' Henri said ushering her along.

Back at the flat Colette managed to persuade Henri to refrain from pilfering from the shop at least until things quietened down. He reluctantly agreed, and Colette felt instant relief, but without those activities, Henri quickly became bored and even more critical of their captors. He railed against the prices in the shop, the living conditions, the fact that people had to bow in the street to soldiers. He would sit at the window watching people pass.

'We're like lambs to the slaughter,' he would say. 'Why doesn't anyone ever say anything?'

'Perhaps because they want to get out of here alive,' Colette muttered, worrying that he was building up to something.

One day, a week or so after the incident at the stores, her fears came true.

Henri was sitting at the open window, brooding as usual, when a Japanese patrol approached.

'Here they come again,' he said to Colette, who went to the window to join him.

A teenage boy happened to be in the path of the patrol and didn't get out of the way quickly enough. The patrol halted, and one of the soldiers stepped forward and began yelling at the boy and slapping his face with a forehand-backhand motion. The boy backed away, and that infuriated the soldier more. He pushed the boy in the chest and the boy went stumbling to the ground. The next second the six soldiers had surrounded the boy and were kicking him in the ribs, the legs. His howls of pain filled the air.

'Hey!' Henri shouted from the window. The soldiers turned to look up at him, but he was up, out of the door, running down the steps and out onto the street. Colette watched, aghast.

'Don't do that to the boy. He's just a child,' Henri yelled, bending down to help the boy up, but then the soldiers had surrounded him too, kicking him, punching him to the ground. He began to yell abuse at them.

'You cowards, you filthy bastards...'

'Please,' Colette murmured under her breath, and ran out of the room and out into the street, but it was too late. The soldiers were beating him with their rifle butts. The boy scrambled to his feet and limped away, but the attack on Henri carried on. Through their frenzied throng, Colette caught sight of Henri's face, bloodied and inert, his eyes open and staring. Finally one soldier drew his bayonet and plunged it into Henri's chest, drew it out and plunged it in again and again.

Colette stood there, shaking from head to foot, screaming at the top of her voice. A crowd had gathered and one woman put her arms around Colette's shoulders and tried to draw her away.

'There's nothing you can do,' she said, but Colette wouldn't move.

The soldiers stopped their attack, put their rifles over their shoulders and marched away. Colette tore herself away from the woman and ran to Henri's inert body, that lay bloodied and battered on the pavement. She threw her arms around him, felt his warm blood on her face, listened to his chest, but he was gone. There was no pulse, no heartbeat.

'Henri, my love. Whatever have you done?' she sobbed.

16

TONLÉ SAP, 1995

C olette walked along the jetty and stepped onto the deck of Achariya's houseboat. Achariya's eyes lit up and she smiled broadly when she saw Colette. Colette was relieved to see that Achariya looked far brighter than she had on the first day. Once again she was dressed in a bright yellow sarong printed with red and orange flowers and now her skin was glowing and there was more colour in her cheeks.

'You're looking lovely today,' Colette said, kissing her friend's cheek.

'It's because of your visit, madam. I've been looking forward to you coming back but I wasn't sure it would be today. Let me put the kettle on.'

'I can do that, Achariya,' Colette said. 'Please sit down.'

'No, I insist. It does me good.' Achariya eased herself out of her chair and moved stiffly towards the kitchenette.

'Well, alright, but do let me know if there's anything I can do,' Colette said, sitting down reluctantly. Perhaps Achariya was right and it was good for her to move about. On the other hand, Colette didn't want Achariya to tire herself out.

'Did you go to the town hall to ask about the land?' Achariya asked from inside the houseboat.

'Yes. I went this morning. A bit of a waste of time, I'm afraid. Apparently, foreigners aren't allowed to own land in Cambodia now.'

'Of course. I should have remembered that before you went. That's the rule nowadays.'

'So, even though nobody wants the land, and the local authority has no use for it, I can't buy it back myself. It's such a tragedy. Henri's grave is on that land.'

Achariya appeared in the doorway, her face solemn.

'I'm so sorry, madam. It's very unfortunate. If there's anything I can do to help...'

'I was wondering...' Colette began. 'If *you* might be able to buy the land for me.'

'Me?' Achariya said weakly. She came and sat down again. 'I'm afraid I cannot do that, madam. Not even for you.'

'But why not? I would provide the funds. We could own the place together.'

'You know I would, gladly. I'd do anything I could to help you, madam, you know that. Only I'm not allowed to own land myself. That's why we live in this floating community. We can own boats on the water, but we can't own land in Cambodia. We are ethnic Vietnamese you see, not true Khmer nationals.'

Shock went through Colette and she looked at her old friend, shamefaced. Of course. She had known that years ago. How tactless of her to have brought this up, to have complained about not being able to own land here when Achariya and her whole community had been denied that right for generations. That was the whole reason for the floating community here on Tonlé Sap. It was their way of getting round the ownership rules.

'I'm so sorry, Achariya. How thoughtless of me. I should have remembered.'

'Don't worry, madam. It's easy to forget when you've been away for such a long time.'

Inside the kitchenette the kettle whistled shrilly and Achariya got up and went in to make the tea. She came out a few minutes later with the tray and Colette got up and took it from her.

'Sit down, please. I will pour.'

'You know, I've just been thinking.' Achariya sat down in her cane chair. 'There might just be a way of purchasing the land. I have heard that there are things you can do. Companies are set up to do that for foreigners... not for us Vietnamese of course,' she added wistfully. 'You could ask a lawyer in the town. It might be possible.'

'Really?' Colette asked, brightening. 'And if I could find a way of buying it, and I had enough money to restore the villa, would you come and live there with me, Achariya?'

She poured the jasmine tea and handed a cup to Achariya. Achariya took a sip before replying.

'That is very kind of you, madam, but I would have to think about it. My life is here in my community. My friends are around me, the medical centre is close by, the market is on the dock so it is easy to buy food. Everything is to hand for me here.'

'Of course,' said Colette softly, a wave of sadness washing through her. Achariya was right, she was probably far better off here in the heart of things than on the other side of the lake in a remote villa, far away from the facilities and everyone she knew. But all the same it brought home to Colette how things had changed between the two of them since they were last together, how their friendship had drifted in the twenty years they'd been apart.

They fell silent then, listening to the mournful cries of the floricans on the water, the engine of a boat powering up the lake, the wash of its wake against the houseboats.

'Did you think any more about how we might find Sophia?' Colette asked, breaking the silence.

Achariya put her cup down.

'I asked my neighbour to ask around. She has a nephew who is a journalist. He knows how to trace people and has helped a lot of families find their loved ones since the fall of the Khmer Rouge. He's recently been up in the north but he is coming home next week. She is going to ask him.'

'That would be excellent. Perhaps I could meet him?'

'I will ask her. But madam, like I said before, no good will come of it. Sophia only ever caused you pain.'

Colette was silent again, thinking about her words.

'Perhaps you're right,' she answered after a while. 'But I still feel responsible for her, whatever happened between us back then.'

'That is because you are a good, kind woman. But she doesn't deserve your kindness. And besides, she will not be young anymore. She is a grown woman – in her forties by now, surely?'

'Of course,' Colette said in surprise. It was hard to imagine. In her mind Sophia was forever young, with her perfectly smooth, creamy skin, her long black hair like a skein of silk and her restless, dark eyes. Those eyes! Every time Colette thought about them they brought those troublesome memories rushing back.

Colette finished her tea and got up to go. She kissed Achariya fondly. 'I will come back in a couple of days,' she said.

'Oh, I've just remembered. There's a lawyer in Street 11 next to the old market if you're interested,' Achariya said. 'He helped some of the fishermen on the lake when their fishing licences were suspended once. He might be able to help you.'

'Street 11?' Colette asked, laughing.

'Yes. The Khmer Rouge banned all the old French street names and gave them new ones. And these names seemed to stick.'

STREET 11 STARTED on the banks of the Siem Reap river and ran north along the length of the old covered market.

'You can drop me here,' Colette told the taxi driver as they arrived at the end of the street. She paid him his fare and got out of the air conditioned vehicle and into the heat. Achariya hadn't been sure of the number of the office, but there couldn't be that many. The market was in full swing and it reminded her of shopping with Achariya in the old days. Shoppers wandered between the stalls overflowing with colourful produce – tropical fruits and vegetables, stacked high in symmetrical piles, herbs and spices displayed in little mounds, their pungent smells wafting towards her, colourful fabrics, silks, batiks and a multitude of household goods. The market was bigger and busier than it had been when she'd known it, but no less atmospheric.

Opposite the market was a row of old French shophouses. Some were still shops, and others had been converted into offices, their fronts glassed over. She didn't have to go far until she found the one with a sign saying; "Angkor Law Offices. All legal problems solved here".

She went inside, thankful of the blast of chilly air that greeted her. She looked around the gloomy interior. An old-fashioned air-conditioner belted out cold air but was supplemented by a fan on the ceiling. There was a desk in front of her piled high with files and papers, overflowing ashtrays and discarded coffee cups. A young man sat behind it, his head down, hair flopping forward. He was writing furiously. Colette cleared her throat and he looked up. He wore wire-rimmed glasses and had an earnest, serious expression.

'Can I help you?' he spoke in English.

'Do you speak French?' Colette asked and he nodded.

'Please take a seat.'

She sat down on the plastic chair opposite his desk.

'How can I help you?'

Colette explained that she used to be a resident in Siem Reap province and that she and her husband had owned a villa on Tonlé Sap.

'I came back as soon as foreigners were permitted to enter the country. I went to see the villa. Sadly the land is all overgrown now and the villa in disrepair. My husband is buried on that land and I would very much like to buy it back so I can restore the place. I would be providing work for local people,' she added, seeing the hostile expression that had crept over the young man's face.

He sat back in his chair and fixed her with a steady gaze. 'I'm afraid foreigners cannot own land in this country any longer,' he said. 'Ownership is only open to Khmer citizens.'

'Yes, I know. They told me that at the town hall. However, I understand that there might be some methods by which it could be possible.'

He leaned forward. 'I'm afraid those methods are not considered reliable.'

'Oh,' Colette was bewildered. Perhaps she shouldn't have come here after all.

'I should tell you that my clients are normally people who are at the bottom of the pile both financially and socially. My work here is to help the local people in their daily struggles against injustice. I am not here to help foreigners exploit loopholes in the Cambodian legal system.'

'Oh, I'm so sorry...' Colette got to her feet, feeling her cheeks heat up with embarrassment.

'I'm sorry I can't help you,' he said, 'There are others who can. Lawyers in Phnom Penh who carry out those sorts of transactions all the time. You might want to look there instead.'

She bid him good day and went out of the office into the fierce heat. Feeling duly admonished, she hailed a passing cyclo. She asked the rider to take her to the Grand Hotel d'Angkor. He began to pedal her through the busy streets and she wondered if what she was doing in trying to buy back the land that her husband had once paid good money for and had nurtured for decades could be regarded as wrong. To her mind it was perfectly natural to want to restore the place that held so many poignant memories for her. Sighing, she settled back in the seat. If this meant a trip to Phnom Penh to see a different lawyer, that's what she would have to do.

17

PHNOM PENH, 1945

They buried Henri's body in a rough patch of land behind the makeshift school, the day after he died. Those prisoners who had died of malaria and dysentery and other tropical illnesses in the few short weeks they'd been interned, had been buried there too, and there was a small forest of simple wooden crosses growing up there amongst the weeds.

The Bishop of Phnom Penh led the service over the hastily dug grave and as there was no coffin available, Henri was wrapped in a white sheet. The Bishop was a kindly, elderly man whose eyes looked tortured at the injustices and brutality he'd witnessed. He had officiated at Henri and Colette's wedding such a short time before in Phnom Penh cathedral, and Colette remembered his kindness then, to a young, naive bride taking her first, uncertain steps in a new country.

Colette stood beside Henri's body, overcome with emotion. Even as he laid there on the ground, through her tears, she could see the blood seeping through the sheet from the terrible wounds he had sustained during the brutal attack that ended his life.

She was still in shock from having witnessed such savagery,

and since that moment she hadn't stopped crying. She hadn't slept all night either. Françoise Fournier had come to sit with her that evening and hadn't left her side. She'd brought water for her and made her drink. She'd tried to get her to eat too, but Colette had pushed the food away.

There was quite a group gathered there on the waste ground to lay Henri to rest. The Bishop articulated the importance Henri had held amongst the French in Cambodia.

'Henri Boissière was a very important member of the French community. As chief curator of Angkor Wat, presiding as he did over the restoration of that fabulous temple, he made French archaeology known for its brilliance throughout the world. But above that, he was a courageous and generous friend to many, risking his life in this camp to make sure others were able to eat, and in his final moments putting his life on the line to protect a vulnerable child. We will all remember him for his bravery and for his unstinting generosity.'

They said prayers, then the men, including Charles Leroux, the Resident, lowered Henri's body into the grave. Colette stepped forward and threw the jasmine sprigs she'd collected from a tree in the camp onto his body, then she bent down and picked up a handful of earth from the pile and threw it into the grave. There was no hollow sound of earth on wood as there should have been. She stepped back and allowed others to do the same.

People drifted away gradually but Charles Leroux came to speak to her, Fleur at his side.

'I'm going to raise Henri's death with the Japanese commandant, the officer in charge of the internment camp. It shouldn't have happened, and the perpetrators shouldn't go unpunished,' he said.

Colette looked into his eyes and saw weakness there. She recalled how Henri had said that Charles would do nothing to rock the boat against the Japanese. She opened her mouth to express the view that Henri's death might not have happened if Charles had been stronger with the Japanese at the outset, but quickly closed it again. What good would alienating him do? Nothing was going to bring Henri back, and they all needed to stick together as one now, didn't they?

Fleur tucked her arm into Colette's. 'Come back to our rooms. We have some whisky. It might dull the pain for you.'

Fleur and Charles had an entire apartment to themselves, the top floor of an old villa. It was comfortably furnished and surrounded by greenery. Colette stifled her surprise when Fleur showed her out onto a spacious balcony. She imagined Fleur and Charles sitting there, soaking up the sunshine, watching the world go by on the street below. Fleur brought a bottle of whisky and three glasses, and poured out generous measures. Colette took a large gulp of hers. The amber liquid coursed warmly through her body, relaxing her muscles, giving her the fuzzy feeling that things might not be quite as bad as she'd imagined.

'I'm going straight out to speak to the commandant now,' Charles said, getting up after he finished his drink. 'Have as much whisky as you want.'

Fleur poured another glass. Colette drank hers quickly and on an empty stomach, she was soon feeling detached from reality.

'Henri was a good man,' Fleur said, holding her glass up. 'We will all miss him.'

'He *was* a good man,' Colette agreed. 'Far too good for me.'

'What do you mean?' Fleur asked sharply. Tears flooded Colette's eyes.

'I almost betrayed him once,' she admitted, the whisky loosening her tongue.

'With Luc Gilbert?'

Shock flooded through Colette. 'How on earth did you know?'

Fleur shrugged. 'I could tell whenever I saw Luc looking at you in the club how he must feel about you. He's a good man, an attractive man, no one would have blamed you if you'd succumbed, I'm sure.'

Colette fell silent, shocked by Fleur's directness. She didn't want to be discussing this now, not when Henri was hardly cold in his grave. She regretted having mentioned anything about it. Even so, her mind was spinning with questions. But she resisted the urge to ask them.

'I saw a whole different side to Henri in this camp,' she said instead.

'He was very brave indeed,' Fleur agreed, 'but a little reckless for his own safety too, it has to be said. He put himself in danger far too much. He sacrificed his life in the end.'

So, the subject moved back to Henri and they spent the rest of the afternoon remembering him and discussing his many virtues. After an hour or so, Charles returned. He was carrying another bottle of whisky.

'The commandant of the camp very much regrets Henri's death and apologised to me. He gave me this to give to you as a gesture of goodwill.' He handed Colette the bottle.

She looked at him aghast, and suddenly, despite how much whisky she'd consumed, she felt stone-cold sober.

'A bottle of whisky? For a man's life? A good man like Henri? A great man even? And you just took it from that Japanese murderer without a word?'

She stood up and her anger made all her inhibitions vanish. She raged at Charles. 'Henri was right about you. You are a coward. He said it right at the start and I always defended you, but he was right. Keep your whisky, it would make me choke.'

With that she left the balcony, moved quickly if unsteadily back through the apartment and down the stairs. Then she walked as fast as she could down the street towards her flat. She was aware that Charles and Fleur must be staring at her from the balcony as she walked past, but she didn't look up once.

After that she avoided Fleur and Charles. Their paths had

hardly crossed before Henri's death so it wasn't difficult. In any case, she went straight back from their place to her room, where she lay down on the mattress and let the sadness of Henri's loss wash through her. Tears filled her eyes and she was consumed by grief. She stayed in that torpid state for several days, hardly moving, hardly eating. Françoise came in and brought her food and, with an anxious face would try to get her to eat. Colette found it difficult to swallow anything. She felt defeated, overcome by lethargy, almost ready to give up.

One day, Françoise took her to task.

'You know, Henri wouldn't want this for you. He was a fighter, Colette. He wouldn't have crawled into bed and given up on life.'

The words hit home, and Colette resumed her routine the next day, getting up early and going into the school. It was difficult, almost impossible sometimes, but she forced herself on, putting a brave face on to mask her grief. Françoise was right. It was what Henri would have wanted for her and she knew that if she didn't she would simply give up and fold in on herself as she nearly had done. It wasn't just losing Henri that was difficult, it was the fact that she had scarcely any money now and she had to ration the food she bought.

Colette found she was losing a lot of weight. She tried to limit herself to one small meal per day to make her money last, but one small portion of rice and vegetables wasn't enough to sustain her. She even thought about stealing from the shop as Henri had done but in the end she simply didn't have the courage.

One day she came home from school and was so weak and lacking in energy, she had to virtually crawl up the stairs to her room. She lay down on her mattress, dizzy and disoriented. She didn't know how long she lay there in her torpor, but after a while she was awoken by someone knocking at the door.

'Who is it?'

'It's me, Madame Boissière, Annie.'

'Annie? What are you doing here?'

Annie was one of her pupils from the school, one of the sweet little girls who brightened up her day. Colette managed to haul herself to her feet and open the door.

'There's someone at the fence on the edge of the camp who is asking for you. She is waiting for you to go to her. I said I would try to find you.'

'Someone?'

'Yes. A lady. She said her name but I can't remember it.'

'I'll come,' she said at once and they went downstairs together. Annie took her along the street and out of the immediate neighbourhood. Soon they were walking through a district that she'd never been in before. The camp was huge, she realised, extending over a large part of the old French Quarter of Phnom Penh.

'It's here,' Annie said, leading Colette down a side street. The end of the road was barriered off by a tall, wire fence, curls of barbed wire along the top. Colette hesitated. Hadn't they been warned not to even go near the fences. Was this some sort of trap? But she looked down at Annie's smiling face, her innocent eyes, and put that thought out of her mind.

'I need to go home now,' Annie said. 'My mother will be worried,' and she melted away.

Colette approached the fence tentatively. She heard a rustling sound in some bushes on the other side. A figure stepped out of the undergrowth and Colette recognised immediately that it was her old friend and housekeeper.

'Achariya! Whatever are you doing here?'

'I have brought you food, madam. I heard that the camp is running low on supplies. I've been worried about you ever since you were taken away.' She was holding a metal food caddy on one arm.

'You are so good to me,' Colette said. 'Did you come all the way from Siem Reap just for this?'

Achariya nodded. 'Yes, madam. The villa on the lake is safe.

Lim is looking after the place. I managed to get a lift to Phnom Penh on a lorry bringing fish from Tonlé Sap to the city. I came yesterday. I am staying with my mother's cousin. I wanted to come here and help you and Monsieur.'

Colette fell silent for a moment, dropping her gaze. Of course, Achariya wouldn't have heard the news.

'I'm sorry to tell you that Henri died a few weeks ago,' she muttered finally. She registered the shock on Achariya's face and lowered her voice. 'He was killed by some Japanese soldiers, for standing up to them.'

'Oh, I'm so sorry, madam,' Achariya said, tears in her eyes. 'That is terrible news.'

They fell silent, contemplating Henri's death, then Colette said, 'He would want you to stay in our villa in Phnom Penh, if you can.'

Achariya shook her head. 'That is not possible, madam. I went there yesterday. It is full of Japanese officers, many army vehicles are parked on the drive.'

'Oh dear. Henri thought that might happen.'

'I will give you the food now, madam and I will come back tomorrow with more. You look pale and thin. You need to eat.'

She bent down and pushed the caddy under a loose part of the fence and Colette gratefully picked it up. She could feel the warmth of the food even through the metal container and her mouth watered at the prospect of a good meal.

'Same time tomorrow?' Achariya asked.

Suddenly Colette heard the rhythmic marching of feet at the end of the road and before she could react, she saw a Japanese patrol moving past. She flattened herself behind a pillar on the wall of the last house in the street and waited until the sound had died down. When she stepped out of the shadows, Achariya had gone.

Colette carried the caddy back to her room and ate hungrily. The food was so succulent and bursting with taste. So different to the greasy scraps and weevil infested rice she'd been forced to survive on. When she'd had sufficient, there was still rice left. She knocked on Madame Leclerc's door and gave the remaining rice to her.

'Thank you, Madame Boissière. You haven't been stealing from the stores yourself, have you?'

'Of course not. A friend gave this to me.'

The next day she went back to the fence in the middle of the afternoon, around the same time as she'd gone on the first day. Achariya was there once again with more food. Colette exchanged the empty caddy for the full one, thanking her friend from the bottom of her heart.

Achariya continued to bring food every couple of days and soon Colette was feeling much healthier. There was flesh on her bones and she had energy again. When Achariya came she would also tell Colette what she knew about the progress of the war. She would listen to broadcasts from remote radio stations on a battered old radio in her relatives' home, and relay what she'd heard to Colette. Colette was surprised and delighted to learn that the war in Europe had ended in May, more than a month before, with Germany surrendering to the Allies. She hoped and prayed that her parents had survived but at least she now knew that Paris was no longer an occupied and dangerous place. Achariya also told her that US forces were advancing in the Pacific and that the Japanese island of Okinawa had recently surrendered. Around a month later, in August, Achariya came to the fence white-faced with shock.

'What's the matter?' Colette asked.

'The United States dropped a bomb on a Japanese city yesterday. It's called Hiroshima, I think. It wasn't a normal bomb, it was an atomic bomb.'

'What's that?'

'It is thousands of times more powerful than a normal bomb. I heard on the radio that 200,000 people had been killed.'

Colette's mouth dropped open. These were civilians, she thought, just like her. Not soldiers. Many must be innocent women and children.

When she went back to her rooms she noticed a new mood amongst the Japanese guards. They were jumpy, distracted, and they weren't taking much notice of the prisoners. Colette wondered how much they knew. Had some of their families been caught up in the bombings?

Three days later, Achariya told her of another bomb that had devastated a different Japanese city, Nagasaki.

'They have to surrender now, surely,' Colette said. 'Or all their cities will be destroyed.'

She passed the news on to all the women she knew in the camp. She thought it best that they be prepared for the end, which must surely come very soon.

They only had to wait a few days. When Colette woke up one morning and looked out of the window, she was astonished to see some unfamiliar soldiers in the street outside. These weren't Japanese soldiers, they were clearly westerners, and when she looked closely at their uniforms she could see that they wore the French insignia on their sleeve. Prisoners were flocking around them, shaking their hands, some of the women were even throwing their arms around them and kissing their cheeks.

Colette pulled some clothes on and ran out into the street to join the celebrations. She could scarcely believe it was over. There was not a Japanese soldier or guard in sight. Looking around at her fellow internees whose pale, tired faces were filled with joy, she felt a tremendous burden lift from her shoulders. But it was tinged with a deep sadness that Henri would not get to rejoice at the end of the war. His life had ended here on the very street people were now dancing on. The tragedy of it made Colette weep tears of bitter regret alongside those for the joy of freedom.

The camp gates had been propped open and people could

now come and go as they pleased. Colette gathered her tattered clothes and put them in her suitcase, reflecting on how much her life had changed since she threw them in there in her bedroom in the villa five long months ago. With sadness weighing down her chest she also packed Henri's few clothes into his case. Then, with a suitcase in each hand, she left the room. Madame Leclerc stood in the doorway to her room, a cigarette in her hand. Colette hadn't seen her smoking for a long time. She must have got it from the French soldiers.

'Are you leaving already?' Madame Leclerc asked.

'Of course. I don't want to stay here a moment longer than I need to. What about you?'

'I'm staying put until it's safe outside.' She blew a long stream of smoke into the air.

'What do you mean?'

'Haven't you heard? There are reports from Saigon that when the French were released from their internment, they were attacked by mobs of natives. Some were killed even.'

'Really? Well I don't think that could happen here. This is Cambodia after all. People are gentle here.'

Madame Leclerc raised her eyebrows. 'I'm surprised you've got so much faith in them. They're all the same in my book.'

'Well, I'm willing to take my chances,' Colette said briskly. 'Goodbye, Madame. And good luck.'

She went downstairs and out onto the street and, glancing over at where Henri had met his death she murmured a quick greeting to him, thinking she would need to come back to the camp soon in any case to visit his grave. Then she turned and walked towards the open gate where the French paratroopers waved her through with friendly smiles.

There were no cyclos or taxis on the street but it wasn't far to Henri's villa. It seemed strange to be out of the camp after so many months of incarceration, and the city felt very different now. The unceremonious departure of the Japanese had left chaos in its wake. Buildings stood empty, doors and windows flung open; vehicles were left abandoned in the road blocking the traffic, people wandered about aimlessly, as if confused by the vacuum left by their captors. After what Madame Leclerc had said to her, Colette walked as quickly as she could, trying to remain inconspicuous, not meeting anyone's gaze. She breathed a sigh of relief when she turned into the end of the road and saw the familiar villa up ahead.

The gates were barred, but not locked, and she pushed them open easily. Then she crossed the drive where weeds sprouted amongst the gravel and pushed open the front door which was also unlocked. It swung back and revealed the empty hallway.

'Hello?' she called, chills going through her as she stepped through the doorway. She had the sudden feeling that there might be a stray Japanese officer left with a gun, wating for her, but all was silent so she moved forward. Her heart sank as she looked around. It appeared that the Japanese had done as much damage to the place as they could before they left. Furniture was upturned, a door kicked in, Colette's best glasses and plates smashed in pieces on the marble floor. She wandered round, hardly able to believe what she saw. In the kitchen, flour and rice had been emptied onto the floor and cooking equipment smashed. A tap had been left running. She switched it off, then stood stock still. She heard footsteps in the hallway.

Taking a carving knife from the drawer, she went to the kitchen door and concealed herself behind it. Whoever it was, was moving around the hall, just as she had a few moments before. She stepped out from behind the door to look and relief flooded through her.

'Achariya!'

'Madam. I came as soon as I heard the Japanese had surrendered. But I'm so sorry to see this. What a mess they've made of the house!'

Colette put her arms around her friend and they embraced,

then she sat down on a chair that wobbled beneath her. She felt like crying but held the tears back.

'Don't worry, madam. We can fix the house up. I will help you, and my cousin is a carpenter. He can come and mend the doors and windows for you. We'll have it all looking as good as new very soon.'

Colette brightened. 'Are you sure? That's very kind of you.'

'Quite sure, madam. I can start today.'

It took them a week to get the villa looking vaguely respectable again. Achariya's cousin came on the second day and mended broken doors and window frames. As Colette worked, she realised that a lot of the damage was superficial. Once they'd cleared away the broken china and cleaned the floor and walls, the place was almost recognisable as the villa Henri had first brought her to in 1939.

On her second week of freedom, Colette felt that the work had advanced enough for her to spend part of the morning visiting Henri's grave. So, she cut some purple bougainvillea that had grown out of control and was smothering the balcony, and some frangipani blossom, and took a cyclo for the journey of a couple of kilometres back to the camp. To her surprise not much had changed there. French people were still occupying some of the buildings, but many of the Cambodian shopkeepers had moved back and opened up the shops on the ground floor. The presence of the locals made the place feel more like a normal district with shoppers moving amongst former internees on the streets.

The waste ground where Henri was buried looked just the same as it had the previous week, but others had been there before her to place flowers on the graves of their relatives. Those were now wilting in the extreme heat and looked shrivelled and brown. She knelt down in front of Henri's simple wooden cross and placed the flowers against it.

'I haven't forgotten you, my darling,' she said. 'I've been busy clearing up the villa. The Japanese left it in a terrible state, you know. I will come back again, but soon I'll need to go back to Tonlé Sap. I will find out if it's possible to move you back there so we can be together.'

It hadn't occurred to her before, but now she was here beside Henri's grave, she realised how difficult it would be to go back there without him. Surely, he would want his final resting place to be in the grounds of the beautiful villa that had been his pride and joy. She would speak to the Bishop about it before she left Phnom Penh.

On the way back home, Colette stopped off at the post office to mail a letter to her parents. She hadn't yet heard from them, but had written to tell them of Henri's death, to say that she was safe and free at last, and to ask for news of them. The post office was working just as it had before the war and queuing up in that tall, cool hall under the ceiling fans, Colette began to feel that some things were at last returning to normal.

Approaching the villa in a cyclo on the way home, Colette was surprised to see a motorbike drawn up at the bottom of the front steps. Had Achariya's cousin borrowed it to cross the city today? He normally came to work on a battered bicycle. She mounted the steps and noticed that the front door was ajar. Had Achariya left it open? She went to push it back and then heard voices.

'When do you think she'll be back? I really need to speak to her.'

'She won't be long, sir, I'm sure. Would you like something to drink?' came Achariya's response.

The familiar male voice made the hairs on the back of her neck stand up. She pushed the door open and went straight in. There he was, Luc Gilbert, standing in the middle of the hall under the chandelier, looking as if he owned the place.

'Ah, Colette,' he said moving forward and taking her hand, smiling, his dark eyes on her face. 'My condolences for your tragic loss. I'm not sure if the Governor General has told you the news. I am to be appointed as chief curator of Angkor Wat to take over from dear Henri.'

She took his hand but could barely meet his eye. So many questions flooded her mind and all she could think of was the last time she'd seen him, in the market at Siem Reap four years ago, talking to some Japanese men. How could he be taking over from Henri? How could Charles Leroux have made such a decision? Perhaps it was to unsettle her after the scene in his rooms in the camp, perhaps Fleur had something to do with it.

'They made the appointment straight after the Japanese surrender and flew me straight out. I'm afraid to tell you that it means I will be taking over this house in due course. There's no hurry for you to leave immediately, the Colonial Service has paid for another week at the hotel, but I will need to move in at some point in the near future.'

18

PHNOM PENH, 1995

It was raining when Colette's minibus arrived back in Phnom Penh from Siem Reap. The streets of the capital were deserted, anyone unfortunate enough to be outside was running for cover wearing waterproofs, or holding umbrellas up against the deluge. She'd forgotten the intensity of tropical downpours and how the rain fell in sheets rather than drops, making normal activities impossible, even at the tail end of the monsoon season. When they drew up under the canopy in front of the Hotel Cambodiana she was glad of the cover it afforded. She paid the taxi driver and went up the steps to check in at the desk. The receptionist remembered her and upgraded her to a suite on the top floor.

'Good view from up there,' the woman said, smiling. 'When it stops raining, of course.'

Up in the room, Colette made herself a coffee and got settled into her new accommodation. It was palatial. The windows looked out over the wide river below, which at that moment was almost obscured by the force of the downpour. She sat down on the bed and put a call through to her bank in France. Her father's business had been successful and he had left her well provided

for, but she needed to find out exactly how much she had available to her and whether, if she were able to find a lawyer to help
her buy the villa on the lake, funds could be transferred to
Cambodia easily.

The bank manager assured her that she had the required
funds in her account, but urged caution.

'You know, buying property in such an unstable market and
fragile economy could be very risky. And I've heard that schemes
for foreigners to do so aren't always operated by the most honest
people. Please be very careful who you do business with.'

'I will find a reputable law firm, don't worry. And in truth, I'm
not really buying this property. I used to own it, you know. By
rights it is still mine.'

'I hear what you say, but that doesn't make any difference to
the actual legal position as I understand it. As I said, please be
very cautious, Madame Boissière. I am always here to advise you,
so call again if you need to talk anything through. We wouldn't
want your father's legacy to be lost to some unscrupulous
chancers, would we now?'

She put the phone down with a sigh. The bank manager had
only said what she knew in her bones to be true, but it was still
hard to hear all the same. She turned her attention to looking for
a reputable lawyer. She had no idea where to start, but there was
a daily paper lying on the desk, the Phnom Penh Post, so she
picked it up and glanced through the headlines – grenades had
been thrown at the conference of a new political party with 35
people injured, another new political party had been formed that
week, three truckloads of people had stormed the offices of a
news agency, and a western doctor was convicted of sexual
assault on Khmer children. Perhaps the bank manager was right
– Cambodia was a risky, unstable place in which to be investing.

Still, Colette was willing to take the risk. The pull of that
abandoned villa was very strong. She flicked through the pages
of the newspaper and found the classified advertisements. There

were several law firms advertising their services but many of them seemed to specialise in criminal or family law. Her finger ran down the column until she reached a large advert that was professionally produced. Khmer Law – offered "robust real estate solutions for every situation". They listed several partners and there was a photograph of their office, in a large, modern, glass-fronted building. This was the sort of thing she was looking for.

She picked up the phone and dialled the number. The receptionist told her that the partner who dealt with property transactions, Aith Chan, could meet her the next morning at ten o'clock.

So, the next day she got a taxi to the business district. The driver dropped her outside a tall, glass building. This area felt as if it belonged in a western capital rather than in Phnom Penh and she reflected on how quickly the city had grown since the fall of the Khmer Rouge. Inside the palatial entrance hall, a stylish receptionist showed her to the lift and on the tenth floor she stepped out into a carpeted lobby. Another glamorous receptionist showed her into a meeting room with a long table and windows with a panoramic view of the city. A man dressed in a designer suit, his hair cut in fashionable western style, entered and shook her hand.

'Good morning. Aith Chan at your service, Madame Boissière.' His French, like his dress sense was impeccable. They sat down at the long, polished table.

'I understand you're interested in buying some land near Siem Reap,' he began and Colette nodded. 'I'm also aware that you lived in Cambodia for a long time. That you first came here in 1939 and left when the Khmer Rouge took over.'

Colette's eyes widened. How did he know all this?

'Your husband was Chief Curator of Angkor Wat for many years. We owe him a great debt for his sensitive restoration of that monument.'

Colette relaxed and smiled. 'Henri was indeed a very talented

archaeologist. It is partly for his sake that I'd like to find a way to
buy the land back.'

She explained that her husband had been buried on the land
fifty years before and she wanted to restore the place to its former
glory, but that she'd been told that foreigners could not purchase
land in Cambodia. Aith Chan smiled.

'That's not quite true. There are various ways in which it can
be accomplished. You've certainly come to the right place.'

He then outlined several different methods that foreigners
had used to purchase land in the country since the law banning
foreigners from ownership had come into force. It was possible to
invest in a land development company with Cambodian ownership, purchase shares in such a company or to use a nominee.

'Each solution has its risks and difficulties, but we have many
foreign clients who have used these methods successfully.'

Colette paused, digesting his words. This sort of transaction
ran against the grain for her. She thought of her father who
would have disapproved of anything like this. She knew it was a
way of evading the law and the words of the lawyer in Siem Reap
came back to her and also those of her bank manager. This
lawyer, Aith Chan, just seemed a little too slick for her liking.

'The next step would be for me to seek suitable investors and
outline your proposal to them,' he went on. 'I would then
approach the local authority in Siem Reap and find out the
market value of the land. We would of course verify that with an
independent surveyor.'

'Look, I'll need to think about it for a little while if you don't
mind. This is a lot to take on board.'

'Of course. Take all the time you need. We can meet again if
you decide to proceed and in the meantime, if you have any questions please don't hesitate to get in touch.'

He stood up and guided her back to the lobby.

'Are you doing some sightseeing while you're in town?' he
asked.

'I'm not sure. I'm very familiar with most of the monuments already. Perhaps I could reacquaint myself with them, though. It might be nice to revisit them.'

'Or you could take a look at some of the new sights.'

'New sights?'

'They are certainly sobering, but there is a museum dedicated to the victims of the Khmer Rouge. It's in a former prison, Tuol Sleng. It's certainly worth a visit.'

'Thank you,' she said with a shudder. 'Perhaps I should go there.'

'Well, goodbye for now, Madame Boissière. Very nice to make your acquaintance.'

Back at the hotel she picked up her guidebook and pored over the Phnom Penh attractions. Her eyes glazed over those familiar monuments that she'd visited many times as a resident – the Royal Palace and silver pagoda, the National Museum, Buddhist temples. She was looking for Tuol Sleng Museum. There it was, tucked in at the end of the pages on things to do in Phnom Penh. She read the text closely. The building was apparently a former school in a cherry orchard taken over by Pol Pot's forces. It became the largest centre for detention and torture in Cambodia during the Khmer Rouge regime. More than 17,000 people had been taken from there to a nearby extermination camp. Chills of horror went through her, just reading about it, but in honour of Achariya and all those who had suffered and died during those brutal years, she felt she owed it to them to at least visit the place.

After lunch a taxi dropped her off in the street outside Tuol Sleng, and she walked into a pleasant courtyard full of trees with grassy gardens in the centre. It was bordered by modern blocks with wide balconies, which when she went closer she realised were covered in barbed wire. She crossed the courtyard and entered the museum which was housed in one of the blocks. She bought a ticket at the desk and began to make her way through the displays.

She was shocked to see hundreds of harrowing photographs of people having been brought in. They were documented on arrival for the Khmer Rouge records. Many of them had a number tag round their necks to identify them. There were men, women and children who looked like ordinary, well-educated, Cambodian citizens. There were some young foreigners too who'd had the misfortune to be captured by the Khmer Rouge. All looked equally terrified. Looking into their pleading eyes, Colette felt profound pity for all these innocent people who had died a terrifying death at the hands of an evil regime. As she examined each one, seeing the same desperate expression in all their eyes, her heart went out to all those terrified people. But in the back of her mind, she was searching for one person as she looked through the photographs, someone with striking dark eyes and perfect skin. Could she have been held here too? There were many young women amongst the ranks of the unfortunate prisoners, but as far as she could see, no sign of Sophia.

She moved on through the rooms. This was where prisoners had been held. Some had been divided up into smaller rooms by crudely constructed breeze block walls. Touring these rooms, she noticed the shackles by which prisoners had been restrained. Out in the courtyard were torture frames where prisoners had been hung upside down and dunked in vats of filthy water to force them to speak.

With a shudder, she entered the final room of the museum. Here were more photographs of victims, but there was one in particular that was different. It was of a group of people seated together. It could have been a family group but for the circum-stances and the expression on their faces. Her eye was caught by a woman at the back, standing a little apart from the others on the back row. Colette looked more closely and her heart missed a beat. Could this possibly be Sophia? The photograph was fuzzy and no matter how hard she looked, it was impossible to say. She turned to the member of staff who stood in the corner of the room and asked him if he knew anything about the photograph. He shrugged his shoulders.

'We do not know the names of that group. The photograph was taken before they were taken off to the killing fields. That is all we know about it.'

'To the killing fields?' she repeated, the blood draining from her face. She found a chair and sat down, her legs suddenly too weak to support her. So that was it, Sophia had been rounded up and taken off to the extermination camp and beaten to death alongside thousands of others who had done nothing to deserve their fate. Poor Sophia. What a terrible way to die, and so young too. She put her head in her hands. Other visitors quietly skirted her chair, averting their gaze while she sat there weeping quietly for the young woman she'd come back to Cambodia to track down.

19

PHNOM PENH, 1945

Colette stood there in the hallway staring at Luc Gilbert. Her mouth had dropped open at the shock of what he was saying, and she was finding it hard to process what was happening.

'You look surprised, Colette,' he said.

She drew herself up in an effort to recover her composure.

'I am surprised to see you. I thought you might be dead. You vanished off the face of the earth without a word. Henri was worried about you.'

Luc gave a short, sardonic laugh. 'I can't believe that. I would have thought he'd have been glad to get rid of me. After all, we never exactly saw eye to eye.'

'But why did you leave? Why so suddenly?'

He came closer to her and looked into her eyes. She wanted to look away but didn't have the strength, his gaze was so compelling. She'd forgotten about the mesmerising beauty of his dark eyes. She hoped Achariya wasn't watching but sensed that her friend had withdrawn discreetly to another room.

'It had something to do with you, actually,' he said, his voice gentle now. 'I waited for you every Friday afternoon for weeks and you didn't come. I thought, after what happened in Ta Prohm that day, that you felt the same way... but it seemed not. I was finding it hard to go on, to be quite honest.'

Colette frowned. 'I find that very hard to believe,' she said, remembering her shock at seeing him conferring with the Japanese men at the market. 'There was a rumour circulating that you had inside information on the Japanese invasion and that you got out of the country in the nick of time before it happened.'

Again, he laughed. 'You've clearly got a very low opinion of me,' he said. 'To be able to believe that I'm a traitor to my country. I may be a lot of things, but I'm not that.'

'I had my reasons,' she said, not yet willing to divulge that she'd seen him at the market.

'I must say you are looking very well for someone who has spent the last five months effectively imprisoned,' he remarked.

'It's been hell,' she said simply. 'And I'm sure I'm not looking at all well. I've lost a lot of weight.'

'It suits you. Your cheekbones are even more attractive now.'

'Please don't,' she said.

He laughed again and cast his eyes around the hallway.

'This is a very nice house. A real bonus. I've hardly been here before and I've never seen upstairs. Why don't you show me round?'

'I don't think that would be appropriate,' she said stiffly. 'And if we are to leave in the next couple of days, I really need to make a start on my packing. I knew I'd have to give the house up, but I hadn't realised it would be quite so soon.'

'It doesn't have to be that soon, Colette. I've just explained that.'

He moved towards the stairs, urging her to follow him with barely suppressed laughter. 'Colette, come on won't you...'

Without responding, she made for the kitchen, where she found a discarded crate and began noisily packing anything that had not been broken by the Japanese soldiers. She had no idea how she was going to get things moved from here to the Tonlé Sap villa, but she wanted something to do so that she didn't have to think about Luc Gilbert. She could hear his footsteps above her head, restlessly prowling around the bedrooms.

After ten minutes or so she heard him on the stairs. He appeared at the kitchen door.

'Thank you for letting me look round. It's a beautiful property. I'll come back again soon.'

'I won't be here,' she said without looking up. 'I'll be going back to Tonlé Sap as soon as I can arrange transport.'

'Well, I'll see you there then, I hope. I will be working at Angkor Wat, of course. And most of the time I'll be living in Siem Reap. So, we'll be neighbours once again.'

She turned to face him. 'Goodbye, Monsieur Gilbert,' she said as coldly as she could.

Two days later, she was sitting beside Achariya and two young Cambodian men on her way back to Tonlé Sap, on the seat of a bullock cart. It was loaded with the furniture and equipment that she and Henri had collected for the Phnom Penh villa. The bullock cart was owned by Achariya's uncle, and the two boys who were helping were part of Achariya's extended family. The journey would take them two days and they would stay overnight in one of the small towns en route, wherever they could find lodgings.

It wasn't a comfortable way to travel, but once they were out of the city, Colette began to appreciate the gentle, lumbering pace of the bullocks, the way they swished their tails from side to side as they walked, and the fact that this way she could see the countryside close up in a way she'd never been able to before. She was astonished afresh by the vivid colours of the lush vegetation in the patches of jungle they passed through, the emerald green of the rice fields, the way the water reflected the blue of the sky, and how villagers waved and smiled from their porches as they lumbered past. For hours they would travel in silence, the only sounds the buzz of insects and the call of jungle creatures, the clip clop of the bullocks' hooves on the road and the rumble of the cartwheels.

They stopped in a small town as darkness fell. There was no hotel there, but Achariya asked around and a householder agreed to cook them a meal and let Achariya and Colette lodge in their room for a small fee. The boys slept on the cart to guard the belongings.

They rose at dawn, setting off as the sun burned the mist off the damp land, and travelled the whole of the next day. It was late afternoon when they finally rumbled through Siem Reap and embarked on the last leg of their journey – the jungle road towards Tonlé Sap. Colette could barely keep the tears at bay anticipating her homecoming and remembering how they'd been driven up this road in the other direction in such different circumstances only a few months before. She couldn't stop thinking how sad it was that Henri had never got to return to the villa he loved. At last, the walls surrounding the villa grounds came into view and her heart soared at the prospect of seeing her beloved home again.

Lim came running to the gates, propped them open and the cart rolled through. When they came to a halt in front of the steps, Colette remained on the seat, unable to move for a moment, taking it all in. The villa was just the same, in fact the garden looked even neater than when they'd left. Lim must have spent his entire time weeding, pruning and mowing the lawn. The house itself looked just as beautiful, with bougainvillea in full bloom climbing over the balconies. At least the Japanese officers hadn't commandeered this house for their quarters.

Lim was smiling up at her, holding his hand out to help her down. When she was on the ground she embraced him and said, 'Thank you for looking after the house for me, Lim. I cannot tell you how grateful I am.'

He smiled broadly but looked relieved when she released

him. The houseboy hung behind him and Colette gave him a
very brief hug, knowing how shy he was.

'No Japanese came here,' Lim said, echoing her thoughts.
'Too far from Siem Reap for them.'

'Thank goodness for that, Lim.'

She turned back to the bullock cart to thank the boys who
had already started unloading furniture, carrying it towards the
outhouses behind the villa for storage.

Then, she went up the front steps and into the cool of the
hall, tears in her eyes. By rights Henri should be here with her.
This was, above all, his home, the one he'd built with love before
he'd even met her. It felt wrong, somehow, returning here by
herself. Everywhere was pristine, the marble floors polished, the
windows sparkling clean, the furniture gleaming. She wandered
through the familiar rooms, running her finger over the smooth
surfaces, touching Henri's precious artefacts. How good it was to
be back here, even though it wasn't the homecoming she'd
longed for while he was alive.

Out on the veranda she sank into one of the cane armchairs
and rested her eyes on the lake. It was just before sunset, the most
beautiful part of the day, and the sky was beginning to darken,
golden chinks of light glinting behind the pink-tinged clouds. A
flock of waterbirds flew past crying their mournful cry. How she'd
missed this, it was what she'd dreamed of for months in that tiny,
stuffy room in the prison camp. It felt empty without Henri but
sitting there overlooking the lake she vowed to overcome that.
She was sure he'd want her to get on with life, to make this place
her home again on her own terms.

Achariya appeared in the doorway. 'Would you like a drink,
madam?'

'That would be nice. Why don't you come and sit with me and
have one too? You must be as tired as I am.'

'Alright... if you're sure?'

'Of course. And Achariya, tomorrow, why don't we take one of the boats and visit the school. It would be good to see the children again and find out if they still need help with their French lessons.'

The next morning, they did just that. The boats had been kept in working order by Lim, and the launch they used to take started straight away. They motored out of the boathouse and onto the still waters of the lake. It felt so good to be on the way to the floating school again. Colette was looking forward to putting what she'd learned in the camp teaching the French children into practice in this local school.

When they drew up at the dock of the floating building, all the children rushed out of the classroom to greet them, waving and calling to them excitedly.

'How wonderful to see you!' the teacher was beaming with joy. 'We have really missed our French lessons these past months. We're glad to see you safe and sound.'

Colette slotted back into the life of the lake smoothly. She found teaching even more rewarding than before. These children were so much easier to control than the French children in the camp. They were quiet, well-disciplined, and eager to learn, despite their poverty and all their disadvantages. She took to going there most mornings, often alone, but sometimes Achariya would accompany her to help. It gave her a boost to know that her contributions to their learning was making a real difference to all these children's lives. And it was good to get out and have the company of other people; she was finding evenings alone on the veranda tended to drag.

During those first few weeks, Colette wrote to the Bishop of Phnom Penh requesting to move Henri's body back home. It took some organising, but eventually permission was granted. She went down to Phnom Penh herself to accompany the body on its final journey. When it finally arrived, she held a short but moving ceremony at the graveside, on the corner of the plot under a banyan tree. It was supervised by the Priest from the Catholic church in Siem Reap and attended only by herself and the servants. She'd had a simple gravestone made on which was carved an image of Angkor Wat. It gave her comfort to be able to go there each morning, lay flowers on the grave and talk to Henri as if he were still there with her.

Occasionally she would venture up to the Grand Hotel d'Angkor to have a drink in the bar and chat with any members of the local French community who happened to be there. She managed to master driving Henri's car after some lessons from Lim on the quiet roads near the villa. Her driving was erratic and sometimes dangerous, but she reasoned that it didn't matter too much on the jungle roads. Before she was confident though, she would park on the edge of the town and walk or get a passing cyclo to the hotel.

Sometimes Françoise and her husband would be in the bar at the Grand, sometimes others who had been interned with Colette in Phnom Penh. They had an affinity borne from their shared months of hardship, and it was good to talk to them and hear how they were coping with normal life again. She always walked into the bar with trepidation though, realising that Luc Gilbert could be there. She'd heard on the grapevine that he'd returned to live in Siem Reap in the house he'd occupied before the war, and that he had started work at Angkor Wat again. She had no desire to run into him and to experience those unsettling and guilty feelings his presence provoked. In the end she enlisted one of the young bell boys, a boy called Narith, to look round the bar and check to see if Monsieur Gilbert was there before she entered. For this she would slip him a large tip.

One day, to her horror, she was upstairs in her bedroom at the villa, when she heard the sound of an engine on the drive. Going out onto the balcony she saw Luc Gilbert's car draw up in front of the house. Somehow, he'd managed to retain the sports car he used to drive before the war and he evidently still drove it in his usual flamboyant style. She rushed back inside and spoke to Achariya who was sweeping the stairs.

'Could you please tell Monsieur Gilbert I'm not at home,' she hissed over the bannisters. Achariya gave her a knowing smile and went downstairs to open the door when the bell went. Colette lurked in the shadows on the landing and listened to the exchange.

'Good afternoon. Is Madame Boissière at home?'

'I'm sorry sir, she's not here at the moment,' Achariya said, in a strong, clear voice.

'Really? I am surprised. Her car is on the drive.'

'She's gone out in the boat, sir.' Colette smiled at Achariya's quick-thinking response.

'Do you know when she'll be back?'

'I'm not sure. Sometimes she stays out for several hours.'

'That's a shame. I can't wait, I'm afraid. Could you please give her these? Some came from my garden, some from Angkor Wat.'

'Of course, sir,' there was a rustling sound as Achariya took the gift.

'You might want to put them in water or they will wilt.'

'I will, sir. Goodbye, sir.'

'Goodbye.'

Colette went through the bedroom and out onto the balcony again and stood out of sight, watching his car roar through the gates and up the jungle road, disappearing round a bend and into the trees. Then she went inside and walked slowly down the stairs.

'He brought these, madam,' Achariya was holding up an enormous bunch of flowers. There were huge, deep crimson and purple water lilies mixed in with a scattering of white frangipani. Colette recognised the lotus flowers as coming from the lake at Angkor Wat where they bloomed in profusion at this time of year. Her heart twisted with longing. She hadn't visited the temple since she'd been back in Tonlé Sap, afraid of running into Luc there, but seeing the flowers brought back to her how much she missed it and how she longed to walk through its echoing passages again.

Something dropped out of the bouquet onto the floor and Achariya bent to pick it up.

'It's a letter, madam.'

Colette rushed down the remaining steps and took it from Achariya. She ripped it open and read it quickly, her heart pounding.

My dearest Colette,

I know we didn't get off to the best start in Phnom Penh so perhaps we could forget that and start again? I was genuinely sorry to hear of Henri's death. He was a courageous man and a great archaeologist. I was telling the truth when I told you why I had left Cambodia in 1941. I had obviously misread the signs with you and I took your rejection very hard. I took myself off back to France to put some distance between us.

I accept now that you don't feel the same way as I do, but since we are neighbours and two ex-patriots living in a foreign land a long way from home, it would be good if we could at least be friends. If you can't find it in your heart to accept my offer of friendship now, perhaps you will at some point in the future. Until that time, I'm at your service if you should ever need me and I will live in hope,

Yours ever,

Luc Gilbert.

Colette read the letter over and over again, going hot and cold, myriad emotions running through her. What was it about Luc Gilbert that provoked such a strong reaction in her? She couldn't pinpoint what she was feeling, all she knew was that any contact with him left her emotions in turmoil.

Over the following days and weeks she often took the letter out and re-read it but she didn't write back or take the car and drive up to Angkor Wat or to his house to see him. She was waiting, she supposed, until she had calmed down and until she could make some sense of her own feelings.

Every passing day was tainted with her ongoing grief for Henri and worry about her parents. She waited anxiously for post to arrive from Paris. Days became weeks, weeks became months and still she'd had no news of them. She even took to driving daily to the post office in Siem Reap to see if something had been sent to her poste restante there, but she was always thwarted. She thought about trying to put a call through to Paris, there was a telephone at the post office, but her parents had no telephone in their apartment.

One day, though a letter did arrive with a Paris postmark. The typed envelope was waiting for her on the hall stand when she arrived home from a morning at the school. She tore it open with trepidation and as she read her hands began to shake and her eyes to fill with tears.

Dear Madame Boissière,

I am acting as your parents' advocate and executor in the matter of the distribution of their wills. I know you have been in Cambodia since before the war and won't have been in touch with them for many years. It is my sad duty to let you know that your parents have both passed away. Your father was arrested by the Gestapo in 1944 for distributing anti-Nazi leaflets. He was held in a prison outside Paris and it was only recently that your mother discovered that he had perished in prison. I'm afraid we do not know of the date of his death or where he is buried.

Your mother passed away a matter of days ago. She had been in poor health since the beginning of the occupation and had been suffering from heart disease. The news of your father's death came as a severe blow to her. She suffered a heart attack recently and died in hospital. Her friends held a funeral in the Basilique Notre Dame du Perpetual Secours and she is buried in Pere Lachaise cemetery in Belleville.

I am very sorry for your loss and for the shock this letter must be to

ANN BENNETT

you. It has taken me some time to find your address, but I have written as soon as I could.

Your father left all his money and property to you, including the apartment on the Champs Élysées and the house in the Dordogne. I await your instructions as to how to deal with those properties. If you should wish to telephone me to discuss any of this, my number is at the top of this letter.

Once again, I offer my sincere condolences for your tragic loss.

Yours sincerely,

Joseph Briande, Avocat.

Colette rushed out to the veranda and threw herself on the settee crying inconsolably. The loss of the three people she held most dear was too much to bear. In that moment of shock and grief, she felt that there was no purpose in her life and that it was not worth living.

'Madame, please, what has happened?' Achariya was hovering over her. 'Shall I fetch the brandy?'

She nodded weakly, then buried her face back in the cushions, wanting the world to swallow her up. In time Achariya brought her a glass of brandy and she drank it gratefully, then sunk back on the cushions letting the alcohol seep through her veins to deaden the pain.

She was drifting off to sleep when she felt arms encircling her body, lifting her gently to a sitting position, then someone was wiping her tears away with a handkerchief. She felt the cushions dip as whoever it was sat down beside her. When she opened her eyes that were swollen with tears, it was to look into those beautiful, dark, mesmerising eyes that were full of sympathy and kindness. And in that moment of deep pain, she had a sudden moment of clarity. She knew where her confusion had come from, it was borne of a deep longing to get to know this man, to understand him better and to let him into her heart.

20

TONLÉ SAP, 1945

Luc sat beside her, there on the veranda, until her sobs had finally subsided.

'I guess you've had some terrible news,' he said at last.

'It's my parents. You can read the letter.' She handed it to him. It saved her from having to say the words. His eyes scanned the lawyer's letter and he gasped as he read.

'I'm so sorry, Colette. You must be devastated.'

She felt his arm around her shoulders and she drew closer to him, craving the warmth and comfort of another human being. They sat like that for a long time. There seemed to be nothing to say. No words could remove her pain, but it was good to feel him there beside her.

After a while, Luc went to speak to Achariya who brought them some food from the kitchen. It was fried fish and salad, one of Colette's favourites but she found she had no appetite and could barely swallow the food. In the afternoon she felt well enough to walk around the grounds, her arm tucked through his. They walked slowly, and Luc admired the garden, the vibrant beds of canna lilies, irises and roses that Lim had tended lovingly.

'You must be very proud of your father. He was obviously an incredibly brave man,' Luc remarked.

'I am. I had no idea he was doing anything to help the Resistance, but I'm not surprised. He hated injustice of any kind, and he would have abhorred living under Nazi occupation. Mother was brave too. She would have supported him in whatever he did. This beastly war. We haven't even been able to exchange letters for years.'

'It's so hard,' he agreed. 'Do you think you will go back to Paris now?'

'I'm not sure. I'm not really thinking straight at the moment. The letter seemed to indicate that I could give the lawyer instructions from here. I need to speak to him about it. But I would prefer not to have to go there. Without my parents there it would be a terrible homecoming. Plus, I would prefer to remember how Paris was before the war, not brought to its knees by years of Nazi rule.'

'So, were you planning on making Cambodia your home?'

'I think so, yes. As long as I'm able to, that is. There's no guarantee that French rule will last here, is there?'

'No, there are already rumblings for independence. The end of the war is a watershed moment.'

They walked on, through an avenue of frangipani trees, the sweet scent of their blossom perfuming the air.

'It's so beautiful here. I didn't realise Henri had such green fingers.'

'He loved the garden but although Henri designed it, it's mostly down to Lim, our gardener. He looked after the place while we were in Phnom Penh.'

'I can see why you love it here and why you'd like to stay. And I must say, I'm overjoyed to hear that for my own selfish reasons.'

She didn't respond, not wanting things to move too quickly, aware that she wasn't in a fit state to make any sort of decision at that moment. They wandered on in silence and soon they were approaching the clump of jungle on the edge of the plot that hid the boathouse.

'What's up that path?' Luc asked.

'Come and see.'

She guided him along the gravel path, through the thick undergrowth. Soon, the bright blue wooden walls of the boathouse appeared in front of them.

'A boathouse? How fascinating. No one would even know this was here,' he said.

She opened the door, switched on the light and showed him inside. He looked around appreciatively.

'What was it used for before?'

'I think the previous owner used it for storage mainly. There are lots of cupboards in the walls, but we have plenty of storage near the house so we just moor our boats here.'

'Shall we go back now? You must be tired.'

'I am, but it's been good to be distracted.'

She closed up the boathouse and they walked slowly back to the villa. Luc was right, even a short walk had exhausted her and she needed to get inside the cool of the villa away from the hot sun.

'Why don't you go upstairs and sleep? I will come back tomorrow and see how you are.'

She agreed and thanked him for everything he'd done. Then he took her in his arms and kissed her chastely on the cheek. She stood on the front step and watched him get into his car and leave, reflecting on the transformation in their relations over the past few hours and how much his kindness had meant to her during those few dark hours.

He came to see her every afternoon for the next fortnight. Sometimes, they just sat side by side on the veranda watching the birds on the lake, sometimes they walked in the garden. Once, she even took him out on the little boat for a tour of the lake. It felt good to get out of the house – she was beginning to feel a little claustrophobic. She took the boat up towards the community of Chong Khneas and showed him the school. As they skimmed the smooth surface of the lake, above the noise of the engine, she told him about her work there.

'I didn't know about that! You are full of surprises, I must say,' he said, smiling, his eyes resting on hers and she smiled back, feeling the warmth of his gaze. She took the little boat right up to the floating school and did a circuit of it. The children noticed her and came rushing out onto the deck, waving and calling, 'Bonjour Madame Boissière,' in unison. Colette couldn't help laughing, despite her sadness.

'It's good to see you laugh again,' Luc said as she turned the boat round and headed back across the lake towards the villa.

'It's the children. They are so spontaneous and generous, you can't help being happy when you're around them. I'd forgotten how much I love going there.'

'Perhaps it's time to go back now.'

'Perhaps. I will go there tomorrow. Achariya went to tell them that I was taking some time off, but I expect they're missing their French lessons. It's been almost two weeks now.'

'Have you made a decision about whether you're going to Paris yet?'

'Not yet. I need to go to the post office and put a call through to the lawyer. Once I've spoken to him, I'll decide what to do.'

'I'll take you up there this afternoon if you like?'

'Thank you, Luc. I don't know what I'd have done without you these past couple of weeks.'

'It's the least I can do. There's no need to thank me.'

They moored the boat in the boathouse and went straight to the drive to get into Luc's car. He drove her slowly and carefully to Siem Reap on the jungle road.

'Your driving's different now, I must say,' Colette said.

'I think you'll find I'm a reformed character in lots of ways,' he said.

It was early in the morning in Paris when Colette got through to the law office from the telephone in the post office in Siem Reap. Joseph Briande was already at his desk.

'I'm so sorry for your terrible loss, Madame Boissière,' he said, his voice sounded faint down the crackly line. 'My letter must have come as a terrible shock to you.'

'Thank you. Yes, it was a dreadful blow. You indicated that I might be able to send you instructions from here rather than returning to France. Is that possible?'

'Yes, of course. I can market the properties for you, to sell or to rent out, and I can ensure the money in your father's account is transferred to you. Whatever you decide. And if you don't want to return to Paris, and I quite understand if you don't, I can do everything for you remotely.'

'Thank you. I'd prefer that.'

'Alright. So, would you like me to sell the properties? The flat in the Champs Élysées would certainly be very valuable. Many businesses are moving back to Paris now the war has ended and are looking for accommodation. That's a very central location.'

'Yes, if you could do that, please, I would be very grateful.'

'And the cottage in the Dordogne? Not as valuable but there is a growing market for weekend places such as that.'

Colette thought for a moment, then said, 'I think I'd like to keep the cottage. I have many happy memories of holidays there with my parents.'

'Very well. I will find a tenant for you. It may be handy to have a residence in reserve in France should you ever want or need to return from Indochina.'

'I was thinking along the same lines. Thank you so much, Monsieur Briande.'

Luc drove her home in the dark. When they arrived back at the villa she asked if he'd like to stay for supper. She saw him hesitate momentarily, before agreeing and she realised that like her, he didn't want to rush things between them. They went out onto the veranda and Achariya and Samang served them with fried rice and seafood.

'Freshly caught from the lake today,' she said. 'Achariya's father is a fisherman and she always brings part of his morning catch. She started during the war when we didn't have enough to eat.'

'She is a real asset to you,' Luc said, taking a sip of white wine that the houseboy had poured.

'She's more of a friend to me than a servant now. She's helped me so much. Do you know, when I was interned, she came all the way to Phnom Penh so she could smuggle food to me. She's the only reason I didn't starve.'

'You obviously inspire loyalty in those who work for you.'

'And what about you?' she asked. 'Who works in your house in Siem Reap?'

'I have a houseboy and a housekeeper, but they keep their distance. I wouldn't call either of them friends.'

There was something in the way he said it that made her look at him quizzically, but it was clear from his dismissive tone, that he wasn't prepared to be drawn on the matter. A few minutes later he changed the subject.

'If you're free tomorrow afternoon, I could take you over to Angkor Wat and show you what I've been working on since I came back from France.'

'Oh Luc, that would be wonderful. I've missed my visits to the temple and I'd love to see the place again. I've decided to go and work at the school in the morning, but I'll be back by lunchtime.'

'Alright. I will pick you up at two tomorrow then.'

The next day felt like something of a milestone for Colette, setting forth in the boat with Achariya, the warm breeze in her hair, the clouds of early morning mist rising from the lake. That day, perhaps for the first time since learning of the deaths of her parents, it felt as though there were chinks of light breaking through her dark clouds. She could appreciate afresh the beauty of her surroundings and even look forward to the day ahead.

The children greeted them enthusiastically as usual, and Colette picked up with them again where she'd left off a fortnight before. The hours flew by, and it felt as if she'd never been away. She left at the end of the morning, as she always did after any time spent with the children, with joy in her heart.

She set off with Achariya in the boat and, realising that Luc would be coming to collect her after lunch, turned the engine up to full throttle. The boat leapt forward and was soon speeding across the water.

Achariya gripped the sides of the boat, her knuckles white. 'Why do you go so fast, madam?'

'I need to get back quickly and have lunch. Monsieur Gilbert is collecting me at two o'clock to go to the temple.'

Achariya said nothing, just stared ahead of her.

'Is everything alright, Achariya?'

'Yes, thank you,' she replied, but her tone was clipped.

'You don't mind me going to Angkor Wat with Monsieur Gilbert do you?'

Achariya turned to her, her face solemn. 'You used to tell me to say you weren't at home whenever he called. Now he is your friend. I don't understand.'

'I'm sorry, Achariya. I shouldn't have asked you to lie for me. It was wrong. The fact is, I think I misjudged Monsieur Gilbert at first. He's been very good to me since the death of my parents. I've changed my mind about him.'

Achariya pursed her lips and said nothing. Colette had never experienced Achariya's disapproval of anything she did before.

'So, he is my friend now, Achariya. I hope that's not going to cause you any problems.'

There was a long pause, during which the boat sped on across the lake, its bow rearing up with the force of the engine.

'I don't think he will be good for you, madam,' Achariya said.

Colette could barely hear her above the roar of the engine but she could read her lips.

'Please let me be the judge of that,' she said, puzzled at Achariya's attitude.

When they got home, Colette tied up the boat in the boathouse, and Achariya hurried away to the kitchen to prepare lunch without a word. When she brought Colette's fish soup out to her on the veranda she retained a tight-lipped silence, and when Luc roared up in his sports car, Achariya was nowhere to be seen. Samang opened the door to him. Colette's heart soared when she saw him. He looked tanned and relaxed in a white shirt and linen trousers. He was wearing sunglasses too. He could have been a film star. He kissed her on the cheek and led her to the car.

'How are you today?' he asked attentively, starting up the engine, and while they drove the few kilometres to Angkor Wat, he asked her all about her morning at the school. During the whole of the journey, while she was telling him about her day, Colette didn't think about her grief once. Her eyes were on Luc's face, watching the dappled sunlight that flickered through the trees play on his skin.

When the temple came into view Colette drew a sharp intake of breath at its beauty, even though she'd seen it hundreds of times before and it was only a matter of months since she'd last been there. But for some reason it felt a lifetime ago since she'd last brought lunch for Henri and his team. She couldn't resist the thought that coming here with Luc felt very different, more exciting, somehow.

He parked the car beside the bridge, and they walked across it admiring the waterlilies on the lake.

'Did you like the ones I picked for you when you first came back from Phnom Penh?' he asked as they leaned on the wall looking at the astonishing display of flowers afloat on the water.

'Of course,' she replied.

'You never said so.'

'Things were different then. I was suspicious of you.'

'And why was that?'

'I told you, the rumours about you being a Japanese spy...'

He burst out laughing and she laughed too. It did seem slightly absurd now, but still, the scene in the market came back to her again. She banished it from her mind. Surely there must be some innocent explanation.

He took her arm and helped her up the rough stone steps and into the first outer corridors of the temple. It was good to be back there, walking through those hallowed stone passages. She knew she would never tire of coming back.

'I'm sure you know the temple almost as well as I do,' Luc said, 'So why don't I take you straight to the part I'm currently restoring? I'm sure you'll find it interesting.'

'I'd love that.'

He guided her through to the central courtyard and across it, past the lake there, this one also resplendent with waterlilies, the still water reflecting the temple towers like a mirror. They reached the other side, and he led her down further passages and into a square, brick built chamber where four or five men were hard at work dressed only in sarongs, their backs glistening with sweat. Some were clearing piles of bricks and rubble from the floor, others were chipping with chisels at a frieze that was emerging on the wall. She took a step closer and saw the astonishing images of horses, kings, gods. It was a tableau of incredible beauty and intricacy.

'The frieze depicts scenes from the Ramayana,' Luc told her. 'You know that Angkor Wat was built to worship Hindu gods and over the course of time became a Buddhist temple?'

'Yes, I knew that. These are marvellous,' she said, walking the length of the frieze, trying to piece together the stories they told. The scenes were full of movement and life, drawing her in.

'I took a bit of a risk uncovering them,' Luc said. 'I discovered some old scrolls in a central chamber under one of the towers. It seemed to show that a false wall had been erected in this chamber, although it wasn't conclusive. I took the decision to take down the wall to investigate. I'm glad I did.'

'So, your risk-taking paid off,' she said.

'For once, yes,' he said, laughing.

They spent a few more minutes looking at the frieze, then walked together round the whole temple complex, completely alone but for the occasional workman or gardener. It lifted Colette's heart to be there again amongst all this beauty and mystery and when they'd finished and walked back across the bridge to the car she thanked Luc for bringing her. He looked into her eyes again and told her not to thank him, just as he had before. For a second she thought he was going to bend forward and kiss her, but he drew back and she realised again that like her, he was determined to take things slowly.

On the way back he alluded to it though.

'I thought about kissing you back there. I had a powerful urge to do so, but I remember what happened before and I want to make sure that you don't reject me again.'

Colette felt colour creep into her cheeks, she looked down at her lap.

'There's something we need to talk about, Luc. I haven't brought it up before, but I feel I need to get it out into the open. Henri told me you were married. That your wife doesn't want to come to Cambodia. I was very surprised.'

He slowed the car down and pulled it onto the roadside. 'Yes, I've been meaning to speak to you about that, but there never seems to be a good moment.'

'So, it's true then?' she asked quietly, still unable to meet his gaze. She'd been hoping that it wasn't, that Henri had his facts wrong.

'Let me tell you about it. Marie and I married young. Our fathers were in business together and we were pushed into it, really. We are very, very different people. Marie is pious, serious and reserved. We never really saw eye to eye about anything. She never wanted me to become an archaeologist, she wanted me to follow my father into the family business. When I did pursue archaeology and I got to travel, she wouldn't come with me, so we've spent more time apart over the past ten years than together. We're virtually strangers nowadays. Last time I was home I told her I wanted a divorce, but she won't hear of it, but she did say we could officially separate and that I was free to be with whom I pleased. She is a devout Catholic and would regard divorce as a sin. So here I am, in limbo, effectively a single man but not free to marry anyone else.'

'What a very sad situation,' Colette said.

'So there you have it. I'd like to be with you Colette, nothing would make me happier, but I could never offer you anything more than my love and my company.'

He started the car and they drove home in silence. He stopped outside the villa.

'Would you like to come in for some supper again?' she asked.

'Of course, if you'll have me.'

They went inside. Samang was standing in the hallway.

'A box arrived for you, madam.'

Sure enough a large wooden crate stood in the middle of the room. Colette examined it and saw from the labels and stamps on the top that it had been sent from Paris.

'Would you get some tools please,' she asked the houseboy. 'So we can open it.'

He disappeared and returned a few minutes later with a hammer and chisel. He handed the chisel to Luc and they both used the tools to prise the crate open. Inside were several cardboard boxes. Colette's heart gave a strange twist. She knew where they'd come from. She ripped open the first one and began to take out the objects one by one. This box contained the contents of her mother's dressing table, her jewellery, photographs, ornaments, even her perfumes and cosmetics. Colette's eyes misted with tears as she examined each item and each one brought back poignant memories. She was so absorbed in the task that she forgot that Luc was there.

At the bottom of the box was a photograph of the three of them; her mother, her father and herself at Nice on a summer holiday. She must have been around fifteen at the time. They were all standing under the palm trees on the Promenade des Anglais, their arms around each other, broad smiles on their faces. They looked tanned and happy and the sun shone on the calm sea behind them. She remembered that day as if it were yesterday. It was nothing remarkable, just a happy summer's day spent enjoying the company of the people she loved. They'd spent the day on the beach and after the photograph was taken had gone to a tiny fish restaurant on a backstreet. She even recalled that they'd eaten mussels. As she looked at it, her hands began to shake and great, shuddering sobs rose in her throat.

Luc's arms were around her in an instant. He knelt beside her and he was holding her tight, kissing her cheeks, her eyes, her neck. She turned towards him and was kissing him too, just as she had longed to do every day for the past fortnight but had held herself back. But now, the need to show him how much she cared for him was growing stronger by the second. She drew away.

'Come upstairs,' she said breathlessly.

'Are you sure?'

'Quite sure.'

So they went, furtively so they wouldn't be noticed, and locked themselves into her bedroom, where she pulled the shutters over the windows and they lay down together on the bed and kissed again. He undressed her slowly, gently, all the time murmuring tender words of love, then he undressed himself and moved on top of her and she pulled him towards her, kissing his face, his lips hungrily, then they were moving together, slowly at first, then more fervently until they were moving together as one.

21

TONLÉ SAP, 1946

A fter that first night, Colette and Luc began to spend a lot of time together. He would often stay over at the villa and in the mornings, if she wasn't going to work at the floating school, she would ask him to take her to Angkor Wat with him. There, she would wander through the temple halls and cloisters soaking up the atmosphere, or sit and watch him at work, endlessly fascinated by his tenacity and the imagination with which he approached the restoration of this hallowed monument. She felt as if his company was helping her heal from the terrible wounds that the loss of Henri and of her parents had inflicted on her. Day by day, although she still felt sadness at her loss, she was no longer overwhelmed by it.

They would bring a picnic table and chairs with them in the car when they went to the temple, and take lunch together. Achariya would have grudgingly cooked it and packed it into a basket that morning. The picnic lunch would be accompanied by wine that they'd kept cold in a vacuum container filled with ice. Those heady days felt very different from the time she used to spend at Angkor when Henri was in charge. Henri had been obsessive about his work and when he was fanatically pursuing a discovery, he would barely acknowledge her presence, whereas Luc remained attentive towards her at all times, beckoning her over to show her something new, asking her opinion on how to approach a task, explaining new discoveries to her. Although Henri had described him as reckless, in Colette's mind Luc was far more measured in his approach to the project than Henri himself, although Luc had flashes of inspiration and brilliance when he would be prepared to take shortcuts to achieve quick results.

One constant sadness for Colette in this time of unexpected joy was that Achariya remained steadfastly against the relationship. Try as Colette might to extract the reasons for the antipathy, Achariya refused to be drawn. She was tersely polite to Luc when he was staying, serving him food efficiently and professionally, but without ever smiling and with barely a word. If he noticed, he never raised the matter with Colette, and she guessed that he was sensitive to the fact that she'd told him how close she and Achariya were.

It was tacitly understood between them that they would spend their time together at the villa and not at Luc's house in Siem Reap. In fact, Luc never once invited Colette to his house. When she mentioned it he would say, 'Oh you wouldn't like it there. It's very bare and functional. A bachelor's residence essentially.'

But he would sometimes go to stay there on the nights before Colette's school days. Sometimes he needed to go to Phnom Penh too for a few days, to stay in the villa there and have meetings at the Ministry. He didn't invite her to accompany him and she didn't ask to go.

'We need *some* time apart,' he would say, kissing her goodbye with the passion that characterised their relationship. 'It makes those times together all the more precious.'

She tended to agree and enjoyed spending time by herself when he wasn't there, going through the boxes of her parents' things, treasuring the memories, in a way she wouldn't have been able to if Luc had been present.

The months slipped by, and the months became years. Colette gradually came to terms with her grief and realised that Luc made her happier than she'd ever been before, even with Henri. He made her feel so loved and wanted and he excited her far more physically than Henri had ever done. But in all this happiness, there was one thing that niggled at her heart.

One day, they were walking arm in arm in the garden when they came once again to the clump of jungle surrounding the boathouse.

'I was fascinated by this place when you showed me before. Could I see inside again?' he asked. They went up the winding gravel path through the trees and Colette opened the boathouse door and switched on the light.

'I've been wondering, do you think I might be able to work in here sometimes?'

'Work here?' she asked, bemused.

'Yes, it's so peaceful here. There's a lot of traffic noise at my house in Siem Reap. I can never concentrate properly there, and the Ministry of Culture has asked me to write a report on my latest findings at Angkor. It's going to be quite a lot of work.'

'Oh, how interesting, Luc,' she said. 'You never mentioned that before.'

'I only got the letter yesterday. I've been mulling over how to approach it.'

She looked around the dusty boathouse sceptically. Geckos scurried up the walls, the roof beams were hung with cobwebs. She was sure that she could see bats hanging up there too.

'There are quiet rooms inside the villa,' she told him with a shudder. 'Are you sure you wouldn't prefer to work in there?'

He shook his head. 'When you showed me in here before, I noticed that there's a little gallery in front of that window above the double doors. There's a small table up there. That would suit me down to the ground. All I'd need would be a chair to sit on. It looks the perfect place to work. There's a view of the lake, and it's completely quiet and undisturbed.'

'If you're quite sure,' she said, shaking her head in amusement at this display of eccentricity.

So, the next day, Lim borrowed a chair from the kitchen, took it across the garden to the boathouse and carried it up the ladder to the little gallery. He swept the place clean for Luc and in the evening, Luc took some books and a notepad and a small typewriter he'd brought in the boot of his car, and spent an hour or so ensconced in the boathouse, working. He didn't go there every evening, but every so often. Sometimes he would go for an hour or two, sometimes for just half an hour. Occasionally Colette would turn over in the night and he would be gone. When he crept back in in the small hours he would say, 'I couldn't sleep, so I thought I would put a couple of hours' work in instead.'

Colette shook her head at his odd behaviour, but she was determined to let him do as he pleased. She wouldn't be one of those women who attempts to control their partner. She understood that Luc was a complex, creative man and that meant he would have flashes of odd behaviour. This would pass, she was sure of it, once he had finalised his report and they would then go back to how they were before. In the meantime, she would not put any pressure on him because she sensed that writing the report was making him anxious enough already.

One morning, she and Achariya went to the boathouse to set off for school. She went to untie the boat and noticed that it had been tied up differently than usual. She frowned.

'Did you go out on your own in the boat?' she asked Achariya.

'Of course not, madam.'

'Do you think Lim did? It has definitely been tied up differently.'

Achariya shook her head. 'It wasn't Lim,' she said, but Colette knew that there was something Achariya wasn't telling her.

'So, do you know who took the boat out?'

'It was Monsieur Gilbert, madam. Samang saw him. In the middle of the night. He took the boat out onto the lake.'

Shock washed through Colette. She felt foolish, having to be told this by Achariya of all people. If Luc wanted to take the boat out by himself, she had no objection, but why hadn't he mentioned it to her?

She said nothing further to Achariya, but she knew Achariya was watching her, wondering how she might react. It was clear that Achariya and the others had been talking about Luc and that made her uncomfortable. Did they all dislike him as much as Achariya did?

That afternoon, when he came home from the temple, Colette confronted him.

'Did you take the boat out in the middle of the night?' she asked. He didn't look surprised by her question. He held her gaze and answered in a steady voice.

'I did as a matter of fact. I meant to tell you, but I didn't want to worry you.'

'Really? Why would I be worried?'

'You worry about me when I can't sleep. A few nights ago, I couldn't sleep and I couldn't work either. I've come across some stumbling blocks in the report. I thought if I took the boat out, it might help me relax enough to unlock the blockage in my mind.'

'Oh Luc, I wish you would tell me about these things. I'm sorry the report is causing you so much stress. I thought it was something that you'd find interesting.'

'I'm sorry. I will tell you if I take the boat out again.'

He took her in his arms and kissed her. She melted to his touch as always and she lifted her head to kiss him back and within seconds the whole incident was forgotten. A few days later, though, he told her in the morning that he'd been out in the boat again.

'I couldn't sleep again. Being on the water relaxes me,' he said. 'When I came back I went straight to sleep.'

Colette couldn't wait until he'd finished the report and things could go back to normal, but the months wore on and nothing changed. Luc continued to spend hours out in the boathouse and to take the occasional nocturnal trip in the boat. It was driving a wedge between them.

One day, Colette decided it was time to do something about it. She was worried about how much time the report was taking him. So, one evening, when he was in the boathouse, she took a torch and walked over there herself. She shut the door quietly behind her and crept up the stairs to the little gallery where his desk was. He was bent over a book and when he saw her he shut it and got up.

'What are you doing here?' he asked.

'It is my boathouse after all,' she said. 'I've come to see if you're alright. And to tell you that I'm going to bed now.'

He drew her close and kissed her hard on the lips. Colette was surprised at his reaction, but at the same time she thrilled to his touch and was soon kissing him back, her arms around his neck, pulling him towards her. Then he was backing her against the wall, pulling her clothes down, kissing her neck, her shoulders, her breasts. Then he lifted her up and made love to her, there against the wall, tenderly, passionately, and as she'd never known it before.

For a time after that, Luc's nocturnal boat trips and evenings in the boathouse were not mentioned, but one day, looking at the calendar, Colette realised that it had been six months since he'd started working on the report.

'Don't you have a deadline for that work?' she asked one day.

'Oh, they keep asking for more at the Ministry. They're being very unreasonable. I'm not sure if they'll ever be satisfied.'

Colette made sympathetic noises, but something occurred to

her in that moment. She might be able to help Luc with this, but she wasn't going to let him know that just yet.

The next day, she went to the post office and put a call through to the Governor General's office in Hanoi. She asked the switchboard to put her through to Monsieur Daniel Grossman. He was the representative of the French Ministry of Culture in Indochina and she and Henri had entertained him several times in Phnom Penh when he'd visited Cambodia.

'Madame Boissière,' he exclaimed, 'what a lovely surprise. What can I do for you?'

'Well, this is a little awkward. I'm hoping to be able to sort something out for my friend, Monsieur Gilbert, and I'm wondering if you can help me.'

'Oh really? I'll do what I can. What is it?'

'I hope you'll be discreet about this because I wouldn't want him to think I'm interfering. He's writing a report for the Ministry of Culture, but it is taking him a very long time and I'm afraid that he's becoming very stressed about it indeed. I'm a bit worried about his health to tell you the truth.'

There was silence at the other end of the line, then Daniel said, 'Report you say?'

'Yes. A report about his findings at Angkor. He was commissioned to write it a few months ago, but it's dragging on rather. As I said, it's making him rather stressed. He is losing sleep over it, actually.'

There was another silence, then Daniel cleared his throat.

'As far as I know, no report has been commissioned from Monsieur Gilbert about Angkor. Not that I'm aware of anyway, but I will do a bit of digging and let you know what I find out. Why don't you call back next week.'

'Oh,' Colette said in a flat, hollow voice, 'Thank you. Until next week, then.'

She put the phone down and sat there in the office for a long time. What on earth had Luc been doing all those hours alone in the boathouse and why had he told her a pack of lies about it? The hairs on the back of her neck stood up as it dawned on her that this man whom she loved and trusted implicitly must have been lying to her for a long time. He clearly wasn't what he was pretending to be.

22

TONLÉ SAP, 1949

Colette didn't breathe a word to Luc about her conversation with Daniel Grossman. Instead, she watched him carefully, trying to understand his behaviour and to work out what on earth he was doing in the boathouse. Although she tried not to alert him to her suspicions, she couldn't help withdrawing from him a little, shrinking from his touch involuntarily, sleeping on the other side of the bed to put distance between them. It seemed a long wait until she could call Daniel Grossman again and the days dragged by. She couldn't wait to find out the truth.

But on the morning of the day on which she was supposed to be making the call, she awoke to the sound of a strange engine outside on the drive. She went out onto the balcony and was shocked to see a large black van pulled up there, several uniformed gendarmes were climbing out of the side door. To her astonishment they were armed with guns. The sight of them instantly brought back the fear of the war years. Trying not to panic, she rushed inside and grabbed her dressing gown. There was a loud rap at the front door and she heard Achariya walking across the hall to open it.

Pulling her dressing gown around her, she rushed down to the front door herself.

'It's alright Achariya,' she said. 'I will get this.'

The district chief of police, Jean Gerard, stood on the top step, beside him a younger Frenchman. She knew Monsieur Gerard vaguely from the bar in the Grand Hotel d'Angkor. He was a portly man with a chubby, genial face. It was difficult to believe he was there to enforce French colonial law.

'Ah! Madame Boissière. I am so sorry to disturb you this early in the morning. This is my assistant Pierre Leblanc. I was wondering if Monsieur Luc Gilbert is staying with you? We've been to his house and his houseboy said he might be here.'

Monsieur Gerard had raised his eyebrow quizzically as he spoke. Colette was aware that the whole French community knew that she and Luc were lovers. Some, inevitably, disapproved. But that didn't matter now. Why was he here asking for Luc? Did this have anything to do with the boathouse?

'Yes, he's here...' she stuttered, trying to remain composed, but all the time reeling from the shock of seeing armed police on her property.

There was a sudden sound behind her. She turned round and saw that Luc was standing at the top of the stairs. He was already fully dressed.

'What's the matter Jean?' he asked, his voice steady.

'We just need to ask you a few questions, Luc, old chap. Nothing to be alarmed about.'

'So, why the van full of armed police?' He nodded over the chief's shoulder where the policemen were now ranged in a row, holding their guns.

'Oh, that's just routine. If you'd kindly come with us, I'm sure we can clear all this up at the station with the minimum of fuss.'

'Of course.' Luc came down the stairs and kissed Colette on the cheek as he passed.

'I'm sure this is nothing, my darling. I'll be back as soon as I can. Please don't worry about me.'

'Can I come too?' Colette asked.

'I'm afraid not, Madame Boissière. You'll need to stay here because some of these men are going to stay behind and search your property.'

Another bolt of shock. 'Why would you want to do that?'

'All will become clear in time,' the chief of police said smoothly.

At that moment, one of the policemen stepped forward and slipped handcuffs round Luc's wrists.

'Is this necessary, Jean? I said I'll come along voluntarily,' Luc protested.

'Just bear with us. Into the van now. Thank you, Madame Boissière, we'll be out of your hair very soon. Monsieur Leblanc will stay and supervise the search. Goodbye now.'

He went down the steps and got into the van, with two of the armed police, one seated either side of Luc. The door of the van slammed, and she watched as it turned round and manoeuvred out of the drive.

'If you could just wait a few minutes I'll go up and get dressed,' she muttered to the young detective.

Upstairs in the bedroom she pulled on some trousers and an old blouse. Her hands were shaking so much it took her longer than usual, and when she looked in the mirror she saw that her face was white, her red-gold hair straggly and unkempt. She pulled a brush through it quickly and went downstairs to face the policeman again. He was standing in the hall patiently, his hands behind his back.

'I don't know what you're looking for,' she began. 'If you could just give me some idea about that, I might be able to help you.'

'Alright,' the young man said. 'We have reason to believe that Monsieur Gilbert has been removing antiquities from Angkor

Wat and the surrounding temples and selling them illegally on the black market. Were you aware of this?'

She sat down suddenly on the bottom step. She felt faint with shock. She shook her head. 'Of course not,' she said weakly.

'We understand you contacted Monsieur Grossman at the ministry in Hanoi about Monsieur Gilbert's behaviour. Monsieur Gilbert was already under suspicion, but that reinforced our investigation. We've done a search of his property in Siem Reap, but we found nothing there. Is there any possibility that he could have been hiding things at your villa? We understand he spends a fair amount of time here.'

She stared at the young man. Things were gradually falling into place now. If she had trusted Luc implicitly she would have defended him to the hilt, but once again her mind went over his strange behaviour in recent months, his reclusiveness, his night-time excursions in the boat.

'He has been spending quite a bit of time in my boathouse recently. Why don't you try looking there?' she said.

'Thank you, Madame Boissière. If you could show us where it is, we will begin our search there.'

'This way, please.'

The young detective, followed by the two remaining uniformed policemen, walked with her through the villa gardens to the clump of jungle at the edge, then down the winding, gravel path to the boathouse. There, she unlocked the door and pushed it back for them to enter. The detective went inside with the two policemen. Colette stood in the doorway and watched them.

Pierre Leblanc went straight up to the desk in the gallery and flicked through a book he found there, while the other policemen began to open the storage cupboards that Colette had never used herself or even looked inside. Before long, they had unearthed a stash of treasures; marble busts, buddha heads, parts of exquisite antique friezes. One by one the policemen took them carefully out of the cupboards and brought them down the steps and out of the boathouse where they laid them gently down on the path.

As Colette watched them her eyes filled with tears. They were tears of self-pity and of shame. How could she have trusted this man, whom Henri had always had his reservations about? How could she have let him into her heart, into her bed, into her confidence? She should have stayed true to Henri's instincts and not succumbed to Luc's flattery and manipulation. He'd been using her all these years. The realisation was hard to bear.

Pierre Leblanc came down the steps from the gallery to join her.

'How long has Monsieur Gilbert been using the boathouse?'

'Around six months, I think.'

'Yes, we gathered that. His smuggling business was sporadic before, but he has been building it up over recent months. Did he ever meet anyone here?'

'Not that I know of. Although, sometimes he used to take the boat out in the middle of the night.'

The policeman nodded. 'He would have been delivering artefacts somewhere remote on the edge of the lake. The perfect cover.'

She shook her head in disbelief. It was hard to take this all in.

'We have finished here,' Pierre Leblanc said, 'but perhaps we could go back to the house now.'

They walked back through the gardens together.

'I can't believe it,' she said. 'I really had no idea.'

'He's a very clever man. We have been closing in on his operation in recent weeks. He has been working with a couple of Japanese dealers and an accomplice in Phnom Penh. A French woman.'

'Who is that?'

'Madame Leroux. Fleur Leroux. Do you know her?'

'Of course.' Once again, the shock of a fresh revelation washed through her.

'I would appreciate it if you could keep all this information to yourself for the time being. Her husband will have to resign from his post as Governor General. The news hasn't come out yet. We only arrested her yesterday. She confirmed that she and Monsieur Gilbert had been working together for a number of years. Their operation was interrupted by the war, but they started soon afterwards again.'

Colette was silent, thinking back over everything. She recalled how Fleur had encouraged her to get close to Luc before the war, the odd comments she'd made after Henri's death, Fleur's extravagance, her love of fine clothes and jewellery. Then she remembered seeing Luc talking furtively with the two Japanese men in Siem Reap and had another bolt of realisation as the truth hit her. Of course. She could see it now. They weren't spies at all, they were his accomplices helping him to smuggle antiquities out of Angkor.

Back at the villa, Achariya brought her and Pierre Leblanc coffee on the veranda while the policemen brought the antiquities across the gardens and laid them out on the drive ready for the police van to return.

'What will happen to Luc?' she asked.

'I'm not sure. We have all the evidence we need now to bring him to trial, but it is more likely the trial will take place in France than here in Cambodia. In the meantime, it is likely that he will be deported.'

She stared out across the lake. The sun was high in the sky now, glittering on the smooth, clear water. She thought of all the times she and Luc had sat here together talking amiably and exchanging news about their days. She reflected that although she was incandescent with rage about the way he'd treated her and about what he'd done, ironically, she would still miss him. She was alone now. Apart from Achariya, of course.

When Jean Gerard returned from Siem Reap in the police van, he came and spoke to Colette.

'No doubt Pierre has filled you in on the details. Monsieur Gilbert is in police custody now in police headquarters in the town. You can visit him there if you like.'

She thought for a moment, then shook her head. 'I don't think so,' she said. 'There isn't anything to say.'

'Well, he's going to be there for a few days, until we can arrange his deportation. If you change your mind at any point, I can arrange for you to visit.'

When the police had loaded up the van with the antiquities and disappeared, saying they may need to visit again in the coming days, Colette sat on the veranda and wept. She wept with humiliation for how easily she'd been taken in by Luc Gilbert, but she wept for her loss too. Achariya came to her and slid her arm around her back. She looked up and blinked away the tears. She took Achariya's hand.

'Sit down for a minute, Achariya,' she said. 'I want to say I'm sorry. I'm sorry for the way I didn't believe you about Monsieur Gilbert. I'm sorry for the distance that's grown between us and I'm sorry I put you in the position I have over the past few years. You were right in the end. He was not trustworthy and he wasn't good for me. I should have listened to you.'

Achariya sat down beside her and squeezed her hand. 'You don't need to be sorry, madam. I understood that you needed time. The truth had to come out eventually.'

'Thank you for being so understanding, Achariya. I really don't deserve you.'

23

TONLÉ SAP, 1949

T he next day, Pierre Leblanc returned. This time he was alone, driving a police car. Colette opened the door to him herself.

'Good morning, Monsieur Leblanc. Please come in.'

'I won't stay, Madame Boissière. I've just brought a letter for you from Monsieur Gilbert. He understands that you might not want to visit him in custody, but he asked me to bring this to you.'

He handed her an envelope which she ripped open. He backed away and headed back to the car. 'Good day,' he said with a wave, 'I'll let you know if we need to speak to you again.'

Colette stood there at the door, watching, as he got back into the car, turned it round on the drive and drove away. Then, she went through to the veranda and ripped the letter open.

My dearest Colette,

I am so sorry to have dragged you into this dreadful business. You have shown me nothing but kindness and love and I owe you an explanation for the trouble I've brought upon you. The fact is, the police have got everything wrong. I brought those artefacts to the boathouse from Angkor Wat to study, and was intending to return them once I'd finished with them. The police have concocted a ridiculous story about me planning to sell them. I am an honourable and professional archae-ologist and to take precious artefacts away from their source perma-nently would be anathema to me and my profession.

The police are determined to deport me to France to stand trial, and I welcome that in order to clear my name. I understand that you might want to keep your distance, but I wish you would reconsider and come and see me before I leave. I would love to rest my eyes on your dear face once more. I have nothing but love and admiration for you, Colette, whatever you might think.

If I am to be deported, there is one thing I would ask you to do for me. That is, my young housekeeper, Maly, will be out of a job now I'm going away. My houseboy is resourceful and capable and will soon find himself another job, but Maly is shy and quiet. She is a long way away from her family in the north. If you could see a way to take her in and give her employment, I would be eternally grateful. I'm sure she would benefit from learning from your own excellent housekeeper, Achariya.

Whatever you may think of me, I have never had anything but love for you, Colette and I am deeply sorry to have hurt and humiliated you by this police investigation. I hope you can find it in your heart to forgive me and that one day, when I return to Cambodia having cleared my name in France, we can be friends once again.

Your ever loving,

Luc.

She read the letter over and over again. It disgusted her that he was trying to hoodwink her with his lies. She had no desire to visit Luc in custody, it would only make her even more bitter than she was already, but she thought about his other request. At first it angered her. How could he ask anything of her after what he'd done? But the more she thought about the young girl, the more her heart softened. She knew of these destitute young women who came from poor, remote villages to work in service for the French. They would work their fingers to the bone and send their entire salary home to the family to save them from starvation. If Maly was out of work, it was likely that her whole family would be starving in some village far away in the north of the country.

So, the next morning, she took Henri's car and drove into Siem Reap. For the first time she went to Luc's home which was tucked away in a back street in the French quarter, not far from the Governor's residence. It was a pretty, yellow-painted colonial townhouse with a tiny front garden. She parked outside, went up the path and knocked on the front door. She had to knock three times before she heard footsteps and the door opened a crack. A pair of frightened, dark eyes peered through the gap at her.

'Are you Maly?' she asked in the native tongue and the girl nodded slowly.

'Hello, Maly. My name is Colette Boissière. Luc... Monsieur Gilbert asked if I could offer you employment now that he has to return to France. I came to talk to you about it.'

The girl opened the door wide and let Colette inside. She showed her through the house and out onto a shaded veranda. Crimson and magenta bougainvillea tumbled over the railings, and lush, ornamental palms provided shade. In the paved courtyard beyond, was a round lily pond. This was really rather attractive and congenial. Hardly the comfortless bachelor's residence Luc had dismissed it as. She sat down in one of the cane chairs and Maly brought her a lemon juice.

'Sit down, Maly,' she beckoned and the girl sat opposite her in the other chair, perched on the edge awkwardly. The girl was probably in her early twenties and, typical of country people she had a wide, innocent face with flawless, creamy skin and dark eyes.

'Where is the houseboy?'

'He has gone,' Maly answered. 'He took his things and left yesterday after the police came.'

'So, you're all alone here?'

Maly nodded.

'As I said, Monsieur Gilbert won't be coming back. He is

returning to France. I'm not sure what will happen to this house, but whoever takes it over might want new servants. Monsieur Gilbert asked if I would give you a job in my villa in Tonlé Sap. Would you like that?'

Maly frowned and dropped her gaze to the floor. She didn't answer the question, instead, at length, asked a question of her own.

'Why is Monsieur Gilbert not coming back?'

Colette took a deep breath. 'I'm sorry, but it's rather complicated. He has to answer some questions the French government have about his work. That means he needs to go to France, I'm afraid.'

Maly looked even more miserable, then brushed her cheek with the back of her hand as if wiping away a tear.

'He was kind to me,' she said. Colette frowned, remembering how dismissive Luc had been about his servants and how he'd said that neither Maly nor the houseboy could be described as friends.

'I'm sure he was,' she said briskly. 'But I'm afraid, as I said, he won't be coming back. You won't be able to stay here too much longer. You could work in my house instead. Would that suit you?'

'What would I do there?' Maly asked after another long pause.

'Well, I already have a housekeeper, so you would be able to help her. Cleaning, cooking, washing up, perhaps. She is very good. I'm sure she would train you well and then you might be able to look for another job.'

'Is it far away from here?' Maly asked.

'Not too far from Siem Reap. Just a short drive.'

'Alright,' Maly said. 'I will come. I need to work. I don't want to go back to my village.'

Colette waited for the girl to pack her things, which consisted of one pitifully small bundle of clothes wrapped in a sarong.

They locked the house up and Maly slipped the key under a plant pot beside the door. Colette contemplated dropping it off at the police headquarters but decided against it. She didn't want any possibility of being coerced into speaking to Luc, and if she went there she knew that could happen. She was doing him this favour regarding Maly. This would be the last thing she did for him and she certainly had nothing to say to him.

When they arrived back at the villa, Colette showed Maly into the kitchen. She'd spoken to Achariya about Maly before she left and now Achariya welcomed the younger woman warmly and took the bundle from her. Soon the two of them were chattering away, exchanging stories about their families. Colette left the kitchen smiling, glad that Achariya was going to accept the new girl without any problems.

For the next few weeks things seemed to run smoothly in the villa. Achariya was teaching Maly the daily routines and at meal-times she would serve Colette her food with a smile. Things were working out better than Colette could have hoped. One day, Pierre Leblanc called in with the news that Luc had departed under police escort for Kampong Som where he would board a ship for Marseille. A huge weight lifted from Colette's shoulders at that news. She could now begin to rebuild her life.

Things quickly settled down into a comfortable routine. Colette went to teach French conversation at the floating school on several occasions. Now she had more confidence and Achariya was busy showing Maly the ropes, Achariya rarely accompanied her. Colette heard on the grapevine that Charles Leroux had resigned as Governor General and that he and Fleur had gone back to France. Fleur was to face trial alongside Luc, but on less serious charges. Colette decided not to go to the Hotel Grand d'Angkor for a while. She couldn't bear the curious looks and the judgemental whispering from her French compatriots. So, she stayed at the villa and kept herself to herself.

One morning, a couple of weeks after Maly had arrived at the villa, Achariya served Colette's breakfast alone. Normally the two of them would serve it together, so this was a departure from the new routine.

'Where's Maly this morning?' Colette asked.

'She's sick.'

'Oh no. I hope it's nothing serious. It's not malaria is it?'

Achariya shook her head and there was something in her look that made Colette curious. After breakfast, Colette went to see Maly. She was lying in bed in her room in the servants' quarters behind the villa. Colette sat down beside her. She looked very pale.

'What's wrong, Maly? Is it something you ate?'

'I don't know, madam. I was sick yesterday too. I feel very weak.'

'Let's see how you are tomorrow and if there's no improvement, I will ask the doctor to come out to see you.'

But the next morning Maly couldn't keep her breakfast down and was so weak she was unable to get out of bed. Colette asked Lim to take the car to town and come back with the doctor.

Colette had known the French doctor, Docteur Allende since she arrived at the villa in 1939. He was an imposing, heavily set man with elaborate whiskers but she knew him to be kind and compassionate. He came with his big, black bag and examined Maly while Colette stood in her doorway watching anxiously. At one point he turned to Colette and said,

'Madame Boissière, it might help if I could have a word with the patient in private if you don't mind.'

Colette took herself off and went to wait anxiously on the veranda. Half an hour later the doctor came through and sat down opposite her.

'There's a simple explanation for this sickness and I'm surprised you haven't worked it out yourself, but you always were very trusting. I'm afraid the girl's expecting, Madame Boissière.'

'Expecting?' Colette felt the colour drain from her face. Maly looked so young, so innocent, how was that even possible?

'Many employers would put her out on the street in these circumstances... but I know you better than that, Madame Boissière. I know I can trust you to let her stay, to not turn her out. She won't have an easy time of it I'm afraid. She has a very narrow frame and she isn't of robust constitution. If you bring her in to Siem Reap to see me once a month I will keep an eye on her for you.'

He got up to go. 'She won't say who the father is, but I don't suppose it matters. Another servant probably who is unlikely to have the means to support her.'

'There was a young houseboy where she was before. Just the two of them I think.'

'That'll be it then. If your gardener would kindly run me back into town, you can settle the bill next time you come in.'

Within a few weeks, Maly was over her sickness and able to work again. She seemed happy to do so and Achariya was grateful to have some assistance again. Soon, her pregnancy became apparent and she began to wear her sarongs loosely. Colette took her into Siem Reap to the doctor's the next time she went in. After examining Maly the doctor spoke to Colette.

'Frankly I'm worried about her. It is a big baby, as far as one can tell at this stage, and she is a tiny girl. I will need to be there at the birth, and you must bring her in weekly from now on.'

On the way back to the villa, Colette glanced over at Maly who in turn was looking out of the window. She seemed to be taking pregnancy in her stride and Colette wondered how much the doctor had told her about the dangers. Colette felt a sudden twinge of envy for this young servant girl who had become pregnant without even trying. She herself had never conceived even though she'd hoped and prayed for a baby. She'd given up hope long before the end had come with Luc. She'd resigned herself to never becoming a mother, but this little slip of a girl would become one when she was barely grown herself.

Everyone in the household was looking forward to the impending birth and as Maly's girth expanded and the birth date drew closer, the excitement mounted. Colette was surprised to note that Lim and Samang were as interested in Maly's progress as she and Achariya were, and both went out of their way to take care of Maly. They would take her arm when she walked in the garden, ensure she had enough shade when she sat outside, bring her drinks and snacks to keep her energy levels up. Colette took her weekly to see the doctor and insisted that Maly only undertake light duties as she became heavier. A few weeks before the birth Maly stopped working altogether. She spent her time resting in her room, or lying out on the couch on the veranda. She was shy about doing that at first but Colette insisted. 'You need fresh air. You can't just stay in your room all day. Please, lie on the couch and watch the lake. The beauty and peace of the scenery will help you to relax.'

By now Maly was enormous. Her stomach was so huge that she waddled rather than walked and had great difficulty getting about. On the last visit to Docteur Allende before the due date, he took Colette aside after the examination.

'I'm very worried about her. The baby will be breech. You know what that means don't you?'

Colette felt ashamed to admit her ignorance. She shook her head.

'It means the baby is lying upside down. It will be a difficult birth. I'm going to try to turn the baby now by manipulation. If it doesn't work, we will have to think again. Would you like to come and hold the girl's hand? It can be a touch painful.'

'Of course.' Colette hurried into the surgery where Maly was lying on the couch. She took the girl's hand and the doctor explained what he was about to do. He then began pressing and pushing on Maly's abdomen and the girl's eyes widened in pain.

Once or twice she cried out and tightened her hold on Colette's hand in a vice-like grip. The doctor was beginning to sweat. In the end, he stepped back and said, 'I can't do it. This baby is too big to turn. We will have to think about a caesarean section. I could perform that here in the clinic.'

He spoke to Maly in Khmer, explaining to her the difficulties and dangers of a breech birth. When he'd finished, she shook her head fiercely. 'I don't want an operation. I want the birth to be natural.'

The doctor tried again to persuade her but no matter what he said, she shook her head and wouldn't agree. In the end he sighed deeply.

'Send your boy for me as soon as she goes into labour. I'll need to be there right from the start.'

On the way home in the car Colette asked Maly why she was so resistant to an operation. At first she wouldn't be drawn, but when Colette persisted she said, 'My father died during an operation. He cut his leg on some old machinery when he was working in the fields and we had no medicine. It became infected. When the doctor tried to operate, something went wrong and my father never woke up. After that, my mother sent me down to Siem Reap to find work. We couldn't survive without my father's wages.'

'I'm so sorry, Maly, how very sad for you,' Colette said, reaching out and touching her hand. 'But it will be different for you.'

She told her that the doctor here was very experienced, that the clinic was modern and well equipped, but to no avail. Maly would not sanction an operation. She was determined to go through with the birth without medical intervention.

Two days later, Colette was sitting on the veranda with Maly when the girl sat forward suddenly, her face contorted with pain.

'Are you alright? Is it the baby?'

'I think so.'

Colette rushed outside, found Lim and asked him to fetch the doctor then she ran back to the veranda where Achariya was already sitting beside Maly, rubbing her back, murmuring soothing words. They persuaded Maly to walk through the house to her room. They made slow progress, stopping every few minutes while she doubled up with a contraction. She bore the pain without crying out but the extent of it was plain to see from her contorted expressions.

When the doctor arrived an hour or so later, he examined Maly and shook his head.

'The baby still hasn't turned. This is going to be tricky,' he told Colette. 'But I'll do my best.'

The hours wore on and the contractions came thick and fast. Soon, Maly was exhausted, lying back on the bed, sweat pouring from her face, her hair plastered to her head. Achariya sat beside her, mopping her brow, talking to her softly. By the evening though, Colette was very worried; Maly seemed to have given up. She appeared unconscious, the pain of each, shuddering contraction passing across her face involuntarily.

It was the middle of the night when the baby started to emerge, feet first. The doctor urged Maly to push, but she was so exhausted she wasn't registering his words. It took an agonising two hours for the baby to be born and as soon as the head slithered out, it was immediately followed by a gush of blood.

'She's haemorrhaging,' the doctor said, cutting the umbilical cord and handing the slithering bundle to Colette. 'It's a girl. This is what I was worried about. I need to get her to the clinic straight away. Help me to carry her to the car.'

Lim and Samang appeared miraculously from nowhere and, together with the doctor, carried Maly through the house. Colette wrapped the baby in a muslin cloth and followed them, alarmed at the thick stream of blood Maly left on the floor as they went. She watched them carry her to the car, where they laid her on a bed of old sheets Achariya had placed on the back seat. The doctor got in beside her.

'Drive!' he said to Lim and within seconds the car was careering out of the gates and heading for the jungle road to Siem Reap.

Colette looked down at the baby girl who was now yelling, testing her new lungs.

'Come on, little one. Let's get you cleaned up.'

She took the baby into the kitchen where she and Achariya bathed her in the kitchen sink.

'She must be hungry,' Colette said, and Achariya prepared a bottle which they'd bought in case Maly wasn't able to feed the baby herself. Colette sat down at the table and gave the baby her first feed. She took the milk hungrily, gulping it down, all the time watching Colette with her beady, black eyes.

It was mid-morning when Lim returned in the car, his face sombre. Colette rushed out to speak to him but she could tell from the heavy way he got out of the car that it was bad news.

'Maly died an hour ago,' he said, stifling a sob. 'The doctor said she'd lost too much blood to survive. She didn't wake up.'

24

TONLÉ SAP, 1950

Motherhood came to Colette in an unexpected way, and although she'd longed for a child for years, she didn't feel prepared or adequate to the task of caring for a new-born baby. Achariya was an enormous help to her during those first weeks. She had many younger brothers and sisters and knew exactly what to do in any situation concerning babies.

But first they had to ensure Maly had a suitable farewell. Colette asked the monks at the Buddhist temple, Wat Bo, in Siem Reap if they would help her, and they agreed to hold a simple cremation for Maly the next day. Colette was aware that in this climate it was necessary for funerals to take place within days, but it seemed very soon to be saying their final farewells. She was reminded of Henri's funeral, hastily arranged by the Bishop of Phnom Penh. That had been the day after his death, when she'd still been reeling with shock at her loss.

Colette, Lim, Samang, Achariya, and Docteur Allende were the only mourners. Achariya's mother looked after the baby while they went to the temple. They made offerings to the Buddha at the altar and placed flowers inside Maly's open coffin. Colette

looked at the girl's face as she laid her flower. Maly looked
peaceful in death, her silken hair as black as night, her skin virtually translucent, but she looked very young too. Far too young to
be a mother, and far, far too young to die. Everyone knelt on the
floor while the monks chanted and prayers were said, then the
coffin was placed inside an inner chamber for the cremation. It
was all too brief and Colette reflected on Maly's short, rather
tragic life. But even in that short life, she had managed to
produce a lasting legacy. Something that Colette herself had been
unable to do.

The next day Colette went back to the temple, and the monk
handed her a small casket with Maly's ashes inside.

'Scatter them somewhere beautiful. Somewhere she loved,'
he advised.

When she got home, Colette took Achariya, Lim and Samang
out on the boat to the middle of the lake. There, they stopped the
engine and scattered Maly's ashes on the still water, saying a
quiet prayer as they did so.

'She loved the lake,' Achariya said. 'She will be at peace here.'

They returned to the house, their hearts heavy. Colette knew
that the best thing she could do for Maly's memory was to care
for her little girl.

The first dilemma was what to name the child. Colette
decided she couldn't just keep calling her "baby". But Achariya
already had an answer to that question.

'Maly told me what she wanted to call the baby,' she
announced. 'It would have been Raksmei for a boy, and Sophia
for a girl. It means "she who is a clever and wise one".'

'Sophia it is, then,' Colette said, relieved that the decision had
been taken for her. 'What a pretty name.'

'It was her mother's name,' Achariya said. Colette thought for
a moment.

'Do you think we should try to contact her family? They may
want to take the baby. She is their flesh and blood after all.'

'I wouldn't know where to start looking. She didn't tell me the name of her village, it could be anywhere in the northern provinces, and I only know the first name of her mother. It's a fairly common name.'

'Hmm.' Colette didn't want to deny Maly's family a chance to bring up the little girl, although from her knowledge of poor villagers they may not welcome another mouth to feed. 'What about the father? Was it the houseboy, do you think? Perhaps we should try to find out who it was and contact him?'

Achariya gave her a strange look, then said quietly. 'I don't think so, no, madam.'

'But whyever not. He might be pleased to know he has a beautiful daughter.' Then she stopped. Achariya had one of those expressions on her face. One that told Colette that she was straying onto dangerous ground.

'What's the matter, Achariya? Do you know who the father is? Did Maly tell you? I know you two became very close.'

Achariya drew herself up. 'I'd prefer not to talk about it, madam.'

'Oh, come on. If I'm going to care for the little girl, I need to know if someone might turn up in the future saying they are her father and that they want to take her from me.'

'She did tell me, madam, but she asked me not to tell anyone.'

'I understand, but things have changed since she told you. She didn't know she was going to die. I think you owe it to Maly and to Sophia to tell me. And if it was the houseboy, we need to find him and tell him he has a daughter.'

'It wasn't the houseboy, madam,' Achariya said, still refusing to meet Colette's gaze.

'So? Who was it? I will keep asking until you tell me.'

'If you must know I will tell you. But please don't be angry with me when I do.'

'I won't be angry with you. Why should I be angry with you?'

'Alright. I will tell you. The father is Monsieur Gilbert. Monsieur Luc Gilbert.'

Shock bolted through Colette like forked lightning. The blood drained from her face and she felt weak, as if she would faint. Nausea flooded her mouth. She couldn't speak, her thoughts all crowded in on her at once. But when the immediate shock had passed through her though, her first reaction was one of denial.

'It cannot be. Maly must have been lying.'

'Why would she lie? She had no reason to. She was telling the truth.'

Colette fell silent, thinking of all those nights Luc used to spend back at his house. 'We need time alone,' he would say and like a fool she'd agreed, even welcomed the space it had given her. Now she recalled those exchanges bitterly. She remembered too, the casual and dismissive way he'd spoken of his servants and of the way Maly had brushed away the tears when she'd heard Luc wasn't coming back. She was clearly distressed at losing him . He'd loved poor, innocent Maly and had used her too. He'd betrayed both of them. It all fitted perfectly now. The girl had been in love with him, pining for his loss.

IT WAS ALL SO PLAIN, so obvious now. 'You're very trusting,' the doctor had said. She clenched her fists and fought back the tears. Had Docteur Allende guessed the truth too? What a fool she'd been. Luc Gilbert had used her from the start. She suspected now that he'd tried to get close to her before the war so he could find out more about Henri, perhaps in order to find a way of discrediting him so he could take the top job at Angkor Wat he'd always craved. And afterwards, he'd preyed on her grief, her loneliness. It didn't matter now to Colette that there had been moments of joy in his company, that she'd loved him, that he'd been kind to her. All that was wiped out now she knew the extent of his betrayal

Instead of wallowing in her bitterness though, Colette threw herself into caring for the baby. But little Sophia wasn't easy to care for. She suffered from colic and would sometimes cry from morning until night and right on through the night too. She didn't like being held by anyone except Achariya for whom she would coo and smile. Try as she might to be positive, Colette struggled to enjoy looking after Sophia. Every time she looked into those dark, restless eyes, she saw Luc looking right back at her and it brought back her pain and her bitterness.

The months passed and once her initial shock was over, Colette decided to write to Luc to tell him about the birth of his daughter. She went into Siem Reap to speak to Monsieur Fournier, the Governor, to ask him how she could get in touch with Luc.

Françoise opened the door to the Residence and greeted her warmly.

'Colette! How lovely to see you. I haven't seen you for such a long time. I hear you're caring for a baby down at the villa nowadays,' she said. 'How wonderful for you.'

'It is… though quite hard work sometimes.'

She was glad to see a friendly face. Since Luc's arrest she'd hardly ventured into Siem Reap, wanting to avoid the judgmental eyes of the French community. Now she realised how much she had missed the company of her fellow countrymen.

'You must come down to the villa and see the baby sometime,' she said to Françoise.

Françoise showed her through to her husband's study. Albert Fournier was sitting behind a leather tooled desk, under a whirring fan, poring over some papers. He'd suffered a great deal under the Japanese occupation and in Phnom Penh and even now, five years later, it still showed in his face. When he looked up from his papers, Colette saw that his skin was sallow and drawn, and he was still painfully thin.

'What can I do for you, Madame Boissière?'

'Thank you for seeing me at short notice, Monsieur. I need to get in touch with Monsieur Gilbert. Monsieur Luc Gilbert. You know he was deported...'

'Of course. Of course. Dreadful business. Have you met the new chap we've installed at Angkor? Terribly nice man. Impeccable references. I always had my reservations about Gilbert, but Leroux insisted on appointing him. Now it turns out Leroux's wife was involved too. It makes you wonder...'

He stared at her vacantly for a few moments.

'I haven't met the new Chief Curator yet,' she answered, thinking she needed to jog his memory as to her request. 'But I was wondering if it might be possible to write to Luc Gilbert? I read he was due to go on trial in Paris, but I have never seen anything more about it. So, is it possible to write to him?'

'The trial never got underway. I'm afraid you won't be able to write to him because unfortunately he was found hanging in his cell on the first morning of the trial. The papers hushed it up for some reason, so you won't have read about it.'

Colette's hand flew to her mouth and once again she felt shock run through her like bolts of electricity. 'How... how terrible. I can't believe it. He said he was ready for the trial, that he wanted to clear his name.'

Albert Fournier shrugged. 'Underneath all his charm and bravado, Gilbert was a weak man. Wasn't confident he would win and didn't want to live with the consequences of his actions. I'm sorry to have shocked you, Madame Boissière. You look quite pale. Here... have a tot of brandy.'

He poured a glass from a decanter on his desk and handed it to her. She sipped it gratefully and was glad of the instant feeling of relaxation that stole over her. She'd been completely unprepared for this news. It sounded so unlike Luc to have taken his own life. She knew he had been working with others who must have been sophisticated criminals. Perhaps he hadn't taken his own life at all, perhaps his enemies had got to him, not wanting him to expose their operation. Or perhaps, as Albert said, the truth was more straightforward; he couldn't face the possibility of going to prison for what he'd done.

Saying goodbye to Françoise, she wandered back to the car and drove slowly back to the villa. Sophia was an orphan now and she knew it was up to her to give the little girl a home. Even though it was difficult, she knew it was her duty and she wouldn't shrink from it.

So, that's what she did. For the next fifteen years, she immersed herself in the task of bringing up Sophia, putting her own life mainly on hold. While Sophia was still a baby, Colette wrote to the Governor General and obtained adoption papers for her. She wanted to make it official, thinking it could only benefit Sophia in the long run if she was adopted by a French woman and thus obtain dual citizenship – French and Cambodian. During Sophia's babyhood she devoted herself to the little girl totally, even giving up her role at the floating school for a few years so she could focus on Sophia. From being a difficult baby, Sophia graduated into being a difficult toddler. She was quick to learn and picked up both Khmer and French with ease, but she had a terrible temper and would throw tantrums at the slightest thing. 'It's normal,' Achariya said, but when Sophia was screaming and raging, throwing things around, throwing herself on the ground, Colette found it hard to accept this was normal behaviour. In those stormy, dark eyes, she saw Sophia's father and although he had never shown his temper overtly, she'd been aware of restless, dark forces lurking beneath the surface.

Sometimes Colette was so exhausted and frustrated, she even thought about walking away. Finding another home for Sophia. Those dark, stormy eyes were a constant reminder of Luc's betrayal. It was almost as if they were mocking her. But in her heart of hearts she knew she would never leave Sophia. She'd committed to her for life, no matter how hard it turned out to be. It felt like a penance sometimes, punishment in a way for loving Luc, for being foolish enough to fall for his charms.

Sophia's first three years was a time of strife and upheaval in Cambodia. The war against the French in Vietnam spilled over the border into Cambodia, and the Vietnamese began to fight the French in Cambodia too, supporting the Free Khmer movement against French rule. Cossetted away in the villa, Colette read the news from a distance. It seemed unreal to her, as if it was happening far away. It was unbelievable to her that French rule in Cambodia could ever come to an end. She'd been there for more than a decade and the Cambodians were peaceful, welcoming people, but outside influences had stirred up latent unrest and before long it appeared that independence was inevitable. In late 1952, the Cambodian King, Sihanouk, who had been put in place as a puppet king by the Japanese, declared martial law and went on a royal crusade against the French and a year or so later, in November 1953 independence from France was declared.

That day, Colette had gone to the bar in the Grand Hotel d'Angkor for the first time in years. She felt the need to be amongst her own people at that difficult time. People sat around morosely, drinking too much, telling stories of their colonial adventures, mourning the passing of French Indochina. Many were speaking about their plans to return to France, trying to put a brave face on it, having spent the greater part of their adult lives serving their country in Indochina.

'What will you do, Colette?' Françoise asked. 'Albert and I are heading home as soon as we can. Retirement is well overdue for us. We're looking for somewhere in the south though, where it's warm.'

'I'm not sure,' she said. 'I haven't decided yet.'

She'd been agonising over it for days, ever since it became

clear that French rule was destined to come to an end. She couldn't imagine returning to live in France after so many years in the tropics. In her mind, life in France would be dull and grey by comparison. What would life be like without the lush green of the jungle, the emerald rice fields, the flaming, vibrant colours of the wild flowers?

But it wasn't just that. There was Sophia to think of too. How would the little girl cope thousands of miles away from her native land? Would she wilt, like a tropical plant transplanted from its jungle home? Colette thought about taking her to the rough village school in the Dordogne where the children of farmers, wine-pickers, poultrymen went. Hers would be the only brown face in the entire school. Would she be accepted by the other children? Would she be happy? Some mornings Colette had taken her along to the floating school and the children there welcomed her and made a fuss of her; the older girls took her under their wing and looked after her while Colette taught the class. It was the first thing Sophia had settled to in her short life and she appeared genuinely happy whenever she was there. It seemed cruel to tear her away from that, just as she was starting to settle down.

'I'm going to stay on in Cambodia if I can,' she said to Françoise at last. 'For Sophia's sake. And for mine too.'

25

TONLÉ SAP, 1965

I t wasn't an easy choice to stay on in Cambodia after the French had withdrawn. The years that followed were turbulent politically, building up to a civil war, and Colette never felt completely safe there again. Her idyllic life became troubled in more ways than one.

Although Sophia was happy at the floating school and was a bright little girl, absorbing her lessons like blotting paper, she was still difficult at home, and Colette found that caring for her was an exhausting, thankless task. She sometimes felt that she was completely unfit to be a mother and it was for that reason that her body had never allowed her to conceive a baby of her own.

When Sophia reached the age of eleven, she graduated to the secondary school in Siem Reap and entered a class of over thirty children. It was then that the real trouble started. It began to dawn on Sophia that her background was different to that of the other children and she started to ask awkward questions.

'Why is your skin white, Maman?'

'Because I come from France. It's a country a long way away from here. It's not as sunny there.'

'Why can't you be like the other mothers at the school? I don't like being different.'

'You're not different. It's not the colour of your skin that matters, Sophia, it's what's inside – whether you're a good person. We've talked about that before.'

After that, if Colette went to collect her at the school gate, Sophia would run away and only come to the gate if it was Achariya who came to collect her. It hurt Colette to be rejected like that – she'd tried to bring Sophia up to appreciate everyone, whatever their background or colour of their skin. It felt as though she'd failed in that task. At these times her mind would turn to Maly and run away with thoughts of her and Luc together, how loving they must have been together, there in his townhouse in Siem Reap, how happy. She couldn't help thinking that Maly would have made a much better mother than she was making. Maly had the sort of natural warmth that didn't come so easily to Colette. She would surely have not made such heavy work of motherhood.

Sophia even rejected her home too, saying she would prefer to live somewhere simple, like her friends, not in a big house a long way from anywhere. She started to misbehave at school, falling in with a group of children who were often in trouble. Colette was frequently called in to speak to the teacher about her behaviour.

'I know you do your best for her, Madame Boissière, but Sophia seems to be a very troubled little girl. I'm wondering if it might help to talk to her about her real parents? She seems very confused about her background.'

Colette agreed reluctantly, and that evening, she sat Sophia down and told her all about Maly and what a sweet, loving person she had been and how she'd looked forward to having a baby. Then she talked about Luc. It was difficult to speak about him without bitterness, but Colette swallowed her pride and reminded Sophia all about his work at Angkor Wat and how much he'd loved working at the temple. They'd already been to the temple several times and Colette had told Sophia how her father had worked there and made many important discoveries there.

But Sophia wasn't interested in hearing any more about her father. 'You've told me all this before,' she said. 'But you've never told me much about my mother. Where did she come from?'

'She came from somewhere in the north of the country. A poor village we think. Her father died and her mother needed her to earn some money so she sent Maly to work in Siem Reap.'

'Did she have brothers and sisters?'

'I think so. Perhaps several.'

'And they are still alive? Why didn't you tell me this before?' Sophia said angrily. 'We need to find them. They need to know about me.'

Colette reached for Sophia's hand but the girl snatched it away.

'It would be difficult to find them,' Colette said, 'We don't know the name of the village, we don't even know what district it's in.'

'But there must be a way.' Sophia's eyes filled with tears. 'Please, Maman, can't we go up there and at least try?'

Colette thought for a long time. She knew that such a trip would be fruitless, but perhaps if it was, it could be the only way for Sophia to come to terms with the fact that she would never know her mother's family.

'Alright,' she said at last. 'If you promise to be good at school for the rest of the term, we can take the car and drive up there in the holidays. If that's what you really want, we will try to find your mother's family.'

After that, there were far fewer incidents at school and it was clear that Sophia was making an effort to behave. At the end of term, they packed up the car and drove north. Achariya came with them because Sophia wanted her support, and because she had known Maly best of all. They headed north towards Preah Vihear Province, the car laden with food, cooking equipment and a canvas tent. They were aware that in that remote province, it was unlikely that they would find guesthouses or lodges to stay in.

Not far out of Siem Reap the roads were not metalled. They became just red dust and progress was slow. On the first day they passed through mile upon mile of scrubby jungle, punctuated by tiny, stilted villages where naked children playing in the dust stared at them wide-eyed as they passed. Sometimes they would drive through small areas of cultivation, rice-fields or maize, but this was subsistence farming, not on the scale it was around Siem Reap.

Occasionally they would pass a temple atop a craggy rock, its seated golden Buddha soaring above the jungle, lending the area a mystical beauty, but mostly there were just subsistence farms and tiny villages, where pigs and chickens rooted in the dust and everyone looked grindingly poor.

On the first night they reached the regional capital, Tbeng Meanchey. It consisted of a series of huts set amongst coconut palms strung along two dusty roads with the occasional shabbily built brick building sitting incongruously on a slab of concrete. They stopped at a roadside tea stall and the owner allowed them to pitch the tent behind his hut. They took tea in the stall once they'd put the tent up, and Achariya asked the owner and the other locals how they might go about finding Sophia's family. The locals all shook their heads and gestured towards the open country that stretched for miles into the jungled hills around.

'Many young girls from these villages are sent off to find work in the cities. If you don't have their name or even the name of their village, it will be difficult, but you can ask around.'

The next morning, having had a scanty breakfast of Khmer noodle curry at the tea stall, they set off in the car on the rutted roads that ran through the jungle into the hills. They passed places where stretches of wild forest had been decimated by logging, all the tall trees removed, the scars of the brutal operation still visible, but mostly they just drove through untamed jungle.

Whenever they came to a group of houses, they would stop the car and ask around to see if anyone knew of a girl called Maly who had come to work in Siem Reap a few years back, and had never returned. Everywhere people shook their heads and turned back to their work. Colette noticed that there were very few young people left in these parts and discovered from the villagers that most of the young women had gone away, like Maly. When they asked about the young men, they were met by silence or vagueness which Colette found curious.

They travelled like this for three nights, pitching the tent either by the roadside or in a village. By the fourth day, Sophia was beginning to look despondent and all three of them were feeling grimy and exhausted from life on the road. That morning, they were approaching a group of houses in a clearing at the end of a narrow, dirt track when Colette slammed the brakes on. Up ahead she was shocked to see an armoured car and soldiers milling about between the houses. She started to reverse, but a soldier stepped out of the undergrowth and banged on the bonnet. Colette felt her hands shaking, any encounter with the military automatically bringing back her experiences of the war years. She stopped the car. The soldier approached and she saw that he wore the uniform of the Cambodian government army, a machine gun slung over his shoulder. He came round to her side of the car to speak to her.

'This area is off-limits for vehicles, madam. You cannot go here. You need to go straight back to Tbeng Meanchey and from there you must go south. You need to leave the region.'

Her heart racing, Colette said, 'Alright. I'll drive straight back there. But what's happening here?'

'It's a very dangerous region. Local communist guerrilla

groups are fighting the government all over this area. For your own safety, you need to leave.'

There was a sudden burst of gunfire ahead of them. The ack ack ack of machine guns. Colette reversed the car out of the clearing at speed, skidded it round to face the opposite direction, then headed straight back to the regional capital. She drove as quickly as she could, understanding now why the villagers had been so secretive about the whereabouts of their young men. They were away from home, fighting with the guerrillas against the government.

Sophia was silent in the passenger seat, but when Colette glanced over at her she saw that her cheeks were wet with tears.

'What's the matter, Sophia darling?'

'We're never going to find my mother's family now, are we?'

'Perhaps we can come back again soon, when things calm down.'

But she knew that it was a vain hope and that even if the region was peaceful, it would be virtually impossible to track down Maly's family.

Back at home, Sophia quickly reverted to her old ways and the weeks and months ground on in the same vein. Colette was exhausted by the conflict. Whatever she did to please Sophia, nothing seemed to work.

'You shouldn't try so hard, madam,' Achariya said one day when Sophia had stormed to her room after a confrontation. 'She doesn't deserve it and she doesn't deserve you.'

Colette looked at her, surprised. Colette had noticed that Achariya had slowly been losing patience with Sophia's behaviour over the past few months, but this was the first time she'd given voice to her growing disenchantment.

'She needs to grow up, madam and understand how lucky she is and how good you've been to her. You should stop blaming yourself.'

'Perhaps you're right.'

Colette went out to the garden and knelt in front of Henri's grave as she had often done down the years when Sophia had tried her patience to the limit. It was peaceful and calming there under the trees, and Colette would talk through her difficulties. This would often have the effect of helping her find a way through them. Kneeling there that day, she realised that Achariya spoke the truth. Perhaps she should stop trying so hard herself and start expecting more of Sophia.

But still the arguments continued, alongside the resentment and the bad behaviour at school. Colette lost count of the number of times she'd been to the school to plead with the teachers not to expel her daughter. In the meantime, alongside her mornings teaching at the floating school, she got another job herself – guiding the dribs and drabs of tourists who arrived in Siem Reap to see Angkor Wat. She'd met the Chief Curator one evening at the bar in the Hotel Grand d'Angkor and hearing of her interest in antiquities, he offered her a job on the spot. It was a way of reconnecting with her past and also with her interest in history and archaeology. She loved those days when she could walk through those hallowed passages explaining the history of the place to a little band of tourists and see the expressions of awe on the faces of those seeing the place for the first time. It reminded her of how awestruck she herself had been the first time she'd seen the temple, and it recaptured those moments of joy for her. And it took her away from worrying about the present and about Sophia.

The next couple of years ground by. The guerrilla fighting carried on in the north, so it was still impossible to go back there and search for Maly's family. But Sophia had stopped asking about it and Colette assumed she had come to terms with the situation. As Sophia grew into her teenage years, she detached herself more and more from Colette and the villa, preferring instead the company of her Cambodian friends. Whenever she could, she would stay over with them in Siem Reap, preferring to lie on a mat in the corner of a simple Cambodian hut than to sleep in her own comfortable bedroom at the villa. By that time she had left school and her days were her own. Colette was racking her brains to think of a way to occupy her, knowing that Sophia needed something to interest her and a way of earning a living.

One day, in the middle of 1966, when Sophia was just sixteen years old, Colette returned from a day of guiding tourists at Angkor Wat expecting Sophia to be at home, but she'd not returned from staying with friends. It was not unusual for her to be late, but this time Colette sensed something was different. She went up to Sophia's room. The cupboards stood open and her holdall and knapsack had gone. She ran downstairs and Achariya confirmed that she'd left with her bags a couple of hours before.

'I'm so sorry. I just thought she was going to stay with someone and that you would know about it,' Achariya said.

Colette sat down, her head in her hands. 'She's taken almost everything. It looks as if she's left home. I'll drive into town and look for her. I'll ask her friends. I'll go to the police if necessary.'

'Let her go,' Achariya said, sitting down beside her and slipping her arm around Colette's shoulders. 'You've done enough. She is almost grown up. If she were Cambodian she would probably have been married long ago. Let her spread her wings and she will come back to you when she's ready. All will be well, you'll see.'

But although she tried, Colette couldn't take Achariya's advice. For the next nine years she devoted herself to searching for Sophia. She started close to home, asking everyone Sophia knew where she might be, but no one knew, or at least they weren't telling Colette. She even told the local police who took down her details dutifully, but she could tell what they were thinking. In their eyes Sophia was perfectly within her rights to go wherever she wanted and Colette was making a fuss.

Everywhere she went, she met with blank faces and passive

resistance. She didn't stop at Siem Reap. Her first thought was that Sophia had travelled north to resume the search for her mother's family, so she drove there herself on an impulse, not even telling Achariya where she was going. But after a hot day on the dusty road, she was turned back by a roadblock. The war with the communists was still raging in that province. Did that mean Sophia had been turned back too? Probably not. She may have slipped through on foot, perhaps with others. Colette had heard of many impressionable youngsters who'd run away from home to join the communists. Was Sophia fighting in those wild hills? Was she putting herself in danger?

She drove up to Phnom Penh and searched there too, walking through the poorest parts of the city where derelicts from the opium dens slept out on the streets. She showed everyone she met a photograph of Sophia, but there, as in Siem Reap, people just shook their heads and looked the other way. She even went to the French Embassy but although the officials there made comforting noises, it emerged that they were unable to help her either.

The years passed and the situation in Cambodia became more and more volatile. Colette's grief for the loss of Sophia was matched by her sadness at the disintegration of the country she loved and had made her home. Soon, the government was fighting a full-blown civil war. The communist guerrillas were supported by the Viet Cong whose own war had spilled over the borders.

One day Lim came rushing home on his bicycle.

'Madam. You mustn't go to Angkor Wat tomorrow. It is dangerous there.'

Colette laughed. 'Whatever do you mean, tomorrow is my tour guiding day. I can't miss it.'

'The temple has been taken over by Vietnamese forces. There has been fighting there today. Please, you cannot go there, madam.'

Colette hunkered down in the villa. It felt like the last safe place on earth. The Khmer Rouge, known to be fierce fighters and ruthless enemies, were soon in control of large swathes of the country. Many people were fleeing from rural areas into the cities to escape the fighting. It became difficult for Colette to survive without supplies and it reminded her of the war years. It was dangerous to go into Siem Reap for food, with sporadic fighting on the road, so Achariya would bring her fish from her family's catch. Colette often wondered what would happen to her if the Khmer Rouge came to her quiet little corner of the region, and one day she had her answer. That was the day that would live on in her nightmares for decades.

That morning she got out of bed and wandered onto the balcony stretching, gazing out over the lake, watching the mist rise from the water in clouds as she had almost every morning for the past thirty-five years. A strange sound came from the jungle and she turned, the hair standing up on the back of her neck. They were already upon her – black-clad soldiers with their red bandanas, jumping over the fence and powering across the grounds, their guns held aloft. For a split-second she was paralysed with shock and fear, but then she sprang into action. She rushed back into her bedroom and grabbed a bag, then tore down the stairs. Through the front windows of the hall she caught sight of them on the drive, approaching the house. They would be through the front door in seconds. She rushed out onto the veranda and climbed nimbly over the rails. She'd had one of the boats tied up there for months. It was the only way she could think of to get away. She started the engine and, keeping the revs low, set off along the edge of the lake, keeping under the cover of the reeds, her heart in her mouth, listening for a shot to ring out that could end it all.

But no shot came and soon she was forced to leave the edge of the lake and strike out towards the floating village. Achariya had told her to go there if the Khmer Rouge ever came for her. She increased the power and the boat began to move more quickly, speeding through the water, creating mini bow waves as it went. The morning was hot and sticky already and her shirt was sticking to her skin. She glanced back at the villa and took a sharp intake of breath. They were on the balcony, climbing on the railings, black figures stark against the white building. They were probably wrecking the place. She hoped fervently that they wouldn't burn it down.

In a few minutes the floating village came into view. She slowed the engine and pottered slowly between the homes, searching for Achariya's hut. All the houses were similar, but eventually she saw it, recognising Achariya's brother's fishing boat, moored up against the deck. She tied her boat up beside it and clambered on board the houseboat. Achariya came to the door.

'Madam! Come, quickly. The Khmer Rouge were here in boats earlier. They could come back.'

Achariya scrambled inside the tiny dwelling, where Achariya's elderly father and mother and two of her brothers were sitting on the floor. They stared at her, wide-eyed.

'I'm sorry,' she said. 'To put you in danger like this.'

'Don't mention it. We want to help,' Achariya said.

There was the sudden sound of a boats' engines moving fast over the water towards them. The houseboat rocked in their wake.

'Come quickly. We have a hiding place.' Achariya beckoned her forward and opened a trapdoor in the middle of the floor.

'It won't be very nice. It's where we store the fish, but they shouldn't find you there.'

Colette slid down into the large, plastic tank, holding her nose. The doors in the floor above her were closed and bolted down and she crouched there, trembling. It was stifling in there and stank of fish. But she was glad she was there. Within seconds one of the boats bumped against the side of the houseboat and she heard voices.

'Good morning, sister, we're looking for a French woman. She came across the lake from the villa over there. Have you seen her?'

'No. We haven't seen anyone. We've been asleep.'

'Whose are those boats moored up here?'

'They belong to us. We are fishermen. Everyone in the family has their own boat.'

There was a long pause, during which Colette, crouching there in the tank could feel her heart hammering against her ribs so hard it was making her nauseous.

'Alright, sister. But if you see a white woman, let us know. We will be staying at the villa over there.'

The engine roared into life and they were gone, powering across the lake towards the villa. Someone lifted the doors above her and Colette scrambled out into the room.

'We'll need to get you away as soon as we can. It's not safe for you here.'

'If only I could get to the French Embassy in Phnom Penh, I would be protected there,' she said.

'I will arrange it. I have some cousins who can help out,' Achariya said.

The next morning, swaddled in a sarong and a turban belonging to Achariya's mother, Colette was taken by boat to the jetty at Chong Khneas where a bullock cart was waiting. The back of the cart was covered with a hooped awning and she and Achariya climbed inside. The boy on the front clicked his tongue at the bullocks and the cart lumbered off, on the first leg of its long journey to Phnom Penh.

'Do you remember our last journey in a bullock cart? At the end of the war?' Achariya asked.

'I have you to thank for that too. Just as I do for helping me now,' Colette said, squeezing her friend's hand.

She stared out of the back of the cart as it made its ponderous progress along the dirt road through the thick jungle. It felt as if she was running away, and she was, to save her own life. Even so, there was something that troubled her about leaving Tonlé Sap and the villa on the lake. If Sophia ever came back, she would have absolutely no idea where to find her.

26

TONLÉ SAP, 1995

C olette thought about that long, arduous journey on the bullock cart to Phnom Penh while her minibus sped in the opposite direction twenty years later. They hadn't been stopped once on that journey back in April 1975, even though the roads were swarming with Khmer Rouge boy soldiers, roaring past them, standing on the back of battered trucks, firing bullets into the air just for the hell of it. There had been a couple of checkpoints as they came into Phnom Penh, when a soldier in a red bandana gave a cursory glance into the back of the cart and seeing two middle-aged women there had nodded them on. Now, she stared out at the flat, scrubby landscape as they neared Siem Reap and reflected on how much had changed in the past twenty years. Although the infrastructure had been ruined by five years of the brutal Khmer Rouge, there had been some rebuilding since they were deposed by the Vietnamese army in 1979, despite continuing fighting. The road she was now travelling on was at least tarmacked.

She thought too about her visit to Tuol Sleng. Chills of horror went through her recalling the photographs of the victims, their eyes wide, their faces bleached with fear, and the one in the last room of a woman she was almost sure was Sophia. Was that where she'd ended up? Had she been taken with the others to the killing fields and beaten to death? Thrown into a shallow grave to rot?

They entered the straggly outskirts of Siem Reap and passed the town hall. She still hadn't made a decision about whether or not to engage the Phnom Penh lawyer to set up a company as a vehicle to buy the villa. For some reason it went against her instincts to get round the law like that, even though he'd assured her the scheme would be perfectly legal. She wasn't quite sure she could trust him completely either. He seemed too slick. If he had a controlling interest in the company he set up to purchase the villa, how could she be sure he wouldn't cut her out somehow. She thought about the words of the lawyer in Siem Reap about such schemes. *I'm afraid those methods are not considered reliable.* Perhaps he had a point after all.

When they reached the Hotel Grand d'Angkor, Colette asked the driver to wait while she checked in again and left her luggage with the concierge. Then she asked him to take her to Achariya's houseboat. She'd told her friend that she would visit her as soon as she came back from Phnom Penh.

Achariya was sitting out on her deck, dressed in a sarong with a colourful red and green pattern. Colette kissed her on the cheek.

'You look better than ever,' she said, sitting down beside her.

'Thank you. You're so kind. How was Phnom Penh?' Achariya asked.

Colette told her about the visit to the lawyer and how she was still in two minds about going ahead with purchasing the villa. Then she told her about Tuol Sleng and the disturbing things she'd seen there.

'There was a photograph of Sophia there,' she added.

Achariya looked at her, shock in her eyes. 'Are you quite sure?'

'Not completely. The photograph was fuzzy, but it certainly

looked like her. I tried to find out the names of the people in that photo, but they said there was no trace.'

'There must be a list of those taken to the killing fields,' Achariya said, deep in thought. 'I'm sure I heard somewhere that the Khmer Rouge documented all their executions meticulously. Perhaps Vanna, my neighbour's nephew, will be able to help you. She came round yesterday to let me know that he is home now. If you like, we could go to her home straight away. She was going to tell him that we were coming and what we wanted to know. Have you brought a photograph of Sophia?'

'Of course. I have it in my handbag.'

'Shall we go then?' Achariya asked, getting up stiffly. Colette took her arm, her heartbeat quickening at the thought that she might be on the brink of finding out what happened to Sophia.

Achariya's neighbour, Sela, greeted Colette warmly. She showed her inside her immaculate boathouse, that was larger and more comfortable than Achariya's.

'Please sit down. I will fetch my Vanna, nephew. He is with the fishermen at the tea stall.'

She bustled off and returned with a slight young man with a serious face, who bowed to Achariya and Colette and sat down on the floor cross-legged. Sela brought everyone jasmine tea.

'My aunt tells me you are looking for someone,' Vanna said, fixing Colette with his intense gaze. 'A young woman, I understand. I've helped many families find their loved ones after the fall of the Khmer Rouge, so I might be able to help, but I can't promise anything.'

'Yes. I'd be so grateful if you could help. It's my adopted daughter. Her name is Sophia Boissière, although she may well have changed it. She wasn't keen on her French roots. Here is a photograph of her. But it was taken over twenty years ago, so she will have changed.'

Vanna took it and studied it, frowning.

'Do you recognise her?' Colette asked.

'I'm not sure,' he said, his eyes still on the photograph. 'I would need to make enquiries. You say she disappeared before the Khmer Rouge came to power?'

'Yes, in 1966. She was sixteen. I searched for her for years but found nothing. And in 1975 I had to leave the country.'

'Those were turbulent years for our country. Many people went missing and have never returned home. It will be difficult, but I will do my best for you. I will need to go to Phnom Penh and speak to my contacts. Can I take the photograph with me?'

'Of course. Let me pay your expenses for the trip,' Colette said, dipping in her handbag for money, but he waved it away.

'No charge at the moment. But if I find her, we will discuss again.'

'Of course.'

'Vanna is very generous with his time,' Sela said. 'And with his money. He often donates to the floating school here. They don't have much money and the classroom is very old now. It is leaking and needs repairs.'

'Is the school still going?' Colette asked. 'I used to teach there when I lived here.'

'That's amazing. I was a pupil there and, thinking back, I think I remember you. You used to come and speak French to us, didn't you?'

Colette nodded, trying to place this stout, middle-aged woman in her memory bank of the children she'd once taught.

'Perhaps you'd like to go there?' Sela asked. 'I'm sure the teacher would love to see you. She was a pupil there once, too.'

'I'd love that!'

Vanna got up from the floor. 'I'm going to pack now so that I can leave for Phnom Penh by this evening's bus. I will call you at your hotel and let you know if I find anything and tell you when I'm coming back,' he said, shaking Colette's hand. 'Where are you staying?'

She gave him a card from the Grand Hotel d'Angkor from her

handbag and thanked him profusely. Sela beamed. 'If anyone can find this lady, Vanna will,' she said proudly.

Colette thanked Sela, who asked her to return the next day for a visit to the school. 'The teacher lives near here. I will ask her this evening.'

Colette guided Achariya home along the jetty. Achariya looked tired all of a sudden. 'Hearing about the old days exhausts me. So many difficult memories,' she said, sinking into a chair. Colette fetched her some food from the food stall on the dock, then kissed her and took her leave.

By the time she got back to the hotel, it was dark. She ate an early supper then fell into bed. Like Achariya, she was emotionally exhausted by the events of the day.

The next morning, she returned to the village, where Sela took her and Achariya in her motorboat across to the floating school. Even as they approached the familiar building, Colette could see that the paint was peeling from the old blue walls, there were streaks of mould where the guttering was leaking and some of the boards were missing from the roof. They climbed on board the deck and the teacher came out to meet them.

'Madame Boissière!' she was full of smiles. 'What a surprise! I remember you well. Welcome to our school once again. I'm afraid you'll find we are a bit shabbier than when you used to come. The old boat needs a few repairs, but we soldier on. Come inside and meet the children.'

The classroom was just the same as in the old days, only there were a few colourful posters on the wall now, a concession to the modern world. The children still sat on the floor and all stared at her as she entered, making her feel a little self-conscious.

'This is Madame Boissière,' the teacher announced. 'She used to teach French at this school when I was here, many years ago. Madame Boissière, would you like to speak some French to us now? The children would love to hear you!'

'Alright...' Colette began nervously and introduced herself in

French. She remembered some of the old familiar phrases she used to say, some of the questions she used to ask. These children weren't as well versed in the French language as her old pupils used to be, but they were attentive and keen to learn.

'They haven't had the benefit of a French teacher for a while,' the teacher explained as Colette continued, getting into her stride, even beginning to enjoy herself, while Achariya sat on a chair at the side of the room, smiling, her eyes full of memories.

'Would you come back and see us again soon?' the teacher asked when Colette had finished.

'I'll try,' Colette promised, realising how much she'd enjoyed being back at the school, but thinking that she really should make some firm plans soon. Perhaps once she heard from Vanna she would have more of an idea of what the future held for her.

Two days later, she received a call from Vanna in her hotel room. She'd just got in from her morning swim and was drying her hair when he called. The line was crackly, but she could tell, as soon as she answered, that he had some news for her.

'Have you found Sophia?' she asked, holding her breath for the answer.

'I have,' he said slowly and Colette's world expanded around her like a balloon being inflated. Everything in the room became distorted. She felt dizzy and sat quickly down on the bed.

'I can hardly believe it,' she muttered. 'How did you do it? Where was she?'

'I can't tell you much over the phone,' he said.

'But did you speak to her?'

'I did, briefly, yes. I'll talk to you about it when I come back.'

'But why can't you talk now, Vanna? Can I speak to her? Can I see her?'

Vanna cleared his throat at the other end. 'Not just at the moment, Madame Boissière. Look, I will be back tomorrow, and we can speak then. I want to talk to you about it face to face.'

She had no choice but to agree to see him the next day. He

said he would come to her hotel at noon. She put the phone down, her mind buzzing with questions. What did it all mean? Where was Sophia? Did Sophia know that it was Colette who was looking for her? Had she refused to speak to her? Suddenly she felt chilled, her wet hair and the air conditioning combining to make goosebumps rise on her arms and legs. She grabbed a towel and dried her hair furiously, then pulled on a bathrobe in an effort to warm up. Once she was dry, she dressed quickly and ran downstairs to take a taxi to Achariya's place. Achariya deserved to hear the news as soon as possible.

Achariya went white when she told her that Vanna had tracked Sophia down.

'What's the matter, Achariya? It's good news, isn't it? It's the best news I've had for almost thirty years.'

'I'm not sure, madam. All I remember is what trouble she was. How she hurt you.'

'She was young then, a teenager. She's a grown woman now. She will be different, you'll see.'

Achariya laid a hand on Colette's. 'I'm worried about you. You seem happy now, contented. I don't want her to come and change that.'

'You're so sweet, Achariya, but finding Sophia again means so much to me. Over the years I've thought the worst about what might have happened to her, and I've always blamed myself. Knowing she's alive means I can stop worrying, whatever she's like now, whatever happens between us.'

'I just think you should prepare yourself for the fact that she might not have changed. She might not have grown up.'

'All right. I will try to do that,' Colette promised.

The next day at noon, Colette was in the lobby of the hotel waiting impatiently for Vanna. She watched the tourists come and go through the hotel entrance, meeting their guides, looking for taxis. She wondered briefly if he'd wanted to come to her so that he could bring Sophia to meet her. She could but hope.

Vanna emerged from a taxi alone and came up the steps. He was wearing dark glasses, his brows drawn up in an anxious frown.

'I'm here, Vanna,' she said waving. He came over to where she was sitting and shook her hand. He looked a little nervous.

'Sit down, please,' she said, and he sat down in an armchair opposite her own.

'Wouldn't you prefer to go somewhere private?' he asked. 'What I have to say is confidential.'

It was Colette's turn to frown. 'Confidential? I don't understand. We could go to my room if you think that would be better.'

He got up. 'I think it might be.'

Mystified, she guided him to the lift and they stood opposite each other in silence as it took them up to her floor. Inside her room she asked him to sit down on the sofa beside the window. She closed the door to the balcony and sat down beside him.

'Now... please tell me what this is all about.'

He leaned forward and looked into her eyes. 'When you showed me the photograph of Sophia at my aunt's place, I had a vague idea that I might have seen her before but I wasn't sure. But when I went to Phnom Penh and started digging, my suspicions were confirmed.'

'Suspicions? What do you mean?' Colette was too perplexed to be worried about what he was about to say.

'Sophia was a member of the Khmer Rouge. She wasn't in the highest echelons, but she was an operative. She was actually a guard at Tuol Sleng prison.'

Shock went through Colette like a bolt of electricity. 'You must have got that wrong. My Sophia? She couldn't have become one of them.'

Vanna leaned forward and touched her hand. He looked straight into her eyes and she could see he was genuine. 'I'm so sorry to bring you this news. I know it wasn't what you were expecting, but I'm afraid it's the truth. It will be hard to deal with,

I know, but Sophia joined the Khmer Rouge at the very beginning.'

Colette shook her head, struggling to take this on board. She thought of that beautiful, innocent little girl she'd cradled in her arms and had always protected and loved. How could she have become part of that brutal, murderous regime?

27

SIEM REAP, 1995

Colette carried on staring at Vanna, watching his face intently, sensing he had more to tell her. Through the window, she could hear other hotel guests in the pool, laughing and splashing. It seemed incongruous at that moment, that people were enjoying themselves.

'I'm afraid it's true, Madame Boissière,' Vanna said. 'Sophia is actually being held in prison in Phnom Penh at the moment. I spoke to her there yesterday.'

'In prison?' this was a fresh blow. She took a deep breath. How could she ever cope with this?

'Yes. Most of the Khmer Rouge leadership were offered an amnesty if they came forward and confessed their involvement before a certain date. For some reason, some didn't. Either they didn't know about it, or they were out of the country at the time. Sophia was one of those.'

Colette stared at him, her mouth gaping open. She was struck dumb. How could she not have considered this possibility? She'd long suspected that Sophia had run off to join the communists in the north, but she'd never thought that she could have become part of the murderous Khmer Rouge. Then she remembered the photograph at Tuol Sleng.

'It can't be right, Vanna. I saw a picture of her in Tuol Sleng. She was with a group of other prisoners. She was a prisoner there, not a member of the Khmer Rouge.'

Again, Vanna shook his head. 'She was a guard at that prison. She might have been photographed with some prisoners, but she would have been guarding them. Perhaps you automatically assumed she was a prisoner because the other thing would have been unthinkable.'

Colette passed her hand over her face. This was so hard to take in.

'Did you tell her it was me who was looking for her?'

Vanna nodded. 'She was surprised. I asked if you could see her, and she was a little hesitant, but eventually agreed. I spoke to the guards about it before I left, and they said that you could go there at any time. She has a hearing coming up, to review her case, so it might be best to go there in the next couple of days.'

'I will go there tomorrow. I can travel up to Phnom Penh this afternoon.'

'If you'd like me to go with you, I'd be happy to do so,' Vanna said, his eyes full of concern. Perhaps he was worried about the meeting, about how Sophia might react to seeing Colette, what she might say?

'That would be very kind of you. I'll probably need some support, and I've no idea where the prison is.'

This time Colette didn't rush over to tell Achariya her news. She decided to wait until she had actually seen Sophia and confirmed the worst with her own eyes. She knew Achariya wouldn't be surprised, and with her low opinion of Sophia perhaps she'd quietly suspected it all along.

They took a minibus to Phnom Penh that afternoon. On the way, Vanna told Colette about some of the people he'd managed to track down, people whose families had virtually given them up for dead, but who just wanted to be sure.

'It's not been easy. The Khmer Rouge forced the whole population out into the countryside. They prised families apart, tore children from their mothers. Many died of starvation or disease on the way or while they were there. Many didn't make it home.'

'I know. It's terrible. Achariya told me her own story. There must be so many others who suffered just like her. How have you gone about finding these people?'

'With difficulty. I started this when I was a journalist working in Phnom Penh. I was approached by so many people who had lost their loved ones that I decided to take it up full time. I go into the villages where people were sent by the Khmer Rouge and interview survivors, trying to build up a list of names remembered. I go to the Khmer Rouge detention centres and killing fields and try to find out who was executed there.'

Colette shuddered. 'That sounds so harrowing.'

'It is, of course, but the work brings its own reward. Seeing families reunited and knowing I've played a part in that is the best feeling on earth.'

Colette thought about Sophia and the mixed emotions that had arisen when she'd discovered the truth about her. On balance though, she decided that she would rather have found out the worst than spend the rest of her life in a state of limbo, not knowing.

When they reached Phnom Penh, Vanna asked the driver to drop him on the outskirts.

'I stay with relatives when I'm in the city. Saves hotel bills. I will come to the Cambodiana at nine o'clock tomorrow morning and we can go straight to the prison from there.'

Colette continued the journey alone. Without Vanna there she began to feel apprehensive about what the next day would bring. How would Sophia react when she saw her? What would she be like now? Since her escape from the villa in 1975 and the siege at the French Embassy, Colette had always been terrified of the Khmer Rouge. Would Sophia be like those soldiers she'd encountered then? With the same contempt for human life, with that evil, murderous glint in their eyes?

At the Cambodiana the receptionist greeted Colette like an old friend and gave her her previous room. But even that incredible view over the smooth, wide river at dusk, with the stunning, ever changing red-golds of the setting sun playing on the water, didn't give her solace. She couldn't bear to go down to the dining room to eat; she didn't feel like speaking to anyone. Instead, she ordered fried rice from room service, but when it arrived, she found she had no appetite and simply picked at the food. She took a bath and went to bed early, but sleep would not come. She was besieged by memories of Sophia, her anger and rages, her rejection of Colette and everything she stood for, her unhappiness, despite all the advantages she'd had. Colette had come to Cambodia to find Sophia, but now she was on the brink of meeting her, she was having serious doubts.

The next day dawned in characteristically glorious form. Colette watched the sun glinting on the river from her window as she tried to force down some breakfast, telling herself she needed to keep up her strength.

Her stomach was doing somersaults when she met Vanna in the lobby at nine o'clock and they set off to the prison in a taxi together. They passed the journey in silence. Colette hardly registered the maze of streets they drove through, but when they arrived outside the forbidding, modern block occupying the entire length of a side-street on the outskirts of the city, she realised that there were marks on the palms of her hands where she'd clenched her fists so hard that her fingernails had dug into the skin.

She followed Vanna into the building, past the security checkpoint, where she showed her passport, and on through several sets of barred, metal gates. An unsmiling female guard strode in front of them, keys jangling from her belt, from which a pistol hung in a leather holster. They went on through endless passages, deeper and deeper into the building. There was no air conditioning here, and Colette felt the sweat run down her chest and back and her clothes stick to her body.

Finally, the guard opened a solid door and showed them into a starkly lit low-ceilinged room with a series of booths on one side.

'Wait there. She will come,' she said, pointing to the first window.

They each sat down in a plastic chair and within seconds a woman appeared in the booth on the other side of the window. She was dressed in a shapeless blue and white striped dress and her ankles and wrists were shackled. Her black hair hung lankly about her shoulders and Colette was surprised to see grey streaks in it. But it was her face that was most shocking of all. It was unmistakeably Sophia, with her high cheekbones and full lips, but her skin was sallow and pale, and she had that dull look in her eyes of someone who has witnessed unimaginable things. Gone was that wild, restless look of her youth.

'Sophia!' Colette had to speak into a microphone.

'Maman,' Sophia responded. Even through the distortion of the sound system, her voice sounded the same as ever and a lump rose in Colette's throat. She told herself she mustn't cry, they only had limited time and she needed to be strong.

'I'm so pleased I found you,' she said.

Sophia sat down opposite them and Vanna got up from his seat. 'I will give you some privacy. If you need me, I will be over there.'

'I'm so sorry, Maman,' Sophia said, and her dark eyes now filled with sorrow and regret. 'I'm sorry for everything I put you through. I know you loved me and only wanted to do the best for me. I was young and stupid and treated you very badly. You didn't deserve that.'

Colette stared at her, stunned. She certainly hadn't expected this.

'I'm a changed person now,' Sophia went on. 'I was caught up by that horrific organisation when I was too young to know any better. I did things I deeply regret now, although I never killed anyone. But every day I meditate, make offerings to the Buddha, try to make amends for my past actions. I know I can never make up for what I did, especially not how I treated you, but I hope that one day you can find it in your heart to forgive me.'

Colette swallowed hard, her vision obscured by tears now. 'I forgave you a long time ago,' she said, her voice catching in her throat. 'If there was anything at all to forgive, Sophia. You weren't happy at home, and as soon as you could, you ran away. You were young, headstrong.'

Through the scratched glass, she looked into Sophia's eyes. Sophia was looking back at her earnestly.

'Thank you, Maman, I thank you from the bottom of my heart. I want to get out of here and make up for what I've done. I want to live a good life, help people, work for a better world.'

'Vanna said you had a court hearing coming up. Might you be released after that?'

Sophia shook her head. 'I doubt it. They provide us with public defenders. They work for the government. They're not impartial.'

'But why are you still here when there was an amnesty?'

'My unit was on the border with Thailand, like so many other guerrilla outfits trying to reassert the Khmer Rouge regime in Cambodia. Our leader was a brutal man and we were just pawns in his evil game. We were kept there long after we should have surrendered. He forced us to continue the fight against government forces. He didn't tell us about the amnesty because he didn't want us to leave. By the time we found out, it was too late. We were captured and brought here. I'm trying to prove to the government that I would have given myself up before the deadline if I'd had the chance.'

Colette was watching her face as she spoke. She saw genuine contrition in Sophia's expression; the regret in her eyes. This wasn't what she'd expected, but her heart went out to her daughter. Was there perhaps a way she could help her, she wondered. Then something occurred to her.

'I met a lawyer in Siem Reap a few days ago,' she said. 'I went to him to ask him to help me buy the villa back, but he wouldn't help. He was too principled. He only works for those he judges to be deserving of his time. I could ask him to help you if you like.'

Sophia's face fell. 'He wouldn't help me. He would still see me as Khmer Rouge.'

'He might. He seemed to be an intelligent man. If you explain how you regret your actions, how you want to make up for the past, he might consider it. Would you like me to ask him?'

'Would you? I'd try anything to get out of here.'

'Of course. I will call him this afternoon.'

The guard banged on the door, then opened it. 'Two more minutes.'

'Thank you for coming, Maman. I've been thinking about you a lot lately, but I never thought I would see you again. I wouldn't have blamed you if you'd washed your hands of me altogether. It's far more than I deserve, you coming here and even offering to help me.'

Sophia held her palm up to the glass and Colette put her own hand on the glass and held it there. It was almost as if they were touching, as if the rift that had lasted for decades was finally beginning to heal.

As they walked away, Colette thanked Vanna. 'Words can't express what this means to me, Vanna. Your kindness is overwhelming.'

'There is no need to thank me, Madame Boissière. Just seeing you so happy at the end of your long search is enough for me.'

THARA PHANG, the lawyer at Angkor Law Offices in Siem Reap was surprised to hear from Colette.

'Madame Boissière! I thought you would have found a lawyer in Phnom Penh to help you by now,' he said.

'No, I haven't as a matter of fact. I'm still thinking it all over. But I have something else I'd be grateful for your help with. Something that might be more in your line of work.'

'Oh, really?' she heard the interest in his voice.

'You said you wanted to help people who really need your help. Well, my daughter, my adopted daughter that is, is in prison in Phnom Penh. She desperately needs a good lawyer.'

'Really? Tell me more.'

Colette explained Sophia's circumstances, and at first Thara was reluctant to help. 'I don't have sympathy with members of the Khmer Rouge,' he said. But Colette talked him round, emphasising that Sophia had been just a child when she'd been recruited into the Khmer Rouge, that she'd been indoctrinated, brutalised, used by its leaders.

'And when the opportunity for an amnesty came up, she was kept in the dark in order to keep her in the hills, fighting. She didn't find out about it until it was too late. She's been refused release, but there's another hearing next week. Would you take her case? It would mean so much to me, so much to her too.'

Five minutes later, Colette put the phone down with a satisfied smile. Thara Phang had agreed to represent Sophia and was coming to Phnom Penh to see her the very next day.

A WEEK LATER, Colette was sitting beside Vanna in the back of a courtroom, under a whirring fan, listening to Thara Phang giving an impassioned plea for Sophia's release. She was so glad she'd remembered him. Once he'd met Sophia, he had taken up her cause completely and had worked day and night to get to grips with the case, see if there were any new angles he could think of, and work out the best way of presenting it to the court. Sophia sat beside him, still clad in her prison uniform. She'd turned round a couple of times to smile at Colette.

Colette had returned to the prison with Thara several times during the intervening days. Each visit had strengthened the renewed bond with Sophia and had reinforced Colette's belief that Sophia was a changed woman and that helping her release from prison was the right thing to do. She hoped fervently that the court would grant it and that she could take Sophia home, wherever that might be. Having Sophia in her life again would be another reason to buy the villa back.

The single judge, seated behind a long bench at the front of the court was listening to Thara intently, seemingly hanging on his every word. Sometimes he interrupted to ask questions or to clarify something. Colette watched his face, trying to get a hint of what he was thinking, but his expression was inscrutable. The courtroom was empty but for a few journalists seated on the front row. The appeal of a minor Khmer Rouge operative didn't generate much interest.

Thara finished speaking and sat down. There was a pause while the judge wrote something down and shuffled his papers. Then he said, 'Thank you, Monsieur Phang. I will go away and deliberate. I will return my verdict this afternoon.'

'All rise,' the court usher called and everyone stood up as the judge left the chamber. There was a general hubbub as people got up from their seats and started to leave. Thara turned round and nodded to Colette and from the look in his eyes, she could tell he was hopeful of success.

It was a tense few hours. Sophia was returned to the cells between two prison guards and Thara came over to speak to Colette and Vanna.

'We could go for a walk,' he said. 'It's rather stuffy in here.'

The court building was ornately beautiful, rather like a temple, with a soaring spire and tiered red roofs. They strolled around the grounds and admired the building. All three were tense and conversation was difficult, but Colette did thank Thara for everything he'd done.

'I don't know what we'd have done without you,' she said. 'I'm so glad I found you that day, even though you didn't want to help me with buying the villa.'

He smiled. 'Have you made a decision about that yet?'

'I'm not sure. I suppose it depends on what happens today. If Sophia is released there's more of a reason for me to stay in Cambodia. Although I don't know what she might have planned. We've hardly had a chance to speak about it.'

'She told me she'd like to return to Siem Reap where she grew up,' Vanna put in, 'Even more reason for you to stay.'

A warm feeling crept through Colette at his words. 'That's so good to know,' she said, swallowing the lump that rose in her throat.

The judge took three hours to deliberate. When they filed back into court once again, Colette tried once again to scrutinise the judge's face, trying to work out what he might say. The air in the chamber was thick was anticipation. Vanna gave her an encouraging look. She could hardly breathe, her nerves were so taut.

The judge began to speak.

'I thank learned counsel for their arguments in this case and I have considered them carefully. It is a difficult and finely balanced case, but my conclusion is that the defendant would have come forward for amnesty at the appropriate time, had she not been precluded from doing so by her superiors. Although there was a hard deadline for registration for amnesty, the statute allows for exceptional cases to be allowed on appeal. I therefore pronounce that the defendant may be released with immediate effect and that any threat of prosecution is removed from her.'

There were excited murmurings from the courtroom and Thanna got up to thank the judge. Sophia turned round and looked at Colette, her face a picture of relief and joy. Once Thanna had finished speaking and the court had risen, Colette left her seat, squeezed along the aisle and took Sophia in her arms and they held each other for a long time, the tears mingling on their cheeks.

'I'm so happy to have you back,' Colette said, holding her daughter tight, never wanting to let her go.

28

TONLÉ SAP, 1995
SIX WEEKS LATER

Colette and Sophia sat in a little boat which was powering across Tonlé Sap towards the villa, the wind in their hair, the sun on their faces. They had come straight from visiting Achariya who was still a little frosty about Sophia returning to live amongst them. But she had melted a little when she'd seen how genuinely contrite Sophia was about her past conduct and how thoughtful and generous the adult Sophia had become. It had helped that Sophia brought her a large bunch of lotus flowers and some traditional sweetmeats, as offerings for the little altar Achariya had to the Buddha on the deck of her houseboat.

As they'd left to find Boran the boatman to ferry them over to the villa, Achariya had grabbed Colette's arm to hold her back. 'She seems different now, doesn't she? She's rather nice,' she'd whispered, as if to compensate for her previous scepticism. Now, sitting in the boat, enjoying the balmy, fresh air and drinking in the beauty of the lake once more, Colette smiled to herself. Achariya had such a generous heart, she was sure to fully accept Sophia before too long.

Sophia had been living with an old schoolfriend since her

return to Siem Reap. Colette was still staying at the Grand Hotel d'Angkor but was hoping to find something more permanent now she'd decided to make Cambodia her home once more. It would be a long time before the villa was approaching anything near habitable, but her heart pounded with excitement whenever she thought of it. That morning, she'd been handed the deeds to the property at the town hall, having paid a considerable sum for the land and the buildings. In fact, it had virtually emptied her French bank account, but she knew it was worth it.

It had been the lawyer, Thana's idea to ask Sophia if she and Colette could buy the villa jointly.

'She's a Cambodian citizen after all. You could buy it jointly with your daughter with a clear conscience.' That man was full of surprises. He'd even offered Sophia a part-time job at his law offices and she'd accepted straight away.

'Are you sure?' she'd asked, incredulous. 'You know I don't have any legal training, don't you?'

'I know that,' Thana smiled, 'But I'm sure you'd be very useful to the practice. You know a lot about the constitution of Cambodia, and a lot about injustice. There's nothing like having experienced the legal system first-hand to give you a unique perspective on how it affects others.'

Sophia had been genuinely delighted. 'It's just the sort of thing I dreamed of doing all the time I was in prison,' she'd said with shining eyes, and she'd turned to hug Colette impulsively as she often did. 'Thank you again, Maman, for making all this possible.'

Now, Colette rested her eyes on her daughter's face. She still had to pinch herself every time she looked at her. Since she'd been freed, Sophia's natural beauty was gradually returning. She had gained a little weight and had lost that sallow look she'd had in prison. Her skin was now luminous and healthy-looking, her dark hair bouncy and lustrous.

Boran slowed the boat and nosed it through the mangroves.

'These weren't here before,' Sophia remarked, looking in wonder at the tangled forest of gnarled tree roots.

'No, they've grown up in the past twenty years. Everywhere is overgrown, sadly.'

They reached the bank beside the villa and Boran helped them to clamber to the top.

'I will wait for you here. Please, take your time,' he told them, then left them to slide back down to the boat.

'It's incredible,' Sophia said, looking around at the profusion of growth, just as Colette had when she'd come here alone a few weeks ago. The jungle had swallowed everything. Creepers with giant, bell-like, white flowers were growing over the walls of the villa and bamboo and ferns had sprung up all around. The villa was as she remembered, decaying and blackened with lichen, the wide, sweeping veranda giving onto the lake, where they'd spent so many happy hours, covered in ferns, collapsing majestically down the bank.

'I'd like to see Henri's grave, but I'm not sure if we could get there,' Colette said.

'We'll have to get some contractors in to clear the under-growth,' Sophia said. 'I'll ask around.'

She parted the bamboo. 'Look, we might just be able to get through here, Maman. Shall I go first?'

Sophia went ahead and Colette followed close behind. She would never have dared do this alone and she wouldn't have been strong enough to hold back the springy bamboo as Sophia was doing. Progress was slow; Sophia broke off branches and pulled out clumps of undergrowth so they could both pass.

'Just to think, this was once poor Henri's pride and joy,' Colette said, 'And Lim's, of course.'

It was barely recognisable as a garden anymore.

'There it is,' Sophia said, pointing in front of her and Colette gasped.

Up ahead, in a patch of long grass, nestled beneath teak trees, was Henri's headstone. Colette went up to it and fell on her knees in front of it. Like the walls of the villa, it was covered in moss and lichen, the inscriptions unreadable, but it was still standing.

'I'm sorry I've been away so long, Henri, chérie,' she said, holding back the tears, 'but we're back now and we will do our best to restore the old place to its former glory.'

She knelt there for a few moments, thinking about the man who had been her rock, had brought her to this beautiful place and had given her so much love. Sophia stood at a discreet distance, waiting for her.

At last she got up and they turned back to retrace their steps through the undergrowth.

'I don't suppose we could get into the villa,' Sophia said.

'I don't think so. We'll have to wait until the undergrowth is cleared.'

'What about the boathouse?'

'Perhaps... maybe that path through the trees is still there.'

Colette looked up and scanned the line of the trees above them. She could just about make out the distinctive line of ancient teaks that surrounded the boathouse.

'It's over there.'

Sophia scouted around amongst the bamboos and ferns and found an opening. They pushed their way through until they were on the narrow strip of gravel path that was left, although even that was covered in grass.

'Shall we keep going?' Sophia asked and Colette nodded. They'd come that far. She was covered in burrs, thorns and moisture from the undergrowth, but was curious to see if the boathouse was still there. They pushed on through, and soon enough there were the old concrete steps leading to the blue door. They made their way up them, pushing away the creepers that were strangling the railings.

The door was rotten and with one kick from Sophia it fell in. They stepped over it and were inside; the dank, musty smell hit

Colette's nostrils and she was reminded powerfully of when she'd come here to ask Luc what he was doing and he'd pushed her against the wall and made love to her. Was that to distract her from what he was really doing there? She sighed. She supposed she would never know the truth.

'Your father used to work in here,' she said now. 'I'm not sure I ever told you that.'

His table was still there, up on the little gallery in front of the window, that was now so blackened with dirt that barely any light came through. Colette had never been up there again, not since they took Luc away and ransacked the place, but now she was curious. She made her way up the steps to the little gallery and pictured Luc sitting there, his head bent forward over a book. His presence was palpable.

'Be careful, Maman,' Sophia said from below.

At that moment a floorboard gave way and Colette stumbled. The floor was rotting away, perhaps she shouldn't have come up here, but something drove her forward. She bent down to look at the rotting floor and even in the gloom she could see something glinting down there, beneath the boards. Intrigued, she bent down to investigate, slipping her hand between the broken boards. Whatever was down there was shiny and solid. Her hand slid around it and brought it up. Her mouth dropped open. It was a gold bar.

'What the...?' she could hear Sophia's feet on the stairs. 'What is it, Maman?'

She pulled the floorboards aside now and there were more gold bars, a stack of them, and a cash box too. She pulled it out and opened the lid. It was filled with United States dollars. Wad after wad of them, neatly packed and wrapped in paper bands.

Luc must have hidden it here all those years ago. It was incredible how much there was. If this was hers, and she supposed it would be after so many years had passed, and how many governments had been and gone in the intervening years, she would have more than enough to restore the villa, help Achariya to lead a more comfortable life, help Sophia get on her feet, and to donate a large sum to the school so they could buy a new houseboat.

She looked up at Sophia who was staring down at the treasure trove, her eyes wide with astonishment. 'Your father must have left all this here,' she said.

'Perhaps he knew we would find it one day,' Sophia said, dropping to her knees beside her.

Colette wasn't going to disagree, not with the love she felt in her heart as Sophia wrapped her arms around her.

'Yes,' she said, 'perhaps he did.'

T<small>HANK</small> you for reading *The Lake Villa*. I hope you enjoyed reading it as much as I enjoyed writing it!

I'd love to hear your feedback either through my Facebook page or my website (www.annbennettauthor.com) where you can sign up for news and updates about my books.

If you've enjoyed this book, you might also like to read *The Lake Pagoda* (a captivating story of love and loss set in wartime Indochina -this time Vietnam). This book is also part of the Oriental Lake Collection and may be read as a standalone story. Please turn over to read an extract.

EXTRACT FROM THE LAKE PAGODA
CHAPTER 1

Arielle, Paris, 1946

Arielle pulled her shawl tightly around her shoulders and stepped out of the entrance to the apartment building and onto the broad pavement of Boulevard St Germaine. An icy wind whipped around her, driving up from the River Seine, funnelled by the tall buildings. She shivered and gritted her teeth against the weather. It was so alien to her, this biting cold air that chilled you to the marrow of your bones. In her native Hanoi, the temperature, even in the cooler months, was always comfortable and she was so used to the sultry heat of that city that this Paris winter was a cruel shock.

Even so, she needed to get out. She couldn't stay inside the stuffy, cramped apartment a moment longer, and while her father was sleeping it was difficult to do anything in that tiny space without disturbing him. So, each morning she left the building to tramp the streets of this alien city, exploring the alleys of the Latin Quarter, the cobbled lanes and churches of the Ile de la Cité, the boulevards and gardens of the Eighth Arondissement. And as she walked, she watched the stylish Parisians going about their business, dashing to and fro in fashionable clothes, getting out of taxis, riding on trams, pouring down the steps of the metro. She was trying to understand her new home, to find her place in it, to find some meaningful connection with this great, intimidating city. And there was something else she was searching for too.

Now, as she braced herself against the wind and started walking along the boulevard away from the apartment, she glanced guiltily back up at the windows on the third floor. She always worried when she left Papa alone. What if he were to wake up and call out for her? What if he had one of his coughing fits? But he always encouraged her to go. 'Go on, explore while I'm resting. You need to get to know the place. You can't stay cooped up with a sick old man all day. I'll be fine on my own.' But still she worried.

She carried on down the road, making for the market in Rue Mouffetard. Cars and buses crawled past belting out fumes. Through the lines of slow-moving traffic wove bicycles and pony traps, army jeeps too. It felt so bleak here and so dull after the vibrant colours of Hanoi; the plane trees that lined the pavements had lost their leaves, their branches stark against the tall, pale buildings, and the sky between them was an ominous slate grey.

She walked past a couple of bus stops without pausing. She'd never yet got on a bus in Paris; she had no idea how they worked and was afraid of drawing attention to herself, even though she told herself it was perfectly safe here to do so. Years of having to keep a low profile in Hanoi had made her fearful of attention from anyone. Not that she need worry here in Paris, people barely noticed her. She could walk in the midst of a crowd as if she didn't exist. And if anyone's eyes did happen to light on her, seeing her dark skin and black hair they would quickly flick away, for she was half Vietnamese and it was as if she were invisible to them; a nobody.

She turned off the main road and walked towards the Jardins

du Luxembourg. She loved these beautiful gardens with their wide-open lawns, broad sweeping paths and the elegant palace that dominated the centre. It reminded her of the gracious French colonial buildings of Hanoi; the Opera House, the Palais du Gouvernement, the Metropole Hotel. Despite the biting cold she would sometimes come here to sit on a bench and stare at the beautiful building; half-closing her eyes she could dream she was back home. But today there was no time. She needed to get to the market and back home before her father needed her.

Putting her head down against the biting wind, she hurried on and soon reached Rue Mouffetard where the market was in full swing, stalls piled high with fruit and vegetables. Despite the post-war rationing, stallholders at this market were adept at obtaining supplies; autumn fruits – apples and pears were piled up on one stall, potatoes and greens on another, yet another was selling whole, plucked chickens and another cheeses from the countryside, oozing and ripe. Arielle went from stall to stall buying what she and her father needed for the next couple of days. It reminded her a little of Hang Be market in the centre of Hanoi, where she used to buy food for the two of them until the war had swept that easy life away. But here there was no exotic fruit or plump, luscious seafood. There was no bartering either and she had to restrain herself from asking for a better price for a kilo of apples or a litre of unpasteurised milk. The stallholders dealt with her stiffly, unsmilingly and sometimes with suspicion, and as she turned away she could sense them whispering about her. It made her feel small, isolated, and a long way from home, but she knew there was nothing she could do about it.

It began to rain as she crossed the cobbles of a little square and carried on into the Rue Descartes. Her shopping bag was heavy now, loaded with produce. It dragged on her shoulder, but it was still quite a way back to the Boulevard St Germaine. She wrapped her shawl more tightly around her, shivering in the chill winter air and looked around for somewhere to shelter until the shower had passed. A bar-brasserie loomed up ahead where the pavement widened out at a junction. It had a red-painted awning above the door. Perhaps she could stand under there for a few minutes? She was far too timid to even think about going inside.

When she reached the building, she sidled underneath the porch and glanced in through the steamed-up window, taking in the polished tables, the elaborate glass and marble bar, the rows of bottles stacked on the shelves behind it. It was just after noon and a rowdy lunchtime crowd was propping up the bar, laughing and joking, calling for more drinks. Arielle saw instantly that they were soldiers. She peered at their khaki uniforms, the dark caps they were wearing. Someone pushed open the door and left, walking quickly away from Arielle along Rue de Montagne, but before the door slammed shut, she caught a burst of conversation and her heart beat faster. The men were speaking English. They must be American GIs, still stationed in Paris after the end of the war, waiting for their transport home.

Her interest piqued, she leaned even closer to the window and stared inside, her hot breath clouding the glass. She was searching for something, someone. She scanned the faces, many contorted in exaggerated laughter, flushed with alcohol, but none were familiar. Then one man turned round and her heart leapt as she caught a flash of tawny hair. Could that be him? She looked closer, not even able to blink, but as he turned towards the window momentarily, she was quickly disappointed. The face was unfamiliar and the hair wasn't quite the shade of flaming red she was looking for. She shrunk back against the wall. The man she was looking for couldn't possibly be here in Paris, she reasoned. If he were here, he would surely have been in touch with her.

Suddenly she wanted to be away from the noisy bar. She was glad when the rain eased off after a few minutes. Leaving the shelter of the porch, she shouldered her bag and carried on, along Rue de la Montagne and Rue St Genevieve, eventually emerging onto the wide pavements of the Boulevard St Germaine.

The concierge was standing in the doorway to her apartment, hands on hips as Arielle entered the hallway.

'Bonjour, madame,' Arielle said with a polite smile, but the woman just nodded curtly and turned away. With a sigh Arielle started the long walk up the steep stairs to the apartment.

Her father was sitting up in bed and as always she was shocked by how gaunt and pale he looked. His lined face was almost grey in the pale light.

'Are you alright, Papa?' She heaved the bag off her shoulder and went to his bedside to peck him on the cheek.

'Of course. How was your walk?'

'It was good,' she said brightly, not wanting to tell him how people shunned and ignored her. 'I bought fruit and cheese, some baguettes, oh and a chicken for supper.'

'You're a good girl,' he said, holding out a bony hand. 'I'm so lucky to have you.'

'Oh, Papa. Nonsense. I'm glad to be here.'

She went into the kitchenette to brew some tea. It was a tiny, windowless room, little more than a cupboard. The whole apartment was small, even though it was in a gracious building with high ceilings and floor-length windows. Her father's cousin had allowed them to stay there when they'd arrived, penniless from Hanoi a few months before. He'd only visited once, to give them a key and show them around, before retreating to his large house in Neuilly.

'The last tenants left it in a bit of a state...' It was true. They hadn't even washed up from their last meal and their dirty sheets were still on the beds, but even though she was dropping with exhaustion from the journey, Arielle had got to work straight away, washing and scrubbing, dusting the surfaces and cleaning the floors.

Now, she took the tea out to Papa and handed it to him,

noticing how his hands shook nowadays. She forced herself to smile but inside she couldn't stop anxious thoughts from surfacing. He was fading before her very eyes. All those weeks on the ship from Haiphong, rolling around on the high seas had taken its toll, lying on a bunk in a cramped cabin, too sick to get out for fresh air. And the terrible months before that locked up in the Citadel. She shivered to think of them now. It was good to put them behind her, but they had left their mark on her father, for sure.

'Will you sit with me and have your tea, Arielle?' Papa asked with pleading eyes.

She shook her head. 'In a few minutes, Papa. I need to get the soup on for lunch first.'

She went back into the kitchenette and peeled onions, potatoes, garlic, leeks and carrots, sweated them in butter in a saucepan over the flickering gas flame. Then she added stock and water and left it to simmer. Wiping her hands, she slipped into her bedroom. It was hardly big enough to qualify as a room, just wide enough for a single bed. There, she felt in her top drawer for the picture. It was hidden under her underwear. She wasn't sure why, but she didn't want Papa to look at it. Perhaps the memories it held for her were too precious to share? She drew it out and placed it on the end of the bed so she could look at it in the weak light from the window. It was a charcoal sketch of the Tran Quoc Pagoda on the West Lake, Hanoi, its many tiered roofs reaching to the sky. It stood proudly on its promontory, surrounded by palm trees, its reflection clear in the still waters of the lake. Just looking at it took her back there, to where so much had happened to her over the years. She could almost feel the sultry air of that city wrap itself around her as she stared at the sketch. And as she looked, the past became real and it was as if he was beside her again, his arms around her, and when she turned to smile at him he kissed her on the lips.

ACKNOWLEDGMENTS

Special thanks go to my friend and writing buddy Siobhan Daiko for her constant support and encouragement for more than a decade. To Rafa and Xavier at Cover Kitchen for another beautiful cover design, to Johnny Hudspith and Trenda Lundin for their inspirational editing, to my friend Mandy Lyon-Brown for her eagle-eyed editing, to my sisters for their help, and to everyone who has supported me down the years by reading my books.

ABOUT THE AUTHOR

Ann Bennett was born in Pury End, a small village in Northamptonshire in the UK and now lives in Surrey. *The Lake Villa* is her thirteenth novel.

Her first book, *Bamboo Heart: A Daughter's Quest*, was inspired by her father's experience as a prisoner of war on the Thai-Burma Railway. *Bamboo Island: The Planter's Wife*, *A Daughter's Promise*, *Bamboo Road*: *The Homecoming*, *The Tea Planter's Club* and *The Amulet* are also about WWII in South East Asia. Together they form the Echoes of Empire collection. She has also written *The Lake Pavilion,* set in British India in the 1930s, *The Lake Palace*, set in India during the Burma Campaign of WWII and *The Lake Pagoda,* set in Indochina during WWII. Ann's other books, *The Runaway Sisters*, bestselling *The Orphan House*, *The Child Without a Home* and *The Forgotten Children* are published by Bookouture.

Ann is married with three grown up sons and a granddaughter and works as a lawyer.

For more details please visit www.annbennettauthor.com

ALSO BY ANN BENNETT

Bamboo Heart: A Daughter's Quest

Bamboo Island: The Planter's Wife

Bamboo Road: The Homecoming

A Daughter's Promise

The Tea Planter's Club

The Amulet

The Lake Pavilion

The Lake Palace

The Lake Pagoda

The Orphan House

The Runaway Sisters

The Child Without a Home

The Forgotten Children

Printed in Great Britain
by Amazon